For Sheila, who is my source of inspiration

SKELETON SECRETS

Dave Uttley

BB

First published in 2023 by Bredbury Books
Sheffield, Yorkshire

ISBN 978-0-9564183-5-7

www.bredburybooks.co.uk

Dave Uttley was born in Cleveleys on the Fylde coast. After working in the Manchester area in IT management, he took early retirement and began painting and decorating, which gave him plenty of time to sketch out his ideas for a story. Many of those thoughts are to be found hastily scribbled on walls behind newly hung wallpaper. They are there for posterity. Dave now lives in Sheffield with his wife, Sheila.

This book draws on his memories of growing up, although all the events and characters are fictitious. However, the reader may recognise some places, past and present.

CAST OF CHARACTERS

Steve Hamshaw	Property developer
Tom Hamshaw	Steve's grandpa
Dorothy Hamshaw	Steve's nan
Rose Hamshaw	Steve's mum
Richard Whittle	Police Inspector
Jill Whittle	Richard's wife
George Whittle	Richard's dad
Enid Whittle	Richard's mum
Gloria Ward	Married to Gary
Don Ward	Gloria's dad
Kathleen Ward	Gloria's mum
Jed Breeze	Amusement Arcade Owner
Terry Breeze	Jed's son.
Gary Breeze	Terry's son. Married to Gloria
Phil Breeze	Terry's son. Ne'er-do-well
Daniel Atkinson	Police Constable
Angie Atkinson	Daniel's wife
Graham Atkinson	Daniel's dad
Irena Atkinson	Daniel's mum
Cora Stone	Detective Sergeant
Barry Crompton	Detective Constable

Jock Crammie	Brickie
Evie	Jock's wife
Lucy	Jock's step-daughter
Arthur Dowling	Bank security guard
Roland Booth	Bank cashier
Becca Boswell	Friend of Gloria's
Valdo Goralova	Fairground worker
Cristian Goralova	Fairground worker
David Leadbeater	Pathologist
Mary Leadbeater	David's wife
Theresa Watson	Friend of Rose
Teddy Watson	School friend of Steve
Margaret Bowler	Snooker hall cleaner
Shirley Baxter	Photographer

Prologue
Tuesday, 19th November 1957

The battered green Ford Thames van eased its way past the back walls of the terraced houses, across the uneven cobbles onto the cinder wasteland, and pulled to a halt. The driver killed the engine and the lights. He sat there in the darkness and silence, contemplating the job that had to be done. He was waiting until anyone who had been disturbed by the engine noise turned over in bed and went back to sleep. It gave him time to reflect on the part he'd played in the killing of a person – a person whose body lay just a few inches behind him on the floor of the van. He felt a sharp pang of remorse.

The night hung dank with a cold, watery mist which rolled relentlessly in off the sea. The kind that soaks into your clothes like it does into a sponge. If there was any moon that late November night, it was shrouded by the fog, and all sounds were muffled in the damp air.

About twenty minutes passed. It was just after three in the morning before the driver's companion, in a broad Glaswegian accent, suggested that it was time to move the body.

They eased the rear doors open and as quietly as

possible, dragged the corpse across the floor of the van. Although the deceased was only five feet ten, he was of stocky build, so the process of lifting him out of the confined space proved difficult even for two people. Eventually, the Scotsman took charge. He bent down and slung the body over his right shoulder. Making sure it was well-balanced, he staggered over the rough ground, trying to avoid the scattering of broken bricks and wooden joists. Twice he lurched forward, tripping over some loose rubble, each time cursing out loud, but each curse was swallowed up by the heavy air. He came upon the gaping hole so suddenly that he almost tottered into it, but he held his stride until the driver caught up and steadied him.

The dead body slid from his shoulder onto the ground at the edge of the hole but he retained control by supporting it under its arms. The driver, who was taller and leaner, grasped the limp legs and together they fed the body into the hole. As its feet touched the bottom, they let go and the corpse crumpled into a heap on the ground below. The Scotsman brought a tarpaulin from the van and together they dropped it over the body and then manoeuvred it with some broken wooden joists that were lying around, until the body was completely hidden from any prying eyes.

The Scotsman would remain in the van overnight until the cement truck arrived the following morning. It would bring the material for the foundations of the house extension that would cover their makeshift burial. The driver nodded in appreciation and sloped off into the murk.

In the adjoining house, a nine-year-old boy, his sleep

disturbed by a nagging toothache, had climbed out of bed and knelt up against the skylight window in his bedroom. Peering through the gloom, he had just been able to make out a familiar van arriving in the back street. He knelt there for five minutes or so, waiting for further movement, but when there wasn't any, he crawled back under the bedclothes and with the pain easing, fell back into a deep sleep.

Chapter 1
Thursday, 6th January 2000

The mini-excavator clawed another bucket full of rubble from the demolished buildings. The operator swung the arm around at ninety degrees and released the contents into the back of a near-full truck. As the debris settled, another cloud of dust erupted. The truck driver was sitting in his cab reading the morning's racing page. He was used to the crashing sounds and the lurching from the truck as each load from the bucket landed heavily. He had his windows shut to prevent the dust and grime from entering his cab, but it didn't prevent some of the rubble bouncing onto his roof, with some sliding down the windscreen.

He glanced up and saw a wooden stick trailing remnants of blue paper. This spent firework reminded him of the big new-millennium celebrations that had taken place just a week ago. Then a larger piece of debris clattered on top of the cab and rolled down the windscreen to join the stick. Two large empty and unblinking eye sockets stared at him from a skull, human by the size and shape of it. The mouth part-filled with clay, had become hooked onto one of the windscreen wipers, giving it a cruel and twisted look. Its nose cavity was pressed against the glass.

The driver leapt from his cab and with a loud, guttural groan, staggered over to a group of bystanders, as if searching for safety in numbers. One of them, who seemed to be in charge, looked up from a large chart to see what the commotion was about. His eyes followed the line of the driver's pointing finger, and he moved swiftly over to the front of the truck and reached up.

He carefully unhooked the skull and lifted it down. He held it in the palms of both hands, but at full stretch – staring at the empty eye sockets. These seemed to stare back, as if challenging him to uncover their secrets. Finally, the boss cleared his thoughts and laid the bone carefully aside on the ground. He hollered at the operator to stop his excavator, took his mobile out of his jacket pocket and dialled a number, not 999, but the mobile number of an acquaintance.

The dialled number was answered almost immediately. 'Rich... It's Steve Hamshaw. You need to get over to number 9, Nuttall Road straight away. We've dug up a body... What? No, it's a skeleton, well, just the skull so far at least. Yes, we've stopped work and I'm getting everyone off site... OK, see you soon.'

Steve Hamshaw ended the call and slipped his phone back in his pocket. He barked at his workmen to stop what they were doing and move off site for an early brew. One of them stared at the skull as he was leaving and suggested that maybe it was one of those skeletons used by medics during their training, but it was said with a voice lacking any conviction. Another replied, rather dryly, that maybe the skeletons were finally coming out of the cupboard.

Steve walked over and peered into the hole made by the excavator. The outline, marked by the ridges of the bucket, snaked its way across the soil to where the skull had been unearthed. A weathered tarpaulin was hanging like a shroud, part of it still trapped by the debris.

Why had he instantly rung Richard when the skull was found? Could it not have just been an old Roman or Anglo-Saxon artifact, or, as mentioned, one a medic would use? But something made him think otherwise.

For a brief moment he was nine again and his brain was filled with a very different picture. The Victorian snooker hall, where the shopping centre was now, the cinder wasteland that had been turned into a concrete car-park, and the van that had been parked in the mist. He shuddered and the vision was gone.

Chapter 2
The same day

Detective Inspector Richard Whittle ducked under the police tape and moved over the rough ground to where a huddle of people were beavering away. The scene of crime team consisting of both forensic analysts and police was hard at work as per normal when a dead body had been found. The photographs had been taken, and because the ground had already been disturbed, the process of collecting bones and other items was taking place. This team would remain on site well into the night until they were sure all possible items relating to the body had been recovered. It would also mean some of the team sifting through the rubble already removed and deposited on a landfill site five miles away. That hadn't gone down well.

Richard ambled over to the edge of the hole and stood next to the owner. He took a packet of extra strong mints from his raincoat pocket and offered one to Steve Hamshaw.

'What was there, Steve?' His head nodded in a gesture to the hole.

'Extension to the original B&B – kitchen, washing room, drying room with an extra bathroom over there,'

Steve replied, pointing in the general direction of the pile of rubble.

'Wasn't this your folks' place, what, thirty years ago?'

'Grand-folks actually, and my mum. Didn't have a dad, at least not one I know of.'

'Oh yeah, I remember.'

They had been at school together, although not really close friends. Richard recollected that Steve had taken a good deal of stick and some bullying as a result of being from a single parent family. In those days it wasn't such a common occurrence as it is today, because such babies were more often put up for adoption. He also remembered that Steve's mum, Rose, had died in tragic circumstances when he and Steve were both fourteen.

'When was this extension built, Steve?'

'They had number 9 before I was born, bought number 11 when I was nine. That would be in '57. My grandpa had them knocked through into one and added these outbuildings.'

'So, who did this construction, then? Someone must have known about it being built and had a chance to put the body in.'

'How the hell should I know, Rich? I was only nine at the time.' Steve was getting irate and very defensive, as he thought of the repercussions from this find. He could remember that his grandpa and Jock Crammie had dug out the footings and then constructed the extension themselves. It was used as a rest area for the staff that his nan needed when numbers 9 and 11 were knocked into one large boarding house.

He remembered running through the empty corridors of the two houses and up and down the stairways when the visitors had left for the morning after their hearty breakfast. To a boy, it was like a castle where all sorts of imaginary games could take place. Steve was an only child and he loved his own company. The place was so big, he could be lost to the world for hours, especially in some of the cluttered attic rooms.

Steve's grandpa and Jock Crammie were builders by trade and he could remember during summer holidays, his nan would give him his grandpa's lunch all wrapped up in greaseproof paper and pack him off to whatever building site they were on.

He'd carry an old battered blue enamel pail, full of hot sweet tea and a thick, crusty bacon sandwich oozing with fat. By the time he'd reached the site the tea was cold and the fat had congealed on the bread. But his grandpa just loved the sandwich that way and a quick balance of the pail on the perpetual fire that burned on site would warm the tea up. They'd sit together in front of the fire, not saying much to each other, but sharing those moments.

Each day Steve would produce the daily paper, delivered too late for his grandpa to take with him. He would turn to the sports pages of the broadsheet and together they would read the county cricket scores. Steve learnt to read well, not at school, but there on those building sites. He'd learn of Wharton, Washbrook and Ikin for his native Lancashire. He'd yearn that Sutcliffe and Hutton would fail for Yorkshire, but his eye would always be drawn first to the exploits of Hampshire, wherever that was.

His hero was Roy Marshall. Hampshire's opening batsman and captain, who strode to the wicket with the aim of demolishing the opposition bowlers before lunch if possible – a swashbuckling West Indian, he used his bat instead of a sword to carve the bowling to the four corners of the ground. Marshall was ably supported by his young protégé, Jimmy Gray, and the dependable, stoic Henry Horton from Hereford, whose bat was so straight and solid that the bowlers would cry out in exasperation at yet another 'dot' ball.

His grandpa would sometimes produce a few chunks of chocolate or a handful of loose toffees for Steve to enjoy. He might also be allowed to remain on site and do some clearing up. Stacking a few bricks, or collecting off-cuts of wood.

But Steve was now remembering, most vividly, the time when his grandpa and Jock built the extension that was now being demolished.

Number 9, Nuttall Road was a three-storey Edwardian end-terraced property of a row of eight, situated just off the busy High Street in the small seaside town of Northcliffe. The town was situated midway between the bustling fishing port of Rossport, and the much larger, and more brash Southcliffe, which is world-renowned as a holiday destination. When they were built, in the early 1900s, these houses were owned by well-to-do families who could afford their own servants. As the trend to move into the countryside became popular, the houses were sold on to become businesses.

During the late 1950s and early '60s, the whole coastline bustled with folk who were brought in by bus and train from the northern mill towns. It was a time of comparative plenty for those folk brought up during, or who had served in, the Second World War. It was a time for workers to take their family away from the hardships and drudgery of factory life for a week of fun and relaxation at the seaside.

Wakes week prevailed for those Lancashire factory towns and whole communities decamped to the same resort to enjoy their week of rest and recuperation on limited budgets. This was the time before package holidays to Spain took off and it was the heyday of the boarding house landlady.

Steve remembered his grandparents allowing him to go and meet the visitors to number 9 from the coach station. He'd take with him a specially constructed suitcase carrier, adapted by his grandpa from an old pram, and a deep-sided orange box. Then, he'd cart the freight to its destination in exchange for an old brass thruppenny bit. In winter time, it became the fastest go-cart in the town as Steve and his mates used them to career down the almost deserted streets.

Those were halcyon days for Steve. He learned the value of earning money and the benefits of hard, honest work. His grandpa had instilled those ethics in him. It had carried forward until the day his grandpa had died from pneumonia, a consequence of the damage done to his lungs on the battlefields in Belgium in the Great War. Steve was eighteen at the time. By then he'd left school a year earlier to join his grandpa on the building sites. But with the death of his grandpa, his world fell apart.

No-one trusted an eighteen-year-old to build their prize homes. He got some work with other builders but it wasn't the same. His nan retired and moved to be with her son Brian, in South Wales, but it was other circumstances that forced Steve to leave not just the work, but the town and the one person he loved. He'd returned thirty years later, literally battle-scarred, but eager to confront his demons. He'd set up his own building business and this was his first project.

Only now, as Steve Hamshaw stood over the scene, he felt like all his new hopes, all that he valued in life, was about to fall down around him. He felt exposed and vulnerable. He didn't know why, only realising that his life would never be the same again. And all because of a pile of old bones.

Chapter 3
The same day

The search of the site took longer than expected. The digger had caused havoc around the probable location of the grave. Richard's boss wanted a complete sifting of the area in case this turned out to be a serial murder enquiry. No more bodies were found, but bits of clothing, the tarpaulin and some old rusty tools were unearthed and bagged for further examination.

Steve spent long moody periods at the site, watching the progress from a distance, expecting at any moment for his grandpa to appear. Sometimes Richard Whittle turned up as well and they stood together, sharing memories of their early childhood.

On one visit, Richard produced a photograph showing a slab of concrete recovered from the site. There were some markings impressed in it. 'This looks like a date and some initials, Steve. Any idea?'

Steve smiled. '1157 SH. That's November 1957 and my initials. Those are my finger marks. I made them the day they laid the base. I wasn't there when the mixer arrived and dumped the concrete. But it was just still wet enough to take my finger-marks when I got home. I'd forgotten about that.'

'So that's the time the concrete was laid, then?'

'Yes. I guess so. Any idea yet whose body it is, Rich?'

'Not yet. We're running a check on any missing persons in the area about that time. But with the possibility of visitors around, it could be quite tricky.'

'What, you think someone had too much to drink and fell down the hole the night before the concrete was laid?'

'Could be. Probably not, though. We'll know more after the post mortem. Steve – I've got to ask this. We'd like a DNA sample. As it's your grandfather's hole, so to speak, we need it to eliminate him from any relevant evidence we might find.'

Steve paused. 'Or put him in the frame?'

'I hope it doesn't come to that, Steve.'

'OK, I'll come down to the station.'

They both continued to stare at the rubble, each immersed in their own thoughts. It was Richard who eventually broke the silence.

'Remember the snooker hall over the back? Did you ever go in there when you were young?'

'I did once, but never again. Too scary. Anyway, I'd have 'got what for' if my nan had found out. My grandpa used to go in there, although my nan never knew. Or at least, she never let on she knew.'

'Your nan knew everything, Steve. I didn't know her well, I only met her when I came round to play or when my dad called round with me in tow, but I always felt she got every secret I had out of me, without me realising. She was a lovely person. But that place over there…' Richard nodded in the direction of where the snooker hall once stood. 'That was a right den of thieves back in those days. My dad used to tell me that.'

Richard had followed his dad into the police force. Sergeant George Whittle was well-known and well-respected in the town by both young and old alike. If you could define an old-fashioned bobby, George Whittle was it. Always ready to help anyone, firm with the kids if they stepped out of line – even admonishing Richard in front of his friends once when they got up to some high jinks – and unyielding with any rogue who caused problems on his patch. Richard adored his dad and had been devastated when he was diagnosed with lung cancer after thirty-odd years of heavy smoking. It was the high regard that the people of Northcliffe held for George Whittle that made Richard join the police force. And it was his father's legacy that had brought him back to Northcliffe, as an inspector when the opportunity arose.

'Did your grandfather knock the snooker hall down as well?'

'No, that was still standing when I left in '66, although it was derelict by then. The shopping mall was built in the early '70s, I think. I wonder if there are any other dead bodies buried under there?'

'We'll not find out until that monstrosity is knocked down. And we'll be long gone before that happens,' said Richard, as he ambled away and left Steve to his own thoughts.

Steve went back to work. At the same auction where he'd bought numbers 9 and 11 Nuttall Road, he'd bid for and won an old chapel in need of a massive renovation, together with over an acre of adjoining land. At least he could immerse himself in another project whilst the grisly goings-on at the back of number 9 were being resolved. His mantra of life was always to strive to succeed, to complete and then move on, not allowing anything or anyone to impinge on his structured and self-contained way.

Except now for number 9, Nuttall Road. This was Steve's history. This place held the only memories he wanted to remember. The grim extension had no attachment for Steve, nor number 11. But number 9 housed all the good memories of growing up, so large and grand to a small boy that it must be retained and restored to its original state.

Steve would complete it and move in. Here he would find the contentment and safety that had been missing for so many years. But the house held a secret that prevented this happening. Why, after securing his purchase and drawing up his plans, was he being thwarted by some grisly act from the past? And was he aware in the dark recesses of his mind, of the reason for and the perpetrator of this act?

So, reluctantly, he moved on to the church restoration project. Strange really, because this was the type of venture Steve dearly loved. But something nagged at his brain and in quiet moments his thoughts always came back to number 9 and the horrific find under the foundations.

Chapter 4
Friday, 7th January 2000

Early the following morning, Richard Whittle made the road journey of nineteen miles to the area's forensic laboratory in the grand setting of Washington Hall in Euxton, just on the outskirts of the county town of Preston. After donning a safety gown, glasses and mask, he was shown into the laboratory. There, presiding over a table full of mismatched bones, he saw the imposing figure of David Leadbeater, the chief forensic pathologist. David had moved from Hull to take charge of the pathology lab two years previously. Over that time, he and Richard had built up a rapport of mutual trust and admiration for each other.

'An interesting puzzle you've set me, Richard. You've surpassed yourself,' David said without looking up. 'Now let's get the preliminaries over with. It's male, best estimate at the moment is late 20s, early 30s. I'll confirm after further testing, but I won't be wrong. His height would have been about 1.8 metres, or five foot ten inches in old money.'

David Leadbeater was a legend in his field and anything he concluded would, almost certainly, turn out be correct.

'The time of death would be around November 1957. But I think you'll have worked that out for yourself, Richard!'

'Yes, I had. Seeing that was the day the cement was laid. Any possibility of a DNA match?' asked Richard, smiling.

'We've sent DNA samples off for testing. The results should be back by tomorrow morning. As it's been in the ground forty years the chances of a match are very slim, but we could possibly get a near profile match with a living relative. There are enough teeth in this skull to do a dental check. But as there were no databases in those days, the chances are minimal.'

'What about cause of death?' asked Richard, leaning over to look more closely at the skull.

'Ah, yes. I was coming to that. Look here. There's severe damage to the occipital bone, the one at the lower back of the cranium. It encircles the spinal cord. There – look. I suspect a blow of some kind.'

'Would you say accidental or intentional?'

'I couldn't say for certain. It could have been caused by using a lot of force, say using a heavy bar, or by falling against something solid. But, as you can see, there's also damage to the temporal bone on the left side, just above, and forward of the ear. Look – see – here. Again, could have been a blunt instrument or hit on falling. But that's for you to find out.'

'Could that blow have caused his death?'

'It's doubtful. It probably would have stunned him. No, the blow to the back of the cranium was the cause of death.'

'Anything else, David?'

'We've scanned the other bones that we've found

already. We've got most of them, so I don't expect any other major discoveries. The scan showed that he'd broken his left arm just below the elbow. If he's local, we may be able to match it with hospital records. But again, hospital records, so long ago, are very difficult to locate.'

'Thanks David. That gives us a good start. Let me know when you have a match.'

'Identifying the body will be the comparatively easy bit, Richard. We've got all this debris from the site to process.' David Leadbeater pointed at a table stacked with plastic bags in the corner. 'It's a pity it wasn't an archaeological dig rather than the work of some ham-fisted workmen. There were bits strewn everywhere. It's going to be difficult to determine which items are relevant to the case and which aren't. But I'll concentrate on the analysis of the tarpaulin as we know that was found covering the body.'

'Afternoon everybody. Right, settle down. Sergeant, let's start with what we know.' The incident room at Southcliffe police headquarters, which served the whole of the Fylde area, hushed into silence and Sergeant Cora Stone rose to speak. Sergeant Stone had been deployed to Southcliffe twelve months previously, after completing her fast-track programme. In two years, she hoped to make the rank of inspector. This was her first murder case and she didn't want to mess it up.

'The skeleton of an adult male was discovered during a builder's excavation behind number 9, Nuttall Road in Northcliffe. We know the concrete was laid sometime in late 1957 by Tom Hamshaw. He was the owner at the time and was extending his boarding house.

Mr Hamshaw died in 1966.

'We've checked the missing person files for around that time and the only individual that meets the age and height profile is a certain Terry Breeze. Breeze was thought to be involved in the famous bank robbery here in the 1950s, 8th August 1957 to be precise,' Cora said, glancing at Richard Whittle, who was known as a stickler for detail. 'Terry Breeze was believed by CID at the time to have scarpered to the Costa Del Sol with the proceeds of his dodgy life to start anew with what would then have become his hard-earned savings.' A titter of laughter rang round the room.

'It would appear now that Terry Breeze could have been lying low much closer to home, and not of his own volition. We've obtained a DNA sample from Terry's eldest son, Gary, a person also well known to us. The results should be back tomorrow.'

'Thank you, Sergeant.'

Now Richard Whittle took centre stage. He removed two photographs of the skeleton from his folder, and attached them to an empty whiteboard. A board that in the ensuing weeks would become the centre for all clues and leads to be documented. Above the photographs he wrote "TERRY BREEZE?"

'Until it's proved otherwise, the chief constable wants us to work on the premise that the skeleton is Terry Breeze. The cause of death, at this juncture, is thought to be a broken neck caused by a severe blow to the base of the skull, either accidental or deliberate. There was further damage to the temporal bone, which again could have been accidental or deliberate. There were no other obvious injuries to the skeleton which would indicate a bullet or a knife. So, we'll work on the premise that he died from a broken neck. We can tie the burial of the body, although not the time of death, to a specific day. Constable Atkinson, you have some information?'

'Yes, Sir.' A young fresh-faced uniformed officer, Daniel Atkinson had already removed his notebook from his top pocket and had it open ready at the right page.

'According to Steven Hamshaw's statement, the footings were dug the day before the delivery of the cement. That would be during November 1957. I phoned my father-in-law because he's in the building trade and he told me the main local supplier of cement at that time was Dodgson and Sons. They sold out to a firm called Castle Cement who in turn were taken over in 1991 by...'

'Constable, we don't need a history lesson, just get to the point,' smiled Richard, as an audible chuckle was heard in the room.

'Sorry, Sir. I phoned their head office and they've been able to locate the docket. It was dated...' Constable Atkinson referred back to his notebook, turning the page over, '19th November 1957 at 7:45am. It was signed for as well, but the signature is illegible. I've got a faxed copy here, Sir', he said, waving an A4 piece of paper in the air. 'They're sending me the original by post.'

'Well done, Constable. Make sure the original docket arrives and you log it in as evidence. We may need a handwriting expert to take a look at it.'

Daniel Atkinson sat back in his chair, elated and rather proud of himself. It was the first piece of real detective work he'd done since joining the Southcliffe force nine months ago. He'd finished his probation period and was enjoying being a "bobby on the beat", but his wife Angie had other plans for him. She was always saying, 'You've been to college, Dan. You're better than those other constables. You can make inspector, no problem. You just need to push yourself forward a bit more, show them you can do the job.'

He couldn't wait to tell Angie when he got home. This time he'd reply, 'I got lots of praise from the inspector. He said I'd done a good job. Could be you're right, Angie, and I'm cut out for this type of work. It's a big case, love. Word has it that they might need uniform backup for this.'

In the briefing room, DC Barry Crompton couldn't hold back any longer. 'Sir, what's so important about this case? A villain's found dead over forty years on. Whoever killed him is probably dead as well. We've got a full incident team set up. They're signing up for overtime like there's no tomorrow, drafting uniform in. Why?'

'I understand your point, Barry, but Terry Breeze, villain or no villain, was possibly murdered and he deserves the same sort of attention anybody else would get. However,' Richard Whittle paused to get the full effect, 'we also believe Breeze was part of a horrendous robbery in our town, the biggest and nastiest in our history. The security guard, Arthur Dowling, was stabbed and died later from his injury. We've applied to retrieve the evidence from the archive and now there's DNA testing available, we should be able to shed some light on it. Forensics have a lot of work on now, but we're hopeful to get a match soon.

'Until we're proved wrong, we assume there is a link between the robbery and Breeze's murder. There were a lot of red faces at the time because the perpetrators weren't identified. A lot of finger-pointing. The bank's still offering a reward and the council are putting pressure on the super to get it solved. There wasn't much money taken. To be honest, it was a bit of a botched job, but it's left a stain on this town that needs clearing up.

'So – yes, the purse-strings have been loosened, but I'm not signing any blank cheques. I want this run efficiently and professionally, and I want a result. The two investigations will run concurrently. Normally the bank robbery would come under the jurisdiction of Inspector Deacons at the Cold Case Unit, but the powers-that-be have said we do it all, for the moment at least. Sergeant Stone, you'll co-ordinate with your opposite number in that unit, so that we keep to the correct protocols.'

The room became quiet as they all absorbed the inspector's words. This was a high-profile case. A lot of hard work, yes, but offering a chance to shine. Rumour had it that Richard Whittle made his way up the ladder on a high-profile case in the Met before coming here. So, it was possible. The silence and the mood were broken by Richard's voice.

'Right. I want to know all associates of Terry Breeze in 1957 and whether they're alive or dead. I want to know who was there when the delivery of cement was made. I want to know who disappeared around the time of 19th November 1957, or just after. Any new characters who came onto the scene about that time. This bank robbery was planned, not opportunist. They messed it up, but they knew the wages were in the safe and the security was not up to scratch.

'Go through all statements and police records, make

a note of anything that looks suspicious. Finally, I want to know anyone that knew Tom Hamshaw and if there were any obvious arguments between him and Terry Breeze. I don't want Steve Hamshaw interviewed, though. I've already spoken to him and I'll do any necessary further questioning myself. Cora, you organise the rosters. Constable Atkinson, you'll be temporarily assigned to the team. I'll clear it with your inspector. Cora, put Atkinson on the police statements and records. He seems to have an eye for paperwork.'

With that he walked quickly out of the room. Richard Whittle needed some fresh air. He was certain that this case would be difficult and would open up old wounds and memories. He also had a big fear that he could be unearthing something that would spiral out of control and undermine everything he believed in. His premonition was soon to come true.

Daniel Atkinson fairly flew out of the room. This was even better than he expected. He'd find that missing link, that vital clue which would open up the case. It'd be somewhere in the police files, it always was. He remembered what they had said at police college after he'd passed out as the top recruit for his year.

'It's the simple things that are missed, even by good coppers. It needs an orderly and conscientious mind to find them. That's what you're good at, Atkinson. That's what the police force wants from you.'

And now it was Constable Daniel Atkinson's chance to prove them right.

Chapter 5

Terry Breeze had been trouble almost from the day he'd been born. His father, Jed, hadn't set him a good example, though. The Breeze family had always veered close to the wrong side of the law. They were often referred to as "loveable rogues". If you didn't cross them, they left you alone. This was the seaside, so in the summer months it would be packed with holidaymakers ready to part with their hard-earned pay in return for some fun and escapism from fifty weeks of dreary, humdrum living. The Breeze family owned the vast majority of amusement arcades in Northcliffe, so were there to help the visitors achieve these goals, but with a view to lining their own pockets. It was a service that they willingly provided. In addition, any minor scam was deemed acceptable – the police often turned a blind eye. It was alleged that some were even given back-handers to look the other way.

The yearly Gala in July was eagerly awaited by the town as the pinnacle of the summer months' activity. The morning procession through the main streets of Northcliffe was a joy for all the children of the town as they dressed up, danced, and sang their way along the streets lined with a mixture of proud parents and holidaymakers. The brass bands brought in from neighbouring areas filled the air with pomp and grandeur. The procession would wend its way through the streets to finally finish at the fields on the edge of the town, where the travellers had already set up their funfair.

Their caravans would have arrived over the previous few days. The travellers would busy themselves setting up their stalls and rides. These ranged from sedate roundabouts of cars that honked, fire engines that rang and buses that went ding-a-ling for the children, up to the whippy, noisy and exciting waltzers and dodgems for the daring teenagers. Copious supplies of coconuts and goldfish were on hand as stall prizes for the excited victors.

The Breezes took a share of the proceeds. They rented the travellers the land for a "generous price" and were instrumental in the Saturday night fight which always took place, pitting the town's youth against the travellers' best.

There was something of an occasion about this annual fight. An unwritten law – men-against-men. Girls safely out of sight. No weapons. The winners were the gang who gained the upper hand. Normally, this was the well-honed travellers as this was to them a weekly end-of-party event. But everyone was a winner. Northcliffe's youth had bragging rights amongst themselves for another year after boasting of their exploits to one another and the travellers left content that their reputation remained intact and that an invitation for the following year was not jeopardised.

But Terry Breeze changed all that. He was fifteen and didn't like to be second-best. He was a bully all through school, but because of his family, no-one ever put him right. The previous year he'd gone with his older brothers to the local end-of-Gala rumble, but watched from the sidelines. He couldn't understand why there were unwritten rules to this ruckus and in the intervening twelve months resolved to change them more to his way of thinking and acting. So the next year, when his brothers included him in the fracas, Terry secreted his flick-knife in his pocket. A knife he had every intention of using. He'd identified one particular young traveller who, like him, had watched from the sidelines the previous year. Terry made a bee-line for this youngster and confronted him.

He goaded the young lad into a fist fight and the lad, once involved, was drawn away from the main ruckus to a quieter area. Once Terry had him isolated, he flicked out his blade and drove it into the youngster's gut. The boy lay at the back of the caravans, losing blood and semi-conscious, whilst the main event went on oblivious. He was found dead later that night and although there was no proof as to who had done the deed, Terry's family knew what had gone on. But they shielded him.

The travellers were enraged and ran amok in the town centre, smashing windows and looting shops. The police, who normally took a back seat, got involved but they couldn't pin anything on Terry either. The Gala continued in years to come, but with a much heavier police presence and an undercurrent of tension. From that year onwards, instead of a touch of sadness at the end of the week, the township was always glad when Sunday came and the travellers packed up and moved on.

So Terry grew up in the safety of the Breeze clan,

but generally he was known as a nasty piece of work. He gathered like-minded thugs around him and created havoc among business owners who sometimes paid back-handers not to have their shops trashed and to keep drugs out of the public bars and burgeoning coffee houses. He married Sally, whom he treated with disdain. There were numerous affairs with younger girls. Many a father would threaten to do for Terry if he came anywhere near their daughter. But it all tended to be pub talk. Terry and Sally had two boys, Gary and Phil, who learnt from their father and carried on the family tradition of being unpleasant people.

Gary was in the same class at both primary and secondary school as both Steve and Richard. There were numerous incidents of clashes at school between Gary and Steve, with neither getting the upper hand. The Breeze family reluctantly respected Steve's grandfather so it wasn't possible for Gary to call on them to back him up in any devious business he got up to at Steve's expense.

When Terry disappeared in 1957, the Breeze clan closed ranks. Word had it, that even they didn't know where Terry had gone. It was generally felt that Terry's dad, Jed, was none too bothered where his son had disappeared to, as now the police would pay him less attention. He'd already decided to make the Breeze family interests more lawful, to leave his grandsons a better legacy. He could see that treating the local bigwigs with respect paid dividends. There was less confrontation so less interest paid to him by the police.

Jed Breeze became something of a celebrity in the town. Many top acts in the entertainment world had summer houses in Northcliffe because they were appearing in the big venues of Southcliffe. He managed to lure some of them to appear in his theatre to draw in the visitors and make them part with some of the cash they would normally spend in the larger resort.

Having said that, Jed Breeze didn't become a soft touch to any ideas of a take-over by any neighbouring would-be thugs. The amusement arcades also became more refined. Bingo took off and that brought the punters in. Jed cottoned on early that a loudspeaker outside the arcade blasting the bingo calls to the passing population was a big draw for anyone hoping to make a winning. Later he took over one of the local cinemas, converting it into a plush upmarket bingo hall where drinks and food were served cheaply to make the punters want to stay longer.

People would say that Northcliffe thrived under the Breeze family and over the years their nastiness dissipated as Gary, now head of the family, strove to keep them legitimate. However, Phil had inherited many of his dad's bad traits and he could still be the cause of isolated bother, unless kept in check by his elder brother.

Chapter 6
Saturday, 8th January 2000

The Whittles were having an early breakfast when Richard got a text from forensics.

It read, 'Interesting finding. Call or come over asap. David.'

'Short and to the point as always,' thought Richard. He rang David Leadbeater straight away but got through to answerphone.

'He's so infuriating,' laughed Richard. 'He always texts me and then walks away from the phone. Why say "call or come over", when he always means, "Richard, come over?" It drives me mad.'

'He may be infuriating, Rich, but he's good at his job and a valued customer of the gallery,' said Jill, sitting across from Richard at the breakfast table.

When Richard was promoted to detective inspector and came back up north, Jill left a prized job she had at a leading art gallery in the centre of London. However, she was so well thought of that her boss decided he needed a presence up north and she was asked to set up a new gallery in Preston town centre, with the task of promoting the talents of local artists. 'There may be a new David Hockney up there that we don't know about,' her boss had said. 'I can leave it up to you to find him or her. We've also got a good number of clients living in the north, so with your skills, Jill, I'm sure it can be a success. Take a selection of paintings you think will interest them to get you started.'

Preston was trying to get "city status', so they'd commissioned a drive to attract new and vibrant businesses to the area. The gallery was one of the first in a new complex that had been built the previous year. It had been a major success after its opening and had the effect of attracting other similar upmarket shops into the same complex. A ladies' fashion shop, a new delicatessen with a lovely tea-room attached and an art-cum-model shop had opened within the first six months. Other independent retailers had followed suit, making the whole shopping experience in this area of Preston much more enjoyable.

David loved his art and was found in the gallery most Saturday mornings, when he wasn't examining a body. He'd be there with his wife, Mary, perusing the latest offerings, with both giving suggestions of new up-and-coming artists they'd heard about. Jill had just started on the preparations for a Spring exhibition to be held the following month, showcasing two artists that Mary had recommended.

Richard rang Cora Stone and asked her to join him at the lab.

'Remind David about the exhibition next month, Rich, if you get the chance,' Jill prompted. 'I'd value Mary's opinion on how to best showcase these artists.'

'I'll try, if I can, love. I think David will want some input on that as well. Drat the man,' Richard said, jokingly. 'He's too good at everything he does.'

'But he won't solve this crime, love. You're the man for that, I know you are. Drive safely and go the scenic route. It helps you think, when you've got problems.'

'You know me too well, Jill. Yes, I'll go the back way. Hope the preps go well. Love you.' Then after a quick kiss, he was on his way.

The drive to Preston was pleasant as Richard took the back route, along two 'A' roads and a cut-through via the agricultural college to get there. And as it was early Saturday morning, the roads were empty of traffic. It gave Richard chance to collect his thoughts about the case and the effect it must be having on Steve. 'I wouldn't have wanted to find a body in a hole my grandfather had dug and filled in,' he thought. 'There may be some other explanation, but at first sight, it looks clear cut. Tom Hamshaw has to be high on our list of suspects, but I can't see any motive. Thank God I had a dad and mum who were always there for me and gave me the love I needed.'

Richard's professionalism soon kicked in and he focused his mind back onto who might be responsible. Jed Breeze and Tom had always had a rivalry, mainly because Tom stood up to Jed despite any intimidation, but this was way off what Tom would do. Maybe David's findings would shed some light on any motive.

His route was shorter than by the motorway and it skirted the town centre, bringing him out on the eastern side where the laboratories were located. Even so, Cora was already there, standing outside the lab in the cold sunshine. They were expected, so were ushered through the reception area and security with ease.

'Right David, what's so important that you need me

here, and why do you never answer your phone?'

'I think you need to hear all this in person, Richard, and good morning to you too. We've had some major findings from the DNA tests. Three big ones actually. Ah-ha, the drinks have arrived.' Two coffees and a decaf tea for Cora were brought in by one of the staff and plonked down on David's desk.

'This looks set to be a long session,' thought Richard, but with the expectation that the case would at last be moving on.

'We took the victim's DNA from the petrous bone which is the hardest bone in the body, sent it off for tests and comparison with the other samples taken at the scene, and the results are in,' said David.

Cora smirked. 'Sounds like the Eurovision Song Contest results,' she thought, but said nothing.

David, detecting that something he had said was funny, but not for the life of him able to figure out what it was, continued. 'We've got three major findings. The first finding is regarding DNA. From that, we've confirmed that it is indeed Terry Breeze's skeleton. That sample gave a 50% match to his son Gary. We couldn't do any testing at the time of the robbery, so it was never done. But now... we have a match between our skeleton and the bank robbery. Breeze's DNA was found on the clothes worn by the guard. It was on the left shoulder of his uniform, to be precise.'

'So...' interrupted Cora, '...that corroborates the witness statement that the person who knifed Arthur Dowling grabbed him by the shoulder before sticking the knife in. So, Breeze knifed the guard.'

'It's looking that way,' commented Richard.

'The second finding,' said David, clawing back

centre stage, 'concerns the tarpaulin that we are assuming covered the body before the cement was poured. It had a number of clear samples on it. We're working through them. Some are from the workmen currently on site and they've already been eliminated. But two stood out. One we can't attribute to anyone registered, but it matches a blood sample that was recovered from the cash till in the bank after the robbery.'

'That's number two robber,' said Richard. 'From the bank cashier's statement, we know that the robber gashed his hand on the sharp edge of the till as he tried to open it. That's very good news.' He glanced at Cora.

'I found that another of the samples taken from the tarpaulin has approximately a 27% match to the sample given by Steve Hamshaw, which would make that person in all probability one of his grandparents,' commented David.

'Tom Hamshaw,' said Richard ruefully. 'Makes sense, as it was his tarpaulin. Could make him a possible suspect in the body disposal, but even if so, I can't see that he was involved in the robbery.'

'Sir, we must keep an open mind. This looks like a falling out between thieves. We know that the witness thought the other two robbers were taken aback by the stabbing. Things went wrong at the bank. Could be, they went wrong afterwards as well.'

'I know you're right, Cora – just thinking out loud. Are there any links between Tom Hamshaw and the robbery, David?'

'None so far, but there was no DNA left by your third bank robber. However, there's still lots more testing to be done,' he said, looking over in the direction of the stack of plastic bags containing material gathered from the site. 'Findings will continue in dribs and drabs, I'm afraid.'

'Right, David, you've given us two findings, and knowing you, you've kept the best 'til last. Let's hear it, then.'

'Yes, you're right, Richard, I have – and this is so left-field!'

Chapter 7
Sunday, 9th January 2000

It had been three days since the digger had disturbed the remains and Steve was getting on with his chapel renovation. He was standing in the centre of the now empty shell with his architect, examining the plans, when he saw a concerned-looking Richard Whittle approach.

'Hi Steve, I thought I might find you here. Have you got a moment? I need to talk to you.'

'Sure, Rich. We'd finished anyway. Rob, I'll get back to you with my changes. Thanks for coming in today.' The architect rolled up his drawing and left.

'So, it's Terry Breeze, is it?' Steve said, turning to face Richard. I thought he'd scarpered to the Costa Del Sol.'

'Word gets around quickly, Steve.'

'No doubt you'll be getting some grief from the Breeze clan. I'd hate to be in your shoes.'

'Yep, they've been making noises, but it's another development that I'd like to talk to you about.'

'Go on.'

'Anywhere we can sit down, Steve?'

Turning away, Steve led Richard across the empty chapel past some full pallets of cement and sand to a small room that had been set up as a makeshift office-cum-kitchen. On the way across, Steve's thoughts turned dark. 'They've found something to link the death to my grandpa.'

He turned and faced Richard, awaiting the bombshell. 'Thanks for providing us with your DNA sample, Steve. We've used the results as a comparison and it's turned up an interesting development.'

'I thought you wanted my sample to eliminate my grandpa from what you found. If it's from the tarpaulin, then it was his stuff. His DNA is bound to be on there.'

'It's not that, Steve. Yes, we got a match on the tarpaulin, but I agree, it proves nothing and we did use it for elimination purposes. But when we have a DNA sample, we have to do further comparisons on all the evidence that's been gathered.' Richard paused and looked at Steve. 'We've got a match with your DNA, but it's not what I expected.'

'What do you mean a match?' Steve was agitated and confused. 'A match with what?'

'Steve, there's no easy way to say this. Your DNA profile doesn't match anything we found at the scene that the killer may have left – but it does match with the tests we did on the skeleton.'

'Sorry, I don't understand. What skeleton?'

'We took DNA from the skull you unearthed. We compared the results from a sample given by Gary Breeze. It gave a 50% match, so the skeleton is definitely his dad, Terry. We then used the results from your sample for a comparison with the DNA from the skull. That was a 50% match as well.' Richard let those last few words sink in.

Steve stood motionless staring at the sun's rays as they cast their bright beams on a stained-glass window, highlighting a face which for a moment looked just like his grandpa's. The words sunk in, slowly releasing memories and visions he had thought he'd forgotten. As he started his reply, he was puzzled, but then his thoughts seemed to clarify those complexities and it all started to make sense.

'Let me get this right. So, none of the items found near the body implicates my grandpa. And my DNA is a match of that bastard Terry Breeze... that means we must be related. That means he's probably my dad.'

'Yep, almost certain he is... You'd no inkling?'

'No – sorry, I've got to...' Steve ran to the door and out into the fresh air. The enormity of what he had just heard hit him forcibly like a solid punch in the gut, making him throw up on the grass outside. The acid bile from his stomach made him gag repeatedly. Sweat oozed from his forehead and he found he was gasping for air. His chest heaved as it tried to fill his tightened lungs with oxygen. Then his breathing became more normal and he stood upright, staring out over the green fields where cows carried on grazing, oblivious to Steve's world being turned upside down.

So after all this time, he finally knew who his father was. Steve remembered his grandpa saying to his nan many times. 'That Breeze family. This town would be better off without them. Especially that lowlife, Terry Breeze. He's the worst. Someone will see him off sooner or later. You mark my words.'

Now someone had killed Terry Breeze. The ramifications of that last thought began to become clear to Steve. Could that someone have been his grandpa?

Chapter 8
Later the same day

Richard left, muttering something that sounded like, 'I'll be in touch,' leaving Steve to process this bombshell.

As he looked across the open fields, Steve found himself reminiscing about his childhood. Behind the row of boarding houses in Nuttall Road there had been an open piece of derelict land littered with pot-holes and covered in sharp cinders. Further over used to be a large, dilapidated, Victorian brick building with a leaking roof and a boarded-up back door.

To any nine-year-old this building looked ripe for exploration. The building was owned by Gloria's dad, Don Ward. Gloria was Steve's childhood best friend. They did everything together. At school they were inseparable and in the long summer holidays they played together every day. Gloria lived with her parents just round the corner from Steve and both their homes backed onto the cinder wasteland.

Neither Steve nor Gloria knew what went on in that eerie brick building. They had both been warned that, on pain of something indescribable happening to them, they were not to go anywhere near that building.

'I remember one sunny day, in the school holidays. We'd had our tea and afterwards we were allowed to play out until bedtime. We sat, looking across the derelict land at this ugly ramshackled building which slowly but surely took on the appearance of a holy shrine awaiting a visit from its two most faithful disciples.

I'm not sure whose idea it was finally to explore, but there and then, we set off on our trek across no man's land, carefully avoiding the deep bomb craters and enemy machine-gun posts, until we made the relative security of the rear of the building. We had already picked out this vantage point from as far away as my grandparents' back yard. It was thickly populated by three-foot-tall stinging nettles and rampant bindweed, all well in flower at this time of year. So, it provided good, albeit prickly, cover from any prying eyes that were hanging out the washing. We'd left behind Gloria's teddy, sitting on a low wall. As usual we'd given it instructions that if anyone came, it was to shout a warning or bang its foot on a metal sheet propped nearby, and as usual, we didn't get a warning so no-one must have come!

We reached the building, aiming for a piece of loose corrugated sheeting which was propped up against the back door. When removed, it revealed a jagged entrance, small enough for two nine-year-olds to squeeze through. On gaining access, our eyes quickly grew accustomed to a dark, dusty, and deserted room. An old painted pine table leant against the wall in one corner. Some chairs were randomly strewn across the floor and there was a distinct smell, as well as droppings, confirming the presence of rats.

We now focused on the bright glimmer of light shining through the glass skylight above the internal door. Creeping quietly towards it, stepping over broken glass, we half-expected the door to suddenly spring open and for us to be set upon by a crack German Panzer Division. There was a muffled echo from the other side which sounded like a series of cracks. Our minds ran wild. Rifle butts bearing down on unprotected skulls, or fingers being snapped by those nut-crackers that you bring out at Christmas. The relative quiet was interspersed with bouts of guttural laughter, followed by more muted conversation.

The door was locked, but one of the pine panels in its frame was split. The gap was too high for a nine-year-old to reach, but by righting a chair which seemed stable enough, we were able to climb onto it to gain a better view. Balanced precariously, we could now see row upon row of green-topped tables filled with brightly-coloured balls, illuminated by overhead lighting. Men were bending over the tables with long pointed sticks, cracking the balls into one another with some disappearing off the corners and sides of the table into some sort of small net. Thick smoke hung in the air, with wisps spiralling upwards, attracted to the lights and hovering thickly under the tobacco-stained ceiling.

Over in one corner some men were drinking from tall glasses whilst swapping jokes. The shimmer of lighting highlighted the tables. Between them was all gloom and shadows. Men emerged, in turn, from this dim world into the bright light to hit a shot and then return to the darkness.

The table just off to the right, but nearest the door, caught my eye. A man must have come to the far end of the table to play his shot. He bent over the table, peered down the length of his cue and as he prepared to play, his eyes locked onto mine. I couldn't turn away. I couldn't do anything but stare. Those eyes were familiar. Those eyes were my family's eyes. They were my grandpa's eyes.

I know now that certain snooker players can hover over a shot for some time before playing it. That it's a game of precision not speed. But the time my grandpa took over his shot was ridiculously long. Instead of looking at the ball, his eyes seemed to look beyond the edge of the table at me. My hair stood on end, my skin tingled with fear and I fought back the tears that welled up in my eyes.

His eyes told me to get down off the chair, go back out through the hole in the wall and back across no-man's-land and report to my Nan as it was bedtime. Gloria, sensing that something was amiss, dutifully led the way back through the hole. I was about to follow when I took a glance into a dark corner of the room. There, staring at me were the scariest eyes I have ever seen. The eyeballs seemed to poke out like sticks from their sockets. The grotesque shape of its face looked set to devour me. I heard a voice in my head telling me not to move. I stood still, froze more likely, trying not to meet its gaze. The eyes seemed to move slightly, as if now looking into another part of the room. I took that opportunity to make a dash for the inviting hole.

Outside, I regained my breath whilst Gloria quizzed me on what had delayed me. I garbled some response like something looked interesting but it turned out to be nothing and we said no more about it. But I knew Gloria didn't believe me, although she never said anything and life moved on.

Chapter 9
Wednesday, 12th January 2000

Steve was standing and staring at the cordoned-off hole at the back of number 9, Nuttall Road, recalling his rivalry with Gary Breeze, the person he now knew to be his half-brother. He was still trying to come to terms with the scale of what had been discovered.

'Hello, Steve.'

The familiar voice brought him back to the present. He turned and saw a slim, blonde woman, about his age, wearing a cosy blue knitted coat and hood to keep off the icy wind. Steve looked shocked. 'Hi, Gloria.' He would normally have been glad to see her. But because she was now married to Gary Breeze, it seemed really strange.

'Steve, I've heard the news. I don't know what to say. Sorry for everything really, I suppose. It must have been a real shock for you. Are they sure Terry Breeze was your dad?'

'They've done a second test and Rich rang this morning to confirm it.' Steve paused and looked up, out to sea, searching for the horizon line. But the sky was grey and that was mirrored in the colour of the sea. He detected a charcoal-like mist that hung across where the two met. Sometimes he felt the urge to swim out there, into that mist and be shut off from all of life's nastiness. For these few moments with Gloria, he suddenly felt that same urge. To be enveloped in her mist again, to not to be able to see beyond the confines of the two of them. That's how it used to be. For him, it still could be. But for her, time and circumstances had moved on.

'I was thinking of all those times when I wondered who my dad was. Mum would never tell me. Maybe one day, if she hadn't died, she may have. I didn't think my grandparents knew either, but now I'm not so sure. I know why Mum didn't say anything now.'

He turned to Gloria and she looked into his eyes. She could see the hurt that he had inside. A pain that was gnawing away at him. He looked so vulnerable, so much in need of comfort. She remembered all too well how she had given comfort to him in the past. How they had seemed so right for each other. But that was a long time ago.

'I always thought my mum didn't know who my dad was. I thought he was probably one of my nan's visitors and one day he'd come back and recognise me. Mum would forgive him and he'd move in and play football with me, teach me sailing – be my dad. I never gave up hope. Even before this, I wanted to find him.' Steve looked at Gloria again. 'Can you believe that at fifty-two, I still wanted a dad? Daft, isn't it? I wasn't after anyone special, nobody famous, nobody rich, just a dad.' Steve eyes latched onto a small fishing boat heading for Rossport, bobbing in the now choppy sea. A low hum emanated from its engine as it crossed behind the pier and out of sight. 'But now. Now I wish I didn't have a dad. I wish I'd never found out.'

'Do you think Terry knew you were his son?'

Steve shuddered. He closed his eyes tight trying to extinguish the vision of long ago. A vision he hoped had gone away for ever. 'You can't rub out the past. You can only put it aside and hope that nothing happens to trigger off a memory. But something always happens that brings it back. It can be a place you see. A glimpse of someone who looks familiar. A smell of someone's perfume. Anything at all, really. Keep busy, that's the key. Keep busy and don't feel sorry for yourself.'

There was a silence, only punctuated by the distant sounds of gulls as they searched offshore for some food. Steve broke that silence. 'When I was young, about ten or eleven I think, my grandpa told me about his time in Belgium during the First World War. He said his friends were killed one by one, but he survived. He could never understand why he came back alive and others didn't. You remember how we used to play at fighting the Germans on that waste ground over there? Sneaking up on them and letting them have it with our pieces of wood made into rifles. He saw me once.

'You weren't there. I was on my own, blasting them with my "Tommy" gun. We sat together in the back yard. He took out his pipe and started filling it from his 'baccy' pouch. I always watched this in a kind of trance. I knew when this happened, that he was going to say something really important. Something that was as significant as the education I got at school. Grandpa always made me wait, though, 'til he'd filled his pipe and lit it. Finally, he took a puff on his pipe and said...

'Me and your Great Uncle Billy joined up together.

"Look after Billy," my mum told me. "See he doesn't get up to any mischief". I was eighteen and Billy was sixteen, but he lied about his age. We both couldn't wait to join up. We wanted to see the world, fight for our country, be somebody. But all we saw was this trench in Belgium. Six months we'd been there. It rained most days. We were up to our knees in mud. It was perishingly cold. Most days I couldn't feel my feet. All day and all night the guns boomed so you couldn't sleep properly. Some days we had no food and we drank muddy, sickly water and blood came out of our pee. We never fired a shot at any of those Germans, although they were only about fifty yards away.

'Me and Billy used to pretend what we'd do to those Germans when we got at them. Fire our "Tommy" guns just like you were doing. Until we heard that next day there was going to be some action at last. I remember, Billy had taken a message down the line and I saw him coming back swinging jauntily along the trench as if he hadn't a care in the world. That was Billy all over. Then I saw a puff of smoke coming out of the side of his helmet. Billy's mouth still held that smile, but his eyes rolled upwards in stark fear. He crumpled to the ground. He was dead all right. A sniper must have got a fleeting view of him and fired.

'I've never forgotten that look on Billy's face. I wanted to die there and then. It should have been me. I was there to protect him, and I didn't. I kept thinking of my mum's last words, "Look after Billy". But I didn't, I let him down. Then the big push came and we went over the top, into the German machine-gun fire. There was mud everywhere. Men and horses were drowning. My gun got clogged up and was useless. All I could do was *shout. For some reason I survived. How I got through the next year, I don't know. I can't remember anything about it. Then I came home.*

'Your nan was here for me and she put me together again as best she could, but I never forgot. I didn't really have any reason for living after that, even with our three children – your mum and your two uncles. But then you came along, young fella, and suddenly I had something real. Somebody I could talk to and somebody I could pass everything I'd learnt of life to. Just remember, when you've got nothing else, there's always something that will happen that gives you that spark to get you going again, so never give up on yourself. Now, get inside before your nan catches you with them dirty hands at the tea table.'

What Gloria had just heard needed a pause, and it got one, whilst both reflected on the sense of Steve's grandpa's words.

'I liked your grandfather. He was kind and I think only you understood him.'

'You did as well,' he replied. 'He liked you a lot, even after you married Gary.'

Steve wished he hadn't said that, as it seemed to drive a wedge between them, so that the closeness he'd just felt had evaporated.

'Do the police think your grandfather killed Terry?'

'I expect he's high up on their list of suspects – it's his hole, he dug it, he filled it in, and... if he knew about me then he'd have plenty of reason.'

'Your grandfather wouldn't kill anyone, Steve, and you know it. So keep faith in him, don't let him down.'

'Yeah, you're right. Somehow, I'll have to do some

of my own digging. Try and find out what may have gone on. Do you think your dad might be able to help? They were good friends.'

'I'll ask him next time I visit. I expect he's high up on the list for Rich to see as well. Maybe I can help with the digging too. That is, if you want me to. After all, you're part of the family now.' She said it in an inoffensive, slightly jokey manner which made them both smile.

'How's Gary taken all this?'

'He hasn't said much. We don't talk much these days, tend to lead our own lives. I think sometimes we just stay together because of the girls. But they're both grown-ups now and have their own lives and families. Anyway, I think any feelings he had for his dad were drummed out of him by his grandfather Jed, years ago. Also, if it's one thing Gary is – he's straight and honest. The shady days of the Breeze clan are well in the past.'

'Gone but not totally forgotten,' said Steve, 'and now back to haunt us.'

'I have to go now, Steve. It's been good to see you again.'

'You too, Gloria, really good. You're looking well.'

She brushed her lips against his cheek and left. Steve trembled at the feeling her lips left behind. He could still feel the imprint as he watched her walk back to the road, get into her car, and drive off. With greater resolve, he looked again out to sea. The sky had taken on a darker hue and the white foam of the waves crashing onto the shore signalled that a squall was on its way.

Chapter 10
The same day

Gary Breeze wasn't happy. He was driving along Nuttall Road and saw his wife in deep conversation with Steve Hamshaw and those old pangs of jealousy came flooding back. Steve and Gloria had always been together even at primary school. They seemed to share some private secrets. Then on through the secondary school years, the teenage dances and even when in a group, meeting up on the beach in the summer months, it was always Steve and Gloria. They were all seventeen, Steve and Gloria were in sixth form studying 'A' levels and Gary had left at sixteen to join his grandfather's business.

Gary fancied Gloria, although it seemed there was nothing he could do about it. But being a Breeze, he had to have her. After years of rivalry, he befriended Steve so he could get close to Gloria, hoping his charms and his sports car would sway her away from Steve. She liked Gary. She found him fun, but it seemed nothing would change her mind, until he hatched a plan.

Don Ward, Gloria's dad, had sold the snooker hall to redevelopers and bought himself a nice little hardware shop on the High Street, selling household goods and good old-fashioned ironmongery to the thriving hotel population. Steve worked there on Saturdays whilst Gloria worked across the road at the bakers. They'd wave to each other across the road and meet up for an early lunch with sandwiches and a cream cake that Gloria had brought from her work. They talked about marriage and they were saving so Steve could build their own house. They'd even opened a joint account and were putting in as much as they could from their Saturday jobs.

The shop was quiet by half past one so 'old man' Ward, as he was known, would stay in the back eating his lunch and checking the racing form for his bets for the afternoon. By then, Steve would be out making some local deliveries of paraffin and logs to nearby customers. It was easy for Gary to sneak in and open the till. He'd take just a bit, two or three pounds so that it wasn't missed and he'd make the corresponding entries on the cash till so that the amount balanced. As his bravado increased, he took more, still making up the balances. He took out a savings account in the name of Steven Hamshaw and made deposits with the money he took. Over a period of six months, Gary continued to steal the money without Don suspecting.

It was only when Gloria was helping her dad do his books for the taxman that she realised he was making less and less money, but only on Saturdays, which should have been the busiest day. The rest of the week's takings looked fine, but sometimes on Saturdays he was making almost nothing. She finally checked the till receipts and knew something was wrong. For weeks Gloria said nothing to Steve. She couldn't believe what she was thinking. Many times, she was about to blurt it out, expecting some simple explanation but something stopped her doing it. She trusted Steve totally, but over time her trust in him began to erode.

Gary was astute and he had seen what was happening. He knew that Gloria had found out about the imbalance and it was now the right time for stage two of his plan. One Saturday night after Steve had been at Gloria's, Gary broke into her dad's house and pushed the savings book down the side of the settee, with just enough showing so it would be noticed.

Gloria found it the next morning. She was devastated and, in a rage, tore it in half. Tears streaming from her eyes, she walked round to Steve's place. He opened the door and she flung the two halves of the saving book in his face.

'Why didn't you ask him for the money? He'd have given it you. My dad would have given you anything. He treated you like a son. You didn't have to steal from him. Why? Why?'

Steve picked up the two pieces, joined them together and thumbed through each page. He saw his name on the first page. He saw the entries on the second, third and fourth pages. He saw the current balance of three hundred and forty-seven pounds, fourteen shillings and ninepence. He saw an interest payment of over eight pounds. He looked at Gloria. She was staring at him. Her face held so many questions, but he had no answers. 'I don't know what to say.' He stopped talking and looked at her.

'There's nothing more to say, Steve, nothing at all.' With that, Gloria turned away from him and walked off down the path and out of his life. Steve stood transfixed, his mouth closed. He had no idea at that moment what to do or say.

Steve never went back to the shop. He wrote Don Ward a letter saying under the circumstances he'd stay away from him and Gloria and enclosed a cheque for the amount in the pass-book. How could he explain? There was no reason for the money being held in his name. How could he say he didn't take it, if he didn't have a rational explanation? At some fleeting moment in the future, he would even believe that he may have taken the money, such was the implausibility of it. Losing Gloria was massive – almost more than he could take.

Steve left school, giving up his places on the 'A' level courses, and went to work with his grandpa. No mention was ever made of his split with Gloria. Neither grandparent broached the subject and he couldn't face telling them about the money. Both had been brought up in an age when it was deemed that if you were old enough, then you made your own decisions and mistakes and you lived by the consequences. Steve always thought that they both knew what had happened, but they kept their own counsel.

He loved the time that he and his grandpa worked together, both as equals – the apprentice learning everything he could from the master, whilst being able to advise on new techniques and building materials that were coming onto the market. Jock Crammie was around as well, adding laughter and fun to their building times together. It was sadly short-lived. The following year, Steve's grandpa died and that really was more than he could take. All the life seemed to be sucked out of him. He went into a shell that no-one could penetrate. He hardly spoke to anybody. He ate only to keep his strength up and the house-build that they had all been working on together was taken on by another firm.

His nan was broken as well. They spent many nights talking about his grandpa and she lost the will to continue with the boarding house. Whilst his grandpa had been alive, it was their project, their life. It seemed so pointless now. She'd seen her husband go off to war full of excitement and curiosity, and come back damaged. She'd seen her elder son go off to war in 1939, and not come back, and she'd seen her daughter, her lovely Rose, destroy herself whilst she, her mother, had stood by, helpless to do anything.

Steve's nan soon sold the business to a couple from Leigh who had been visitors to the boarding house every year for the past ten years. She moved to live in South Wales with her younger son, Brian, and his wife, where they converted a room so she could have her privacy. Steve agreed it was the best course of action for her, but to lose both his grandparents and his lovely Gloria in the space of a year was hard to take.

With nothing to keep him in Northcliffe, Steve took the train to Manchester. He got a job with the Manchester Guardian newspaper and his life moved on.

As soon as Steve left, Gary took his chance. He was a great comfort to Gloria. At first, she wouldn't go out, but he'd go round to her dad's house and sit in with her watching television or listening to records. Finally, he managed to coax her to The Doors' concert in Manchester – a rock group from Los Angeles who were so popular that their first UK tour made tickets hard to come by. Gary, through a friend, had managed to get front row tickets for the gig and a pass backstage. The concert was fantastic, the atmosphere electric and Gloria loved every moment. Then afterwards at the reception party, they got to meet the members of the band. Jim Morrison in particular had a massive effect on them both.

'Wow, Gary, that guy Jim Morrison is amazing. His music is so emotional and it's given me a massive buzz.'

'Might be the smoke in the room that's giving you that buzz,' Gary laughed. It was that night that Gloria realised there had to be a life after Steve, and when Gary asked her to marry him six months later, she agreed.

'I'm very fond of Gary and that will be enough,' she said to her best friend and bridesmaid Beth, on the eve of her wedding. 'After all, what did love bring me? Nothing but tears. I trusted someone once and let him into my life and look how he repaid me.'

It was only her dad, 'old man' Ward, who said she was making a big mistake. He never thought that Steve had taken the money. He always made out it was his bad head for figures that had made the mess-up. But he was unable to explain the savings account. He always said the money didn't matter and that his Gloria and Steve were made for each other. But Gloria married Gary Breeze on 18th November 1967, exactly ten years to the day after Terry Breeze had been killed.

But now Steve was back. 'It's time to face up to things,' he thought. 'Northcliffe is still my home and the place where my happiest memories are.'

Chapter 11
Thursday, 13th January 2000

'Hi, Steve. Sorry to call by so early, but I need to ask you a few questions.'

'Come on in, Rich. There's a pot of coffee on. D'you want a mug?'

'Yeah, I'll join you, thanks.'

They sat round Steve's large pine kitchen table in his townhouse across the road from the promenade. His spacious kitchen was above the ground-level garage. From a large window he had a panoramic view across the promenade and out to sea. The second floor housed Steve's lounge and was off limits to most visitors. It was Steve's personal hideaway.

'How're you doing?' asked Richard.

'So-so. Trying to keep busy. Trying not to think too much, about... well, you know.' Steve found it difficult to speak of his circumstances directly. 'And you – how's the investigation going, well, what you can tell me of it anyway?'

'It's the concrete delivery I've come about, Steve. We've got the docket from the supplier. This is a copy. Is that your grandfather's signature?'

'Could be – I can't tell, but probably not. He wasn't there when the concrete was delivered.' Richard's eyebrows rose in surprise. 'I know, you're asking how I'd remember that far back. I'd been awake most of the night with toothache and Grandpa took me to the dentist first thing the following morning. It was an emergency appointment. I got my first filling that day. I remember it 'cos I was really looking forward to the mixer arriving that morning. Grandpa told me over breakfast that Jock would be supervising the delivery.'

'Jock? I remember, he worked for your grandfather for a few years. But I can't remember his second name.'

'Crammie – Jock Crammie.'

'Is that Jock as in John, Steve?'

'Dunno. I only knew him as Jock. I think we called all Scotsmen Jock in those days. Could have been John or James, or even Richard for that matter. Good bloke, a wee bit rough, but he was an important part of my early life.'

'Any idea where he is now?'

'Last time I saw Jock was at my grandpa's funeral in '66. He disappeared straight after that. I remember asking my nan once if she'd heard from him. She said she hadn't. That he'd moved out of the area. That's all I can tell you.'

'Thanks Steve. I know it must be hard for you at the moment, but we need to try and piece everything together. If you want to talk to me, as a friend?... Well, you know where I am.'

'OK. I know you're only doing your job. It's just a lot to take in at the moment, Rich. Did your dad never say anything to you about Terry Breeze's disappearance?'

'No – nothing at all. We're trying to get a feel for what action, if any, was taken when Breeze disappeared.

Not much by anybody, it seems. Terry's dad, Jed, filed a missing person report, but didn't really kick up any fuss after that. So the police probably thought he'd just scarpered. There were a couple of files on crimes he was possibly involved in at that time. I can't tell you anything else. But there was no police national database then, so somebody could easily have left the area and disappeared off the radar.'

'Yeah. OK, thanks, Rich. I appreciate what you've told me. But it doesn't make me feel any better.'

Later that afternoon, Richard walked back into the station. Before he'd reached his office, he was accosted by an excited Constable Atkinson.

'Sir, I've found something that may shed some light on the relationship between Tom Hamshaw and Terry Breeze,' said the constable, almost breathless, waving a police report in his right hand.

'In my office, Daniel, please.'

Richard had just come from a meeting with the chief super who wasn't at all pleased with the lack of progress and the mounting manpower costs.

'We don't need a handwriting expert at the moment, Richard. What we need is a breakthrough. Something I can tell the chief constable. Action, Inspector. Action!'

'I hope it's worth it, Daniel. I need some good news.'

'Yes, Sir, I think it is. I've been looking through past police reports around the time of the murder. I started at that date and worked back day by day, until I found one dated 6th November, just two weeks before, at two-fifteen in the afternoon. It wasn't so much an incident, more a disturbance that seemed to have been broken up before it escalated into something more serious. But it did seem that the policeman concerned thought it prudent to log a report even though no charges were brought or discussed.'

'Well, come on, constable, what was this disturbance?'

'Oh... sorry, Sir, it was... well, it was an argument between Tom Hamshaw and Terry Breeze. It took place in the old Anvil Snooker Hall. I think it was where the new shopping precinct is now. It seems Tom Hamshaw had his hands round the throat of Terry Breeze and was threatening to finish him off. That's according to the policeman's report. The report said also that Don Ward was a witness. He was trying to pull them apart, but he was such a slight figure, he stood no chance on his own.'

'Good work, Daniel. That's just the kind of breakthrough we need at this moment. Now, who was the policeman? Let's hope he's still alive or at least compos mentis. He might remember more than he was willing to write at the time.'

'That's just it, Sir. He's dead, Sir. His name was Sergeant Whittle, George Whittle, Sir. I believe he was your father.'

Richard heaved a short sigh, his mouth creasing upwards into a broad smile. 'Yes, that was Dad,' he thought. 'Dad would make a report on it, just in case.'

Richard could still remember his dad's words on the day of his passing out ceremony – "Son, if something out-of-the-ordinary happens, make sure you make a note of it. You're a policeman now. You've got a responsibility to the badge and to the public. Make sure you don't let them down. An incident, however trivial, a word, however insignificant, is just a piece of the jigsaw.

You fit them all together and the whole picture is revealed. That's what a detective needs, us 'bobbies' to provide the pieces.

"I wasn't clever enough to put them all together, but you will be, Son. You'll make a detective, one day. It's inside you, it's what you're born to do."

That's exactly what happened. Richard had always wanted to join the Met in London, where he felt he could make the most difference. There, he did his learning on the streets and housing estates of Hammersmith and Blackfriars, in places where drug pushers, petty thieves and prostitutes plied their trades. Places where racial tensions built and exploded two or three times a year and then settled down – to not quite harmonious, but acceptable levels for the rest of the time. At eight years old, youngsters would be initiated into gangs that frequented the tenement blocks. Gangs whose rules and values a youngster would be expected to respect for the rest of his life, inside or outside of jail.

Richard watched and learnt, never afraid to ask or add his own opinion, but always deferential to his superiors. Like Constable Atkinson, Richard got his chance to move to CID, and he took it. It was the spring of 1972, and he'd been drafted onto an enquiry into the murder of an eight-year-old boy. The young lad was found strangled and naked on some wasteland near where an old electrical components factory had stood. It had closed down due to the recession, being unable to compete with the rising tide of cheaper and better Japanese imports.

Most of the local residents of the '60's high rise flats had worked at that factory and the vast proportion of them had no skills or in some cases no desire to find further work. So families lived off benefits. Their kids, leaving school with little education, went straight onto benefits as well. Men hung around on street corners, their meagre allowances being spent on booze and the horses, but as with any society with little to offer except fellowship, they looked out for each other.

Tommy Simpson grew up within these harsh surroundings. His father drank and gambled. He beat both Tommy and his wife, Tommy's mother, and that was looked upon as an accepted part of normal life. But when he was sober, Billy Simpson was a jovial, wholehearted man, who loved his wife and his son and tried to look out for those in his neighbourhood. He was also a petty villain, dealing in stolen goods, driving a van from one side of London to another with a cache on board. After all, what else was he any good at? On Saturday nights he'd spend what was left of his benefit money, or his ill-gotten gains, or, if he was lucky, any winnings from the 'nags', on beer and fags at the local Ferris Wheel pub.

The night usually ended with a good punch-up, which turned even livelier when the police arrived. Each 'bobby' gave as good as he got and Billy Simpson was always at the front making sure he got the first blows in. Every six weeks or so, a bit like clockwork, he'd be singled out for some heavy treatment or carted off with the others to spend a sobering night in the cells, before appearing before the magistrate the next morning. Bound over to keep the peace and a small fine was usual. Sometimes he would be sent to prison for a couple of weeks, but always got out after a few days. It was a life. Not much – but it was all Billy had.

Tommy Simpson had been missing all day and all

night. The day hadn't been a problem. He'd left for school at eight-thirty. Whether he turned up for lessons or not, no-one seemed to care. He'd go off down to the river bank or to play on the old factory sites. As long as he turned up back home about four-thirty, which he always did, then all was well. No-one ever asked him what he did at school or whether he'd actually attended. The 'welfare' seemed to have long since stopped caring about his truancy.

But that night, Tommy never came home. His parents ate their tea, Billy cursing him and threatening him with a sound beating as soon as he put his head round the door. But it went dark and still Tommy didn't appear. Billy Simpson stayed sober that night and with twenty or so cronies searched the streets and nearby wasteland for his missing son.

In the early morning sunshine, a local dog-walker made the grisly discovery of the small boy's body. The murder squad was called out. When Billy was told of his son's death, he went berserk, smashing a poor WPC's nose with his heavy fist and battling with three other constables before he was subdued and carted off to the cells. Chief Inspector Turnbull disliked thugs and villains, particularly those who beat their own kids. Billy Simpson was in the frame for this murder. He was known to hit his son and he had no alibi for that day.

Turnbull put forward his theory. 'Billy Simpson found out that Tommy was bunking off school. So, he followed his son and when he saw that the young lad was playing truant, he confronted him and gave him a good thrashing. There were recent marks on the body to indicate this. But his short temper gave way, he couldn't stop himself and so he strangled the little lad. He then hid the body and took off the lad's clothes because they probably had spots of his own blood on them, and then callously acted as if he knew nothing about it. He won't say where he was or who he was with that day. That's because he wasn't with anyone. He laid low until tea when he could carry out this pretence of care and affection. For God's sake, he was sober. When have we ever known Billy Simpson to be sober? He'd realised what he'd done and it shocked even him.'

So Billy Simpson became the one and only suspect. He was arrested and interviewed. He couldn't give an alibi because he'd been driving a load of 'hot' electrical goods over to the south of the river. His employers demanded one thing, total silence. Billy Simpson knew about honour amongst thieves and he didn't need to think twice, no matter what happened to him.

'We don't need to tie up our stretched resources too long on this case,' Turnbull addressed his team. 'There are real villains out there we need to catch, those that cause distress to people who matter, not some two-bit crook and his useless son. Constable Whittle, you're on secondment to this. Do the rounds of the neighbours, get some statements of how the bastard treated his son. Make sure no-one saw him the day the lad went missing. Have them on my desk the day after tomorrow. Right, let's get back to some real crime solving.'

With that, the team was dismissed, Richard sat there shell-shocked, unable to grasp what had just happened. 'This isn't real policing,' he thought. 'It doesn't stack up.' Those next two days Richard Whittle became the detective his dad anticipated he would become. Billy Simpson, for all he was, just wouldn't remove his lad's clothes, including even his underwear, and leave young

Tommy naked. No father in his right mind would do that. And Tommy was strangled, so where would the blood have come from?

Richard asked around the neighbourhood, he read police reports, contacted the welfare and probation services and talked to Tommy's teachers. A known child molester had just been released from 'the Scrubs' in the past week, into the local area. One teacher had seen someone loitering outside the school gates several times. Another witness had seen some man down by the river talking to a young lad on the day that Tommy had disappeared. Richard wrote up the statements.

He asked around in the streets on his beat. People who would normally run a mile rather than talk to a copper now wanted to help. Finally, Richard got a breakthrough from one of his sources and tracked down the current address of his suspect. Armed with this information and the statements, Richard presented it to Turnbull, but with enough caveats so that the chief inspector could take any credit. One thing Turnbull hated more than anything was a 'perv' on his patch. They organised a raid at the address and during the search found some of Tommy's clothing in the dustbin.

There was no formal acknowledgement of Richard's crime-solving skill, just a begrudging and private 'Good work, constable' from Turnbull and Richard found himself back on the beat. But Chief Inspector Turnbull was no mug. He hadn't got to his rank without others' help and he saw in Richard Whittle a helper rather than a challenger – someone who would shun the plaudits and give them to him in exchange for the inner satisfaction of a job well done. Richard Whittle was moved to CID two weeks later.

'Sir... Sir, are you all right, Sir?' Constable Atkinson's voice penetrated Richard's thoughts, and the vision of his dad receded. 'Sir, what shall we do?'

'Follow the clues, Daniel, that's what we'll do. That's what we always do. There's only one person left who we can talk to about this incident between Tom Hamshaw and Terry Breeze. We're going to see Don Ward.'

As he picked up his jacket, Richard reflected, 'I haven't seen Don for years, but I know he's still alive. My auntie sees him and Kathleen out shopping sometimes. They always have a word.'

Chapter 12
The same day

Don Ward and his wife, Kathleen, lived in sheltered accommodation in Rawcliffe, a village eight miles away over an old toll bridge and surrounded by farmland and market gardens. The area had originally been littered with salt mines, with no traces on the surface, as they were hidden underground. Rock salt had been extracted since the 1890s to feed the now defunct chemical factory, producing large amounts of chlorine. Rumour had it that the vast caverns had housed mustard gas produced for the First World War offensives and now there were talks of them being used to store vast quantities of natural gas purchased from Russia.

The weather inland was much less harsh and well-sheltered from the strong, cold breezes coming off the Irish Sea. Nowadays, salad crops and root vegetables flourished under glass and many growers had got rich before the large supermarkets started squeezing suppliers on margins and requiring tasteless but uniform and unblemished produce.

The advent of growing organic crops meant that some farms were now making a comeback, whilst others had sold land during the property boom of the '80s and

'90s, ending up with new box-like housing estates. Some developers had gone so far as to predict the explosion of sheltered housing for the elderly as the percentage of people retiring to the coast increased year on year.

One such development was Thurnham Grange, which had the ring of a stately nineteenth-century mansion, but in reality, was a new-build estate of retirement homes. Built in 1996 in the grounds of Thurnham Hall, Thurnham Grange was a retreat for like-minded over 65s. Don and Kathleen Wood had been one of the first couples to get a place. They had been able to select one of the better units, slightly away from the others and with the best views across the fields to the distant fells.

The units wanted for nothing. They had one spacious bedroom with an en-suite, a roomy lounge with French windows opening onto a secluded, well-stocked and well-maintained garden and a modern fitted kitchen-diner with all appliances, including a dishwasher which Don always maintained was the most important appliance ever created. For in his words, 'What could be worse than enjoying making a meal, then enjoying eating the meal, only to have it all spoiled with a sink full of dirty pots.'

Richard and Daniel drove out there in torrential rain. When it rained on this coast, the wind invariably blew strong as well. Casual visitors to this area of the north-west would comment that the rain would soon blow over. Locals, however, knew better. Once the rain came in from the Irish Sea, it could persist all day, and was more than likely heavy. So when they arrived at the Grange, they both had to rush to the door and try not to get too wet.

'Come in, Richard. Get yourself out of the rain,' said Kathleen, 'and you, young lad, as well. Get yourselves inside, I've got a hot cup of tea ready for you both.'

'Thanks, Kathleen. This is Constable Atkinson – Daniel if you like.'

'Daniel it is, then. Get those wet things off and come through.'

Don Ward was sitting, in what Richard reckoned was his favourite chair by the window. He didn't look well. His face was drawn and pasty. Richard didn't like to ask, but Don volunteered his doctor's diagnosis. 'Pancreatic cancer, I'm afraid. I got diagnosed a month ago. But I'm fine, otherwise.' Don laughed and said, 'I'd be better if it stopped raining, though.'

Don welcomed Richard like a long-lost son and was at pains to find out about how his career had progressed. 'Old George would have been proud of you, Richard. He always said you'd make a fine copper, and to know you'd come back to his old stomping ground, well, that would have made his day. I miss George. We had some great discussions. We were both pig-headed enough not to give way, but we never fell out.

'Kathleen and I don't get many visitors. Our Gloria's here most days, of course, popping in to fuss us, but it's nice to be able to talk to someone else other than the old fuddy-duddies that live in the Grange complex. Anyway, Richard, you haven't come all the way out here for a friendly chat. You've got something on your mind, haven't you?'

With that, Kathleen got up and headed for the kitchen.

'I'll leave you men to your chat. Don't tire him too

much, Richard, will you, please?'

When she'd gone, Richard turned to Don. 'It's actually my dad I want to talk to you about, Don. You'll no doubt have heard by now that we've found Terry Breeze's body. So we're trying to piece together his final days. You called my dad to an incident that happened in your snooker hall back in 1957...'

'6th November at 2:15pm,' interrupted Daniel Atkinson. 'Sorry, Sir…' Daniel glanced sheepishly at his inspector. Richard and Don both grinned.

'He's keen, your constable, isn't he, Richard?' Don smiled, then turning to see the fast-reddening features on Daniel's cheeks, said, 'There's nothing wrong with that, young lad. I remember some other fresh-faced 'bobby', just like yourself, and he's sitting not a million miles away. He didn't do too bad, in the end. I've heard about you finding Terry Breeze after all this time. Now, what's this about an incident, Richard?'

'It was an argument between Terry Breeze and Tom Hamshaw. You must have felt it was getting out of hand, so you rang the police, and my dad came. What was the argument about?'

Don paused for a few seconds, then said, 'Richard, I ran a snooker hall. They were rough places where men went to drink after a hard day's work, but they also attracted riff-raff – Terry Breeze and his like. There was a fight of some sort every day, mostly about nothing. You can't expect me to remember one specific one. It's over forty years ago.'

'You rang for the police, Don. This was no ordinary fight. You were scared somebody would get hurt. You were a great mate of Tom's and I expect you thought he was going to do some serious damage to Terry, maybe even go too far and kill him. So you rang the police and my dad came. What was it about Don?'

'You think that Tom Hamshaw killed Breeze, don't you, Richard? Tom was a hard man, but if he'd wanted to kill Terry, he'd have done it then, no matter how many policemen had come. Tom wasn't a man to have waited and done it sneakily.'

'Did the argument concern Rose, Tom's daughter? Was it about Terry and Rose? Had he found out that Terry was Steve's dad?'

'I'd heard about that. Gloria told me and Kathleen the other day. How is the lad? He must be distraught, finding out after so long. Kathleen and I always thought Steve would become our son-in-law. But it wasn't to be. Gloria married that wastrel, Gary Breeze, instead. Do you know, he's never visited us here? Gloria and the grandkids come regularly. But Gary? He can't do it. Too much guilt. It's always a Breeze who gets in the way, isn't it? So, how's Steve taken the news about his dad?'

'Steve puts on a brave face, but he's taken it badly. That's why we need to know who killed Terry Breeze. It'll torment Steve until he knows. So if you've any information that helps get Tom Hamshaw off the suspect list, tell me now, Don.'

'Richard, leave things be. It's been over forty years. You've got better things to do than dig up the past. You might dig up something you don't want to find.'

Richard knew that this was the end of their conversation. If he wanted more, he'd have to drag Don Ward down to the station and interview him formally. He didn't want that, and he'd no proof that Don knew any more than he'd already told him.

But there was something being held back, some

secret that Don was either refusing to tell or refusing to remember. Richard knew that this could be the key to help him solve the murder of Terry Breeze, but would it mean that a good man like Tom Hamshaw had his name besmirched and with it, his grandson Steve? If that was the price, then would justice have been served, or as Don had said, would it be best to leave well alone?

Maybe no-one knew at the time who Steve's father was. That is, except for Rose Hamshaw, who may have kept her secret until she died. But there were still two weeks between this fight and Terry Breeze's death. That was enough time for Tom Hamshaw to quiz his daughter and get this information from her. Yes – Tom Hamshaw was still a suspect.

Richard had no doubts. He was a policeman who believed in the law, and this case should be no different than any other. He promised himself that he would solve the case, no matter what secrets were unveiled or reputations damaged.

Don Ward sat in his favourite armchair staring intently out across the fields. Often, he'd rue the day he took on the snooker hall from his father. Dark things had happened in there and he'd breathed a sigh of relief when it had finally been demolished, hoping that all the bad things and bad memories would be taken away from Northcliffe forever with the rubble. But rubble can be disposed of and forgotten. Memories are only suppressed and can be triggered when least expected. And these kinds of memories can gnaw at your mind and continually torment you.

Chapter 13
Friday, 14th January 2000

'Is there any match on the other DNA from the tarpaulin yet, Cora?'

'Nothing yet, Sir. We've still just got Tom Hamshaw's. Daniel's trawled all the national databases, births, deaths, employment etc. and found nothing at all. I've got some requests out with Interpol and we're waiting for them to get back to us.'

The investigation team had gathered for the morning briefing. Richard turned to face Daniel. 'Keep going on the DNA link, Daniel. It's tenuous, I know, but it may lead us somewhere. We've precious else to go at. What about the bank robbery, Cora? Refresh our memories, please.'

Cora walked towards the sparsely populated whiteboard. Seven days into the investigation and not much new evidence was on display. Pointing to a floorplan pinned to the whiteboard, she said, 'On 8th August 1957, the National Bank on Corporation Street, Southcliffe was robbed. At 11:35am, three masked men entered the branch. There were no customers inside. The only staff present were a cashier, Roland Booth, twenty-two years old, who had just nipped into the manager's office to make a cup of tea, and the bank guard, Arthur Dowling, aged forty-seven. The bank manager, a Mr Tubbs, had been called home to an emergency, fifteen minutes earlier. This turned out to be a false phone call, probably made by the robbers to get him out of the office. Dowling, the guard, was on the customer side of the counter and he was unarmed – that was the usual case in those days.' There were murmurs from the audience.

'Yes – it wouldn't be like that today. One of the robbers pointed a gun at the guard as the cashier emerged from the office with his cup of tea. Together with the guard, he was ordered at gunpoint back into the office. As they approached the office, Arthur Dowling made a lunge towards the panic button located below the counter. One of the robbers, who we now believe to be Terry Breeze, caught hold of him and knifed him between the ribs, just missing his heart by millimetres. Panic ensued. Another of the robbers vaulted the counter and emptied the till of four hundred and ninety-two pounds in banknotes, some cheques, and some worthless paying-in slips. They beat a hasty retreat, leaving behind an untouched safe in the manager's office containing a large amount of cash. Altogether a botched robbery. For those interested, the sum stolen equates to about seven thousand pounds in today's money.

'It wasn't a massive amount, I'll grant you, but enough to make a mark on a town like Southcliffe. And not without repercussions as well,' commented Richard. 'Arthur Dowling didn't die that day, but after a long illness, he took his own life two years later. He walked out in front of a train. That's why we need to nail the crew that did this.'

'How did we finally link Breeze to this, Sarge?' Barry Crompton enquired.

'Forensics did a comparison between Breeze's DNA sample from the skull and a sample found on the left lapel of Arthur Dowling's uniform. It turned out it was a match.'

'What was the sample on his uniform, Sarge?'

'Snot!'

A roar of laughter from the team broke the silence and the tension. 'Aha! He wasn't called a snotty-nosed kid all those years for nothing, then,' sniggered Barry.

'Forensics have also looked at the old photos of the entry wound on Arthur Dowling's body, and although it wouldn't stand up in a court of law, it's a dead ringer with the photos taken from an earlier body in August 1947. An unsolved traveller's death after the Gala weekend. The knife used in both stabbings had a bit broken off. As I said, it's not concrete proof but it's probably enough to solve an old outstanding crime.'

'My old man used to tell me about those Gala fights, when I was growing up,' chirped up Crompton. 'That stabbing spoiled it for everyone. After that the coppers... us, I mean...' He paused, just beginning to realise what he was saying. 'Well, let's just say – that he said things weren't the same ever again.'

'I can never understand why men get such a kick out of beating each other up,' Cora said, shaking her head.

'It was just after the war, Sarge. There wasn't much else to look forward to at the time. Young blokes back from the war, some had hardly worked before getting conscripted. We've got it lucky – our generation. Kids are too soft these days.'

'Blimey, Barry. I didn't think I'd ever hear you say

anything so sensible. I see you in a new light,' laughed Cora, slightly mocking him.

'OK,' said Richard, trying to get everyone to refocus. 'Good work all round. But there's still a lot of proper police work needed to find the other two robbers and the link, if any, to Breeze's death. Daniel, can I see you in my office? Cora, can you come too?' Then seeing the look of horror on the young constable's face, Richard added, 'It's nothing to worry about, constable.'

Once seated in the inspector's office, Richard said, 'Daniel, I want you to concentrate on finding the identity of robber number two's DNA. There's no outright distinct match in police records, but start by matching percentage-wise, you know, fifty percent for parents, siblings etc. Let's see if we can find out who this guy is.

'I've also been talking to your chief inspector. I've requested that your assistance is put on a more formal footing and he agreed. So, from today you're seconded to the investigation team for the duration of the inquiry. If you agree, Detective Constable Atkinson?'

'Yes, Sir. Thank you, Sir. I won't let you down.'

'I know you won't, Daniel. Just keep doing what you're good at. We need your skills on this investigation.'

As Daniel got up to leave, Richard added, 'Oh, and Daniel. Make sure you come to work in civvies tomorrow.

'Right, Cora, you and I are off to see the bank cashier, Roland Booth. He's living 'Over Wyre' in Knott End. I know it's a long shot, but we'll see if anything jogs his memory.'

Chapter 14
That afternoon

Richard always enjoyed his trips 'Over Wyre', a reference to what the locals called the salt marshes on the other bank of the river Wyre. The easiest way to get there was by yet another toll bridge, now free after recent government legislation. The new bridge had replaced the old one in 1993 and it had taken away some of the magic he felt when crossing it. Back in his childhood, Richard remembered his dad often driving him, Steve and a couple of other lads across, at a cost of a thruppenny bit, return. The toll man always tried to wave George through as a favour, but his dad always paid.

'I'll be beholden to nobody,' George would say to Richard. 'That way I don't have to look the other way if someone asks me to.' They'd go across when the tide was out and find a flattish area of short grass, shoo the sheep away and set up for their cricket match. They only had a tennis ball, so it used to fly in all directions. George always gave pointers on the correct batting and bowling techniques.

Many a time each session, the ball was hit into one of the shallow trenches carved out by the strong tides.

That usually meant a wet foot or two, but because it was a tennis ball, it never sank out of sight. The constant running around soon dried any wet feet.

Sometimes Steve's grandfather came as well. He was not as young and energetic as the others, so he tended to either keep wicket or bowl a few gentle off-breaks. After a good game the boys went off playing deeper into the marshes, taking care to avoid any quicksand areas. George would light the primus stove and heat up a kettle of water for some sweet tea accompanied by buttered scones he'd made earlier in the day. Richard smiled at those memories, every time he crossed that bridge. Happy times indeed.

They reached Knott End High Street. There was only one main road which petered out at the entrance to the old lighthouse, but it was named High Street to announce its importance. Two cul-de-sacs split off from this street and down the first one, Wyre View, they found a 1970s-built bungalow belonging to Roland Booth and his wife. Richard had phoned ahead, so, with the kettle already boiled, he and Cora sat down to a freshly-brewed cup of tea.

They looked at each other and grinned. It seemed that every house they went to, they always ended up with a cuppa. It would be churlish to refuse, and it did put those that they were interviewing in a more relaxed state. Many times, the tea would be left untouched, but today, Richard was thirsty and just needed a boost of caffeine. He picked up the cup from its saucer and took a good gulp. Cora, taking his lead, automatically followed suit, whether she wanted a drink or not.

'Thanks for seeing us at such short notice, Mr

Booth. As I mentioned on the phone, there have been some developments in the bank robbery case back in 1957 that you were involved in. I'd just like to go over some points in the statement you gave. If that's OK with you?'

Roland Booth had been twenty-two when the robbery took place. He'd been deeply traumatised afterwards, but as with most things in those days, people just got on with their lives, put it behind them and carried on. Roland had risen to become bank manager in the very same branch. He'd seen the advent of better security, grilles and then bulletproof glass partitions, panic buttons linked directly to outside security and bigger and thicker-walled safes for the storage of money. He never experienced anything like the robbery attempt in all the following years. Now retired, he could enjoy the peace and tranquillity that he and his wife had found in this haven.

'If I can be of help, Inspector, I will. It's over forty years ago since that robbery, but I can still remember details of that day as clearly as yesterday, even now. When things like that happen you never forget. But I'm sure my statement at the time was totally accurate.'

'I'm sure you haven't forgotten, but I'd like to query a couple of entries in your statement if I may?' Roland Booth nodded and Richard continued. 'You only saw the robbers first when you came out of the office with a cup of tea, so the bank was empty except for you and Arthur Dowling?'

Roland nodded again, 'Yes that's correct, but I did hear someone talking whilst I was putting the milk in. I thought it must have been a customer.'

'That's not in your statement. Are you sure?'

'Are you certain it's not in my statement, Inspector? It's something I can remember even now. I'm not imagining it. He sounded foreign.'

Richard and Cora exchanged surprised glances. 'The notes on the robbery indicate that one of the robbers was foreign, but it doesn't say that you said it. Again – are you sure?'

'Yes. I thought I'd told the police that, but maybe I hadn't. I can still hear his voice in my head. I couldn't make out the words, but it did sound foreign to me. I thought at the time, maybe he was Russian, but I didn't mention it because I wasn't sure. I was only twenty-two, and had hardly been out of Southcliffe.

'I'd never heard many foreign accents before. Now there's a good few in the town and in retrospect I'd be more prepared to describe it as Eastern European. When I saw him, I felt that he was in charge and when that other one stabbed Arthur, well – the foreign one, the boss, pulled him off smartish and bundled him out the door. Him and the other bloke – the one who raided the till – were totally shocked at what the one with the knife had done. It didn't seem part of the plan. Poor Arthur. I always thought that he wasn't much of a guard, but he was a lovely bloke and didn't deserve getting stabbed.'

'This chap who you thought was in charge, Mr Booth. Did you notice anything else that was strange about him at all? Anything unusual?'

Roland paused. Richard could see him, thinking carefully. Making sure any answer was properly thought through. 'I thought at the time that he might have been bald. I don't know why, as they all wore balaclavas, but by the shape of his head he looked bald. That may sound daft. They, the police at the time, that is, laughed it off. I remember the sergeant laughing and saying, 'You mean he'd had a Yul Brynner?' That made me feel a bit stupid, but I know what I saw. I don't think they took me seriously because I was making a cup of tea whilst a robbery was taking place.'

Once they were sure that Roland had nothing else new to tell them, Richard and Cora gave their thanks and said their goodbyes.

Outside the bungalow Richard blew out his cheeks and said, 'Blimey, shows how interview techniques have moved on since the '50s. No way would that mess-up have happened now. Not on my watch, at any rate. If they'd put Roland Booth at his ease and actually listened to him, they might've solved the case there and then. So, we have possibly an Eastern European male, maybe bald, who was around Northcliffe forty-three years ago. It's not much to go on, Cora, but it's better than what we had half an hour ago. Come on, let's get back to the station.'

Cora was quiet in the car as they left Knott End High Street and made their way back over the marshes. Richard assumed that she was deep in thought about the case. Finally, she turned to Richard, and asked, 'Sir – who's Yul Brynner?'

Chapter 15
That evening

Daniel Atkinson was on cloud nine. This was what he wanted – a proper investigation, some way to show off his talents. For as long as he could remember, he'd always wanted to be in the police. He'd left school at sixteen and had gone straight into the area's police training college, located in Hutton, just outside Preston. There he excelled, particularly in the detection area, where his persistence and eye for detail meant he graduated with the year's top marks. He could go anywhere. Join any police force in the country, but he loved the seaside and particularly Southcliffe, plus his childhood sweetheart had all her family there. So he settled on serving his probation year in his home town, married Angie, and started to build his career. That decision was ready to bear fruit.

Angie, a primary school teacher, was already home, when he literally flew through the door, with a broad grin on his face. 'I've been seconded onto the "Skeleton case", as it's become known in the town. Inspector Whittle has made it official. I'm on it until it's solved. It's plain clothes from tomorrow, Angie. I can hardly believe it. I'm a detective constable now.'

'I'm not surprised, Dan,' said Angie, hugging him. 'You've proved your worth to them already by finding the cement docket. It's just taken them a week to realise it,' she said with a broad smile. 'I'm really proud of you – well done! Now give me another hug and tell me all about it over a coffee.'

'I'm sorry Angie, I got so excited. How's your day been?'

'My day was fine, nothing different, but don't change the subject. You've got the good news today. Come on, tell me what you can.'

Daniel told Angie everything as none of it was restricted information. They had had this discussion some time ago and agreed that sometimes Daniel would have to withhold information from his wife. It came with the territory of being a police officer's spouse.

When he'd finished, Angie gave him another big hug. 'Well done, Dan, it sounds as if they need someone with your skills. Your college tutor told you the same – remember? Use your strengths. Anyway, just to bring my dear husband back down to earth, there's that PTA meeting at school this evening. Do you remember me mentioning it? We're finalising the details of the panto. You will be able to help again this year, won't you, love?'

'Oh no! I'd forgotten that you always have the panto after Christmas,' groaned Daniel. 'OK, but is there a small detective role that's more in keeping with my new-found status? After last year, playing the pumpkin in Cinderella, I feel that my acting skills need to be taken a bit more seriously.'

It's a pantomime, Dan,' Angie laughed. 'I can't find any panto that has Sherlock Holmes in it. Anyway, as much as I love you, you don't possess any acting skills and you know it's true. Not that acting skills are any criteria for our production. But you're ace at helping me direct on the night. Last year's production went down brilliantly.'

'I know, and I enjoyed it. I'll help with whatever you want done, but on the proviso that this case will have to come first.'

'Of course, love. I understand. When I'm out this evening, why don't you pop round and see your dad to tell him the good news? He's always believed in you and a lot of your doing well is down to how he and your mum brought you up. Now, let's finish making tea.'

Daniel was the only child that Graham and Irena Atkinson were blessed with. His dad was in his late 40s and his mum in her mid-30s when he was born. His birth was a difficult one for Irena, and she never fully recovered from that. Although she was a wonderful mum, she was very frail and died when he was twelve. She never got to see him join the training scheme. She never got to see him graduate. But Daniel always felt that she was watching over him, and would be immensely proud of her 'little boy'.

Daniel had no other close living relatives, as both his parents were orphans. There was some talk of an uncle living in Canada, his mum's brother, but there had never been any contact. So the Atkinson family grew up as a close-knit unit. His dad, Graham, ran a successful furniture and carpet warehouse in Southcliffe. He'd also opened a smaller establishment in Rossport and it was doing quite nicely.

Daniel used to love going with his father to the warehouse on Sunday mornings, when it was shut to the public. Whilst his father did his books, Daniel would run up and down the aisles of carpets, dodging in and out, tracking criminals and apprehending suspects. Time would just flash by in his quiet and vast realm of dreams.

Graham was well-thought of in the community and had stood, successfully, to be a town councillor. After many years of service, he was given the honour of becoming the town's mayor and more recently had taken on the mantle of the Chair of the Police and Crime Panel.

After hearing about the unearthing of the skeleton and the possible link to the armed robbery all those years ago, Graham had rung the chief constable immediately and urged him to do whatever it took to finally solve the crime that had left a dark stain on the town for over forty years. Graham had also offered any of the council resources, if needed, and had agreed for extra cash over and above the police budget to be made available, to help bring this sorry case to a close.

Daniel breezed into his dad's kitchen as Graham was finishing the washing up. 'Dad, I'm officially seconded to the "Skeleton case". Inspector Whittle says the case needs my type of skills. I'm on it 'til it's solved.'

'That's terrific news, Daniel,' his dad replied, turning and shaking his son's hand. 'Well done. I'm so proud of you. All that extra studying on police detection you did at college can now be put to good use. Come on through to the lounge and tell me all about it.' They got settled down in two comfy chairs overlooking a spacious garden that bore the ravages of a harsh winter.

'I spoke to the chief constable this afternoon, but he didn't have many facts he wanted to divulge at this time.

It's understandable, so don't tell me anything you aren't comfortable with, son. But it's great news. Your mum would have been ever so proud of you.'

'There's nothing secretive at the moment, Dad. As everyone knows – the skeleton belongs to Terry Breeze and it's been confirmed that he was part of that bank robbery team in 1957. We're trying to locate a person called Jock Crammie who took delivery of the cement load at that time, but we've had no joy yet. I'm trawling the different databases, but it's still early days.'

'Whoa, son, don't tell me any more. You're so excited, you'll blurt out something confidential if you're not careful. I'll be getting regular updates from the chief constable. So I'll find out in due course. Just tell me how you're doing. How are they treating you?'

'Sorry, Dad. Yes. I'm getting a bit carried away. Everyone's being great. I think it helps that what I'm doing – trawling through statements and databases – is what I enjoy most, and it's what most of the others really hate about the job.'

'Just like your mum. She loved attention to detail. That's why the business is doing so well. Always listen to the customer, she'd say, because they're never wrong. They can't be wrong, because they're the ones who are spending the money. She put me right when it was needed.'

'Right, I'd better get back, Dad. It's just a fleeting visit. Angie should be home from the PTA meeting soon and I should find out my fate in this year's panto.'

'Anything will be better than last year's pumpkin, Daniel. I look forward to seeing it.'

'Yes, it will be, and I'm glad you still want to sit through another panto.'

Chapter 16
Later that evening

'Hi Steve, I was... just passing and saw your light was on. How are you doing?'

'Gloria! I'm OK, surprisingly. I've come to terms with it a bit more, since we last spoke... But, come in, don't stand on the step. You look frozen.' Steve led Gloria through the hall and up a flight of stairs into his kitchen.

'Sorry about the mess,' he said, staring at a sink full of washing-up. 'I don't often get visitors, but I'm glad you've come. I could do with some company. Tea, coffee, or something stronger?' he asked, brandishing a bottle of Chianti. 'It's from a small vineyard in northern Tuscany. I stayed there when I was covering the Peace Conference in Florence about ten years ago. I got to know the owner and his family very well. Signor Ricasoli sends me a case of his finest reserve every year.' He paused. 'I'm showing off, aren't I? Sorry, it's just I'm a bit lost for words, and not good at small talk, as you know.'

Gloria laughed and said, 'No, you're not showing off and yes, I'd love a glass of wine, especially one from a bottle of Signor Ricasoli's finest reserve!'

'Touché,' said Steve as he poured Gloria a glass and handed it to her. 'I deserved that, but it's good to see you. My head's been spinning ever since I got the news about Terry Breeze being my dad. I keep thinking of him with my mum and every time I get physically sick. But then I ask myself – would my grandpa actually kill Breeze if he'd found out? And I'm convinced that no, he wouldn't – I'm sure of that.'

They took their drinks up a further flight into Steve's spacious lounge. Here it was tidy and warm, but sparsely furnished. At first sight, Gloria thought that it didn't really have a lived-in feel to it. She crossed over to the large picture window which totally filled one wall of the room. It opened up a panoramic view across the Irish Sea. The last wisps of sunlight were disappearing beyond the horizon, leaving behind a dull red glow against a darkening sky.

Gloria scanned the room again, and noticed that the furnishings, although initially looking scant, were of Scandinavian design. The wooden chairs had smooth, round edges with curves that looked like the rolling waves of the sea outside. On the walls hung vibrant, modern paintings against a pastel background, bringing the room together and complementing the Nordic style. She was no expert in this kind of art, but she could tell that they were originals and quite well-painted. 'I could do something with this room,' she thought.

She turned to face Steve and smiled nervously. 'I wasn't sure if I should come, but when we met last week, I left rather abruptly. I know that I'd like a sympathetic ear if I'd gone through what you're going through, so...' Gloria shrugged her shoulders.

She set her drink down on the oval coffee table and

couldn't help but notice a cardboard box full of black and white photographs. She picked one up from the top that caught her interest.

'That's me – there – look.' She pointed to an image of a small girl standing at the front of a group of smiling people. 'And that's you, Steve, standing next to me.'

'You're on a lot more of those photos as well. You always seemed to turn up just as they were about to be taken. My nan always had a group photo of our visitors taken every Saturday morning in the summer months, just before everyone left to catch their coaches home.'

'I remember, but I didn't realise it was every week! Are you on all of them?' she asked, picking up a few more at random.

'Yes, on every one. It was a ritual my nan had. She'd call all the visitors together, just after breakfast, whether they wanted to or not. There were always some moans, but I think secretly they all looked forward to it. Everybody was included on a photo – there's my nan and grandpa on that one, and my mum.'

'I remember now. Your nan would bang the gong that sat on her hallway table.'

'Oh yes. The gong,' replied Steve. 'The gong that was rung at breakfast-time, at lunch-time and at dinner-time that made our guests scurry from their rooms to the dining table.'

'I remember, Steve, you once rang the gong as a dare.'

'That was your fault, Gloria. You were the one who dared me. I never did it again, though. My nan gave me a right telling-off. Although the visitors and my grandpa thought it was very funny.'

'I wouldn't have liked to have got on the wrong side

of your nan, Steve.'

'She was OK, was my nan, I miss her.'

'Who took all these photos?'

'That was my Uncle Brian. He'd just got himself a state-of-the-art Brownie 127 camera. Before he left school, he had a butcher's round on Saturdays. Used to ride around town on a carrier-bike, delivering meat to the local boarding houses. He saved up everything he earned to buy that camera. I remember, he'd never let it out of his sight.'

'Didn't your uncle take photos of people on the High Street as they walked past?'

'Yeah, that's right. He was cunning, was my Uncle Brian. He'd pretend to take a photo of some passing holidaymakers and then give them a slip of paper with a number on – like a cloak-room ticket. Then, if they took the ticket and showed interest, he'd offer to take another one because of some excuse, like the wind was blowing their hair or someone walked in front of them. With the proper photo taken, they'd come and see him later in the week to collect it and pay him.'

'That's the entrepreneurial spirit of the '50s in a nut-shell,' joked Gloria. 'Did he end up as some big business tycoon?'

'No, he became a television engineer working for Warings in the square. He just loved fiddling with electronics. He got married and they moved to South Wales. That's where my nan ended up living as well, until she died. Anyway, he'd get the photo developed and my nan would send a copy to each family as a memento of their, hopefully, happy holiday by the sea. There must be over a hundred photos in there, and she would always write the date and year on the back. I was looking through them, hoping to find something that explains all this, but I kept getting side-tracked by remembering the good memories.

'Some of these families came back the same week every year. You can see the kids growing up and you can see us growing up as well.' Steve laughed. 'I hated it sometimes, particularly when I got a bit older, you know, twelve or thirteen. I started getting pushed back in the line-up as I got taller – and you stopped being on them as well, so it was never the same.'

Had he crossed the line there? He wasn't sure. Would the events that came between them resurface? Not really, as for him, they had never been buried. There was a moment's silence, before Gloria laughed.

'You were pretty gangly then, for your age. You seemed to shoot up overnight – and when your voice broke, it scared me for a while until your nan explained it. Look at this one, Steve, you're nearly twice my size.'

'Yes, but you soon caught up with me. They were good times, weren't they?'

Gloria looked across at Steve with a serious face. 'Yes, they were the best.' There was another interlude while each absorbed what had been said, or unsaid. 'What was your nan like, Steve? I never really knew her.'

'My nan – I don't think anyone really knew her, except for my grandpa. That generation never let their emotions spill out. She was half Maltese. She would always say, she was a Malteser – round, smooth on the outside, but with a crunchy, sweet interior that melted in the mouth. Grandpa would add that having tasted one, people would always want more.

'My great-grandfather went over to Malta in 1875 I

believe. He was a baker working in the Naval bakery making bread and stuff for the Navy. He met my great-grandmother over there. She was from a well-to-do Maltese family, supposedly going back generations. They fell in love, married and had three children whilst over there – Dorothy, my nan, was the eldest girl. They came back to England in the early 1900s and settled in Leigh, where my family came from. Anyway, my great-grandfather opened his own bakery shop. It's still there now, but it's not in the family any more. Nan was very loving and caring towards me. I often thought of her as my mum, and grandpa as my dad. My real mum – well, you know.' Steve paused, trying to find the right words. 'My mum was never well, not that I can remember, anyway. I think I can understand a lot more why, now.'

'Your mum always seemed troubled in some way, Steve. She was lovely with me, but seemed to disappear inside herself often. I do remember your nan always being on hand to comfort her.'

'Nan would say to Mum, every Saturday morning, without fail. "Rose, are those bedrooms spick and span? The first visitors will be here within the hour." Saturdays were super busy for me as well. But Nan was always there, that's the thing. My nan always seemed to appear when something wasn't right, and then she made it right. She loved her visitors arriving. Called a lot of them her family.

'I can remember going to see her at my uncle's in South Wales, one Christmas. She had about two hundred Christmas cards and she knew who'd sent every one of them. "Test me," she used to say. "Point to one and I'll tell you who it's from." And she did. She knew their names, all the children's names and how many grandchildren they had. What their favourite meal was, which room they stayed in and whether they were noisy. She left me these photos after her death with a note that said, "When you're down and need answers, get these photos out and remember those good times we all had, that will help clear your mind." That's my nan, all over.'

'It seems we should take your nan at her word. Who knows, we just might get some inspiration,' said Gloria.

They each took a sip of wine and started looking at the photos together. Somehow sitting in such close proximity just felt so natural to both of them.

'That's Harry,' Steve said, holding a photo and pointing to a small boy standing next to Gloria. 'You must have been seven or eight then. Do you remember, he followed you around all week? He had a massive crush on you.'

'Oh yes, I think he was all of six, much too young for me. I liked them a bit older. That chap there, standing next to your grandpa. He seems to be in a lot of these photos and he looks familiar. Who is he?'

'That's Jock, grandpa's brickie. They worked together as long as I can remember. Jock was one of the family, really. He lived in one of the attic rooms all year round. He'd be there even at Christmas, always carried the tree in and took charge of decorating it. He worshipped my grandpa. He'd do anything for him. Jock had been in a military prison during the war, I seem to remember, I don't know why. Grandpa took him on, knowing that, and he'd told me once that he'd never regretted it.' Steve's thoughts went back many years, to when he was younger. To a Scotch accent, whispering out of a dark mist. But then the thought faded.

'Who's that – half-hidden behind him?' asked

Gloria, pointing at a partly visible figure in the back row behind the bulky frame of the Scot.

'I'm not sure,' said Steve, taking the photo from her outstretched hand, to get a closer look. 'He's a bloke who did some work for Grandpa around the sites. Not brickie work, more labouring. You know, climbing the ladders to the next floor, carrying wooden joists, hauling bricks up – that sort of thing. He was around for a few years on and off. He used to share Jock's room when he was working. I can't remember his name, but he used to give me the heebie-jeebies.'

'He does look a bit sinister, Steve. He's wearing one of those bobble-caps without the bobble – I can't remember their proper name – and it's summer.'

'It's called a watch-cap. He always seemed to wear it, whatever the season. I remember he would wear it even at breakfast. Strange that – my nan would never normally allow anyone at the breakfast table with something on their head.'

They checked other photos, getting them into date order. Steve held up one of them to show Gloria. 'This is the last one that this mystery man appears on. It's dated 28th August 1957. That would be the last week of the Wakes Week holidays, so there wouldn't be any more photos for that season. And there are no others with him on in all the following year's photos. So maybe he just moved on.'

'Or had to move on. Steve, don't you see what this means? He could have killed Terry Breeze and then scarpered. He'd know that the hole was there. He was friends with Jock. You've already said that your grandpa wasn't there when the concrete was laid. They had the chance to do it. We should tell Richard.'

'I don't know. I can't think Jock had anything to do with it. It's only a photo. This chap may have left town at the end of August and have had nothing to do with it. I can't bother the police with an old photo and a crazy idea that this person's involved somehow. We can't just wish something to be true.'

'Then let's find some more proof. It's worth a shot, isn't it? What else can we do?'

Steve looked at Gloria and saw the teenager that he had loved so much, all those years ago. 'We're doing this together,' he thought.

'You're right. It is worth a shot,' Steve heard himself say.

'What do you remember about him, Steve? Can you think of anything at all?'

'He was foreign – I think. He had a bit of a soft spot for my mum and used to flirt with her a bit at breakfast-time. Made her laugh when he said strange words. I asked her once and she said he was probably Russian, but that could have meant any nationality in those days. I don't think many people in Northcliffe would ever have heard the Russian language before, anyway.'

'Russian. Well, that's a start. We can do something with that straight away.' Steve looked at Gloria in surprise.

'Becca… From our school… Don't you remember, Steve? Becca was in our class. She's Russian. Her dad ran the Russian Club on Bloom Street in Southcliffe. It closed down years ago. But Becca's still around. We can at least ask her. If he was Russian, he'd most likely have been to the Russian Club. Becca's dad might know who he is.'

'Yes… Right… Becca. I remember, you were good

friends with her at school, weren't you? Do you know where she lives?'

'No, I don't, but I know where to find her. She took over from her mother when she retired. Becca's there every day during the summer. But as Southcliffe is now an all-year-round resort, I bet she'll be there most days in the winter too.'

'Where, Gloria? Stop keeping me in suspense.'

'On the prom near the Pleasurebeach. In her little cabin.'

Steve was laughing now. 'What, you mean she's the Laughing Man?'

'No, you berk – but you're close. She's the one and only Gypsy Rosa Lee!'

'No!' exclaimed Steve. 'Really? Wow! So, are we going to have our fortunes told?'

'Couldn't do any harm, could it?' Gloria smiled. 'Might be nice to find out what our futures hold.' They stared at each other, neither wanting to say more. Steve thought Gloria looked as lovely as ever. He desired her. He wanted her. Did she feel the same?

'Stay,' he heard himself say.

Chapter 17
Saturday, 15th January 2000

Steve woke the following morning and glanced over to the other side of the bed. It was empty, as it had been last night after he'd said goodnight to Gloria when she left.

'Stay,' he'd heard himself say to her. She'd looked at him, really looked at him, the way she used to do, as if she knew him totally.

'No,' she'd said quietly. 'I want to – I really want to, but our lives are complicated – too complicated for this at the moment. We'd both regret it in the morning.' She kissed him lightly on the lips, lingering a little longer than expected, as if remembering a past pleasure. 'I have to go. I'll ring you when I've spoken to Becca.' With that she slipped her coat on, and headed for the stairs. She stopped briefly and taking Steve's hand said, 'Don't come down with me, otherwise I might not go. I'll see myself out.' With that, she smiled and was gone.

Steve lay there, with good memories of their times together as teenagers floating through his mind. But those memories began to turn sour as he recalled what he had always called his cowardly leaving of both Gloria and Northcliffe.

Steve had waved his nan goodbye as she set off for her new life in South Wales. He was still only eighteen, but his nan knew that he was worldly-wise enough to make it for himself. With a promise that he would visit as soon as she had settled in, he made his plans. He didn't say goodbye to anyone and he spent the next forty years regretting that. He'd hurt people, Gloria in particular. He'd no answer as to how the money had ended up in his account. He'd no answer as to why his mum had left him when he was young, and he'd no answer as to why his grandpa had died. So he ran away, and he wasn't proud of that. And now he was back in Northcliffe, and he'd no answer as to how his dad was found dead in a hole that had been dug by his grandpa.

Steve had gone to Manchester and taken a job, washing-up in a restaurant in the bustling Chinatown area. Then he'd answered an advert for a general dogsbody at the Manchester Guardian newspaper. Steve's initial tasks were to tidy up in the print-room and to make sure that new spools of paper were always there and ready for loading. But he was soon entrusted with franking the envelopes to go out each day in the post.

He got some cheap 'digs' in the nearby suburb of Sale in a large boarding-house with three other lads of similar ages. The meals were sparse and tasteless, the coal they were given each night for the fire, by a stern-looking landlady, only lasted until nine o'clock. This encouraged them all to take early nights. But Steve felt content. He was used to being on his own and always felt happy with his own company. He avoided small-talk. Some days he would hardly exchange a word with anyone and the months flew past.

One day, the print room manager, from his lofty perch, shouted down for Steve to come up to the office. The two of them had always got on well, so Steve wasn't particularly worried.

'Steve, there's a job going with one of the photographers out in the field. They want someone to carry the equipment, run errands and such like. They asked for someone reliable and enthusiastic. That's you, isn't it? It's a great chance. The previous lad wasn't up to it. It's only part-time, two days a week so you'd be back here the rest of the time. But it's a good opportunity. Just be yourself and don't blow it.'

So Steve reported next day to the photographers' office. He had been told to knock on the door and wait for an answer before announcing who he was.

'Get yourself in here,' said a female voice.

Steve opened the door and went in.

'Are you the help? Do as I say and we'll get along just fine. I just hope you're better than the last one they sent me.'

That was Steve's introduction to the infamous Shirley Baxter, a legend in the field of photography. That same morning, he loaded the camera gear on his shoulders and they made their way into Salford, a city in its own right but slap bang next to the city centre of the more populated Manchester. Shirley's home turf was the subject of her photographic project. There she photographed life in the slums. Candid and spontaneous photos of the local people, both old and young, as they went about their daily lives.

She photographed mothers hanging washing across the back alleys, chatting to each other in the summer sun. She photographed children running, shouting, and playing in the heaps of debris that littered the old bombed-out sites, not yet cleared. They reminded Steve so much of his young days, playing on the cinders behind number 9, Nuttall Road – he and Gloria, and sometimes some others, imagining they were their equivalent of today's superheroes.

Steve took to the job with total commitment. Soon he was hungry for more. In fact, he'd work weekends for nothing and into the late evening, any time when Shirley asked. He'd point out possible sites and views for a particular photo and with his ear to the ground sniffed out places where demolition was due to take place.

Shirley warmed to him. 'I lecture at Salford Art College to would-be photographers,' she said after one particularly successful photo-shoot. 'I've checked your 'O' Level results and although you haven't got the 'A' Levels to match, I think I can swing a place on the evening course for you. That's if you want it? You'd have to do it in your own time, but I reckon you've got all the makings of a good photographer.'

Steve was overjoyed and his broad smile gave it away. 'Are you still living in that hovel, by the way?' asked Shirley. Steve nodded. 'Well, we've got a spare room in our house doing nothing. You can use it if you want. It'd mean I wouldn't have to drive all the way over to Sale to pick you up when we've got something urgent on.'

So Steve moved to leafy Didsbury on the southern edge of Manchester and went to Salford Art College every Wednesday evening. He loved his time living with Shirley and her friend, Jean. They both made Steve welcome, immediately he set foot in their rambling, Victorian semi. Shirley and Jean loved to entertain and they were well known in the area for the lavish dinner parties they hosted. Steve was always invited and he was soon rubbing shoulders with actors and producers from the Granada TV studio located nearby. There were always two or three actors from the successful Coronation Street drama sat around the dinner table and they were keen to hear his take on the slum removal going on in Manchester and comment admiringly on some of his photographs.

It was a wonderful time in Steve's life. Shirley and Jean owned two dogs, Wilf and Honey – both Bedlington Terriers that were spoilt rotten. Steve was allowed to take the dogs on long walks down by the river Mersey. He'd always take his camera with him, an old Zeiss Ikonta 531, given to him by Shirley. Whilst the dogs were off their leads, Steve would snap anything he saw, whatever the weather. Wilf and Honey soon became two of the most photographed dogs in history. He'd spend hours of his own time in the newspaper's dark room, developing his film, looking for the one perfect photo.

Soon, Shirley got him some photographic work of his own, capturing the slum clearance in Hulme, a Manchester suburb and the emergence of the replacement high-rise flats which were to be a scar on the skyline for decades to come. In that environment, Steve learned to talk to people about their everyday life. Events that were important to them. They were fearful of leaving their familiar, albeit dilapidated homes for a soulless replacement. He soon realised that a good photograph needed context and taking an understanding approach opened up new feelings in him. The shy, insular lad of old was gradually being left behind.

Steve graduated from his course with top marks and he was now working on his own projects. It was the mid-1970s and he was told to go over to Ireland. To East Belfast, specifically. It was the predominately Protestant area of the city. He was not there to record the troubles, but to photograph ordinary life as the slums were bulldozed to make way for redevelopment on a massive scale. Previous British governments had thrown money into the Catholic West Belfast area, to clear their slums and try to earn peace that way. But now they were facing a backlash from the Protestant East and needed to even things up. Areas were changing daily and family life was being constantly disturbed or destroyed. Steve captured the very essence of life in those times.

Then he was sent to cover life affected by other conflicts. He was in the Falklands in the '80s living with the ordinary farming communities, capturing their existence whilst the horrors of war took place not far away. Then in the '90s, the Bosnian War brought home first-hand the atrocities that man could inflict on man, neighbour on neighbour. It was impossible during that war to find ordinary life to photograph, when carnage was taking place in the same village.

Up until then, Steve had thought of himself as just an independent observer. His job was just to document what he saw. He didn't allow himself to make judgements on right or wrong. But in Bosnia, he couldn't help but be involved as the terrible events unfolded. He'd race to the scene of yet another act of brutality when it was discovered, half of him wanting to ignore it, but the other half needing to capture it in its raw horror for all the world to see.

The carnage he saw in Bosnia took its toll on

Steve's health. He couldn't sleep without having nightmares about some atrocity that he'd witnessed. He lost weight and became lethargic. Back in Manchester, he didn't pick up a camera for six months. Until one day after a lot of badgering and encouragement from Shirley Baxter, he went back to photographing wildlife in the local parks and river areas. Thus regaining his love for it.

Then three years later, whilst trawling the internet about current goings-on in Northcliffe, he saw a local estate agent had put number 9, Nuttall Road up for sale. A change of life beckoned. He had unfinished business in Northcliffe. He was ready to put things right. To confront his demons. Except the one demon he hadn't expected to face – the discovery of who his dad was.

Chapter 18
Monday, 17th January 2000

There was a general buzz of excitement in the room as Richard entered, closely followed by Cora Stone, with Daniel Atkinson bringing up the rear, clutching a handful of paper. The noise subsided and Richard took centre stage. 'Right, we've had a major breakthrough in this case and it's solely down to DC Atkinson's tenacity. So, Daniel, come forward and tell us what you've found.' Richard beckoned the shy constable forward, still clutching his papers close to his chest. 'OK, Daniel, take us through the process you followed, because I think we can all learn something from this.'

'Right, Sir – right – erm,' he stuttered. 'First, I'd been tasked with locating Jock Crammie, but I'd exhausted all possible options – police and national databases etc. Which was a bit weird. Jock Crammie didn't seem to exist. Then the inspector put me on trying to match the blood DNA sample from the bank robbery, which was the same as that found on the tarpaulin. In the police DNA database, I found a 3.125% match with our sample. It was a Ben Talbot who did six months in prison for joyriding back in 1997. He lives in Stevenage so I rang him and – well, he was a nice lad and wanted to help, if he could.'

A titter went round the room. Daniel had become known as a bit of a romantic and could find the good in everybody. He continued. 'His sister had drawn up a family tree and Ben emailed me a copy. It took a lot of searching, ringing quite a few of those on there and I wasn't sure I was getting anywhere.'

Daniel glanced at his inspector, in case he thought he was wittering too much, but Richard looked back intently and the whole office seemed transfixed. 'Anyway, then one name jumped out at me – John Cameron. He was, or is, Ben Talbot's second cousin twice removed. That means…'

'That means someone who's been thrown out of a wedding twice!' blurted out Barry Crompton to roars of laughter.

Richard laughed too. 'Sometimes it's good to have a wise-crack in the room when it's a tense time. Just as long as it doesn't get out of hand,' he thought. 'Go on, Daniel,' he said, encouragingly, 'tell us the more sober reason.'

'Yes, Sir. It means they share the same great-grandparents. In fact, John Cameron is Ben's grandmother's second cousin'.

'Whoa,' laughed Richard. 'Too much information now – you're baffling us all. Get back to John Cameron, can you, Daniel, please.'

'Right, Sir – John Cameron. He's Scottish, born on 20th April 1927 in Govan, a suburb of Glasgow. I pulled his employment and medical records and even found a copy of his identity card, which everyone was issued with after the war. Everything points to him living and working in and around Northcliffe at the time of both the robbery and the death of Terry Breeze. I managed to track down an old school friend of his, who is still living in the same street in Govan. He said that there were two John Camerons in the same class at the secondary school. So, he started calling himself Jock Crammie. That's why we couldn't trace him.'

'So,' confirmed Richard, 'we already had a probable DNA match between the robbery and the death of Terry Breeze. And now, both can be linked to John Cameron. For the purpose of this investigation, we'll continue to call the suspect Jock Crammie, and Daniel, you've found him, I believe?'

'Yes, Sir, I have and he's still alive – but only just. He's in a hospice in Perth. That's Perth, Australia, not Scotland. He's got lung cancer and I've spoken to his doctor, who says that he's not got long left.'

'Well done, Daniel. Maybe this is the breakthrough we need. Any idea how long he's been out there?'

'The local police reckon it's about thirty years, Sir. We're checking emigration records from around that time.'

Richard Whittle looked up at the crime board. The links were beginning to fit into place. Terry Breeze for definite was part of the bank robbery team. Jock Crammie was now in the frame too and also a good bet for being involved in Breeze's death. That left the other one, the ring-leader. Maybe Crammie would be ready to talk, seeing as he wasn't long for this world.

'Well done, Daniel, excellent police work. We need to get over there to talk to Crammie as soon as possible.'

'Shouldn't we get the Perth police to interview him, Sir?' asked Barry.

'Normally yes, Barry. But bobbies from Southcliffe might be able to get more out of Jock than our Australian friends. Plus, I think I need to be there to ask the right questions.'

Then Richard started the applause which was quickly taken up by the rest of the team. Daniel stood at the front, bright red, but really proud of himself. The briefing broke up after some other tasks were allotted to members of the team. As they left the room, Daniel was inundated with back slaps. He still had words of congratulation ringing in his ears when Richard beckoned him over.

'Hope your passport's up to date, Daniel. I've booked us two tickets on a flight this evening from Manchester to Perth. We need to get there quickly. We'll go via Kazakhstan if necessary.'

'You mean, you want me to go with you, Sir?'

'Yes, I do. Sergeant Stone is in court tomorrow on the drugs ring case. So, seeing as you're familiar with all the background and have done most of the work, I want you along. It'll be good experience for you. Anyway, you've already spoken to an old friend of Crammie's and some of his relatives. It might just make him open up a bit easier.

'This is no holiday, mind. Don't pack your swimsuit! We'll be there and back as soon as we can. You'd better liaise with the guys in Perth, just to make sure it all goes smoothly when we get over there. Do that and then get yourself home and get packed. Cora, can we have a word about the case? See where we're up to. Daniel, I'll see you later this evening.'

Daniel Atkinson could hardly contain himself. It was the

break he needed to take his career upwards. To be part of both a murder and major robbery investigation and to be working alongside Inspector Whittle was just what he'd dreamt of. When he got home, his wife Angie was already in from work and she had a visitor. It was his father.

'Angie, we've got a breakthrough. I've located Jock Crammie and we're off to see him, and guess what, he's in Perth in Australia.' He then blurted out the rest of it to them, including everybody clapping him at the end.

'That's great news, Daniel. Well done, lad. I'll be talking to the chief constable later this afternoon. Clearing this robbery up after so many years is very high profile for the town. It's as important as this murder enquiry. Are you sure that this Crammie was involved in both?'

'Looks like it, Dad. He was definitely there when the body was dumped and the same DNA linked him to the scene of the robbery. Hopefully he'll come clean and lead us to the third man in the robbery. The inspector reckons that they both must have seen off Terry Breeze. Maybe Breeze got greedy – it wouldn't be the first time by all accounts. Anyway, me and Inspector Whittle are booked on a flight tonight from Manchester.'

'Tonight!' exclaimed Angie. I'd better get you a case packed. You always forget something, so I'll do it for you, love. How many nights do you think you'll be away?'

'It's going to be five, I'm afraid, Angie. We have to change in Zurich and Singapore both ways. They were the only economy seats we could get at short notice. The inspector says the budget won't stretch to business class.'

'I'll do it now,' said Angie. 'But I promised your dad a cup of tea about an hour ago. Can you make it for him please, love?'

'Never mind that, you two, you've got lots to do and your goodbyes to say, so I'll get off. Good luck, Daniel. You know that I'm really proud of you, don't you? You've done well, I can see that.' With those words ringing in Daniel's ears, his dad left.

Daniel beamed. He loved it when his father said things like that. He'd always looked up to his father as he grew up, always wanting to please him. 'Atkinson and Son has a certain sound to it,' was what his father would always say. Daniel had been expected to take over the business at some point and he had often felt that by joining the police he'd somehow let his dad down. But after hearing that praise from his dad, Daniel had no doubt that he'd made the right decision.

'I'm worried about your father, Dan,' said Angie, out of the blue, bringing her husband back down to earth. 'He's not been himself lately.'

'What do you mean, Angie? I haven't noticed anything.'

'Dan, these past few weeks you haven't noticed much, other than work,' she grinned. 'It's OK – I know you've got a lot on, but I wonder if your father has some business problems that he'd like to talk over with you. He's been over here a lot more often, lately.'

'Yes, he has, now you come to mention it. He might just be lonely, Angie, but... yes, as soon as I get back, I'll have a talk with him. Is it too much to ask that you keep an eye on him whilst I'm away? I would be really grateful.'

'How grateful is that, constable?'

'Oh, very grateful!' replied Daniel. 'The packing can wait for a couple of hours. As my father said, we have a lot of goodbyes to say!'

Chapter 19
That afternoon

'Is everything on track for tomorrow, Cora? Any last minute hitches?'

'Nothing so far, Sir. We've got the witness under protection. As long as he doesn't get cold feet, then it should go well.'

'Good. There's a lot riding on this, Cora. This is our chance to do some damage to the drug trade round here. It's not going to go away, until Phil Breeze is behind bars. Which is a big ask. At least by busting this drugs ring we should be taking some of his top people out of the frame.'

The drugs problem in Southcliffe was no different to that in any other popular seaside resort in England. The bosses that ran it were protected by a hierarchy of underlings who were too frightened to squeal on pain of reprisals, even if they were in police custody. Information had come to the attention of Cora's team from a middling boss who wanted to get out. He'd been recruited into the gang as a teenager, he now had a young family and was particularly aware of the damage that drugs did to children who got hold of them in their early teen years.

The county drugs squad had got involved and Cora had been seconded to the team because of her local knowledge. It had led to a painstaking investigation over the past six months to uncover the money trail and they had finally been alerted to an upcoming drug consignment due to arrive in the town. With the county police team based outside of the town, there was less chance of information being leaked, or sold from within the police force, something that Richard was all too aware happened on a regular basis. The police operation went without a hitch and some important members of the gang were apprehended. The court case against the ring-leaders was due to start at Manchester Crown Court the next day and Cora was to be called as a witness.

'Strange that it's the Breeze family again that's causing us all this bother, Sir.'

'Yes, but this family's been around since my dad was a boy, and they're not likely to go away anytime soon. They've cleaned up their act a lot. That's not to say that their proceeds from crime didn't give them a head start. But if it wasn't them, it'd be someone else. At least we have control over most of them. It's Phil Breeze that's the problem. Even his brother, Gary, can't really control him.'

'Seems like it's Phil that's inherited his father's bad genes, Sir. What was their mum like?'

'Pat? She was a lovely person. What she saw in Terry Breeze, I've no idea. She brought the two boys up, helped by their grandfather after Terry went missing. She kept them in check during their school days. Both of them were always a bit wild, but it was in his late teens that Phil began to show his nasty side. He's been trying to prove himself ever since. A bit like his dad did, all those years ago, it seems.'

'Maybe someone will put him in the ground as well, Sir. Save us the trouble. And then our successors can dig him up in forty years and try and solve another who-dunnit.'

'Don't say that Cora, even in jest. We don't want any vigilantes here, however much it may make our life a lot easier.'

'Is that what you think happened to Terry Breeze, Sir? The police didn't put him away, so someone else did?'

'It's a strong possibility, Cora. Very strong. Terry Breeze wasn't liked, even by his own family, and then there are the other two robbers. He messed up, by all accounts. So they had to scarper. They'd be none too pleased about that.'

'And did Tom Hamshaw know about Terry fathering his grandson? That's still a strong motive, Sir.'

'Thanks for reminding me, Cora. I can always count on you to keep me professional. Much as I don't want to believe it's true, it's still a viable possibility. Anyway, good luck for tomorrow. I'm certain you'll handle it well. Keep to the facts when you're in the witness box. It's a strong case. Now, talking of cases, I need to get home and get packed. I've just got one more visit to make before I do. Daniel and I have a long journey ahead of us. Here's hoping it's a fruitful one as well.'

Chapter 20
Early evening

Number 9, Nuttall Road was still sealed off by police tape, so work there was out of the question. Instead, Steve turned his energies to his other project. He'd bought the chapel in the same auction as his boyhood home. It came with just over an acre of waste land and was an impulse buy. The chapel had been the last lot in the auction and Steve had stayed on until it came up, more out of curiosity than an intention to bid. But the price was low, and he was the only bidder.

So the old chapel now belonged to him. Steve remembered the chapel from his childhood, cycling past it every day on his way to school. He saw it as an ideal project to do his bit, to help regenerate a part of his town that had fallen out of favour. He intended to use the adjoining land to build small, affordable housing for local families, to give them a start in life. It wasn't easy in England's coastal towns to get a foot on the property ladder. Low wages from seasonal work, together with the influx of retirees, meant that young families were squeezed out of the market.

Steve remembered his days of photographing around the slums of Manchester. He remembered the squalor that families had to contend with daily. But also the happiness that children found from these tight-knit communities. Maybe it was his way of giving something back and Steve was excited at the prospect. He was also in early discussion with the council to do a joint project for regeneration of a row of houses close by.

After his successful purchase, Steve had done some research. It was, to be accurate, a non-conformist chapel, built in 1876 by one of the early benefactors of Northcliffe as the village began to be developed into the seaside resort of today.

Major Nuttall was a war hero from the Crimean War. He had led his brigade as part of the allied expeditionary force. With startling success, given the odds, they overcame the Russian forces in the notorious Battle of the Alma in 1854. The major was born and raised in nearby Wesham. He built this chapel as an incentive for his Welsh workforce. They were encouraged to bring their families up from the valleys, to set down new roots in Northcliffe. Many of the buildings in the town and a good deal of the overall layout have been attributed to Major Nuttall's ambition and drive.

Located near the chapel were some run-down houses, originally built to accommodate the workforce. In their day, these houses buzzed with the excitement and neighbourliness of their inhabitants. Today they were shabby and dilapidated and in need of total regeneration.

The chapel was the key, however. Finish that, and then sell it on, in order to create the funds required for the other renovations to take place. He'd got planning permission granted to convert the ground floor into three-bedded accommodation with a fourth bedroom and second bathroom on a mezzanine floor. It was still in the early stages and today he was meeting a glazing expert who was to undertake the careful removal of the ornate stained-glass windows ready for cleaning and repair.

Steve loved the windows. They weren't the usual religious scenes. They were abstract and impressionist. The mid-1800s saw a revival in Gothic architecture and from America came a brand-new technique in glass manufacture, invented by a painter called Louis Comfort Tiffany. He'd been experimenting with glass to create new textures and depths. Major Nuttall was enchanted by this and commissioned the best craftsmen available to make similar window displays for his chapel. 'These were not made by Tiffany, but were Tiffany-style,' thought Steve. 'Otherwise, they'd be worth millions and would've probably gone walk-about before now.'

'Oi! Hamshaw. I want a word with you.'

Steve turned round and saw the lanky figure of Phil Breeze silhouetted in the doorway. 'Hello Phil. I was expecting you to turn up sometime.'

'Expecting, or dreading? Dear step-brother, I thought I should come and meet the latest addition to our family.'

Steve didn't really know Phil personally, only by reputation, and that reputation wasn't good. Phil, it's fair to say, was like his father – mean, aggressive, selfish – generally not a nice person to cross. He'd gained that reputation under the umbrella and safety of the Breeze clan. Gary ran the businesses and tried to keep his brother in check, but fast cars, impressionable women and shady deals were Phil's forte. This visit, Steve surmised, was not a social one.

Phil, followed by a couple of his blokes, walked into the chapel. Steve immediately thought, 'This looks like trouble.'

'Nice place you've got yourself here, bruv,' said Phil, with a strong accent on the word "bruv". 'It'll look good, if it ever gets to be finished. Kind of place I'd like to live in, but not too keen on the standard of neighbours, if you know what I mean.'

'Selfish brat,' thought Steve. 'What do you want, Phil?' Steve asked. He eyed up each of the lackeys in turn, trying not to look too intimidated by the overwhelming odds.

'I just wanted to warn you off, bruv. You're no Breeze, not part of this family and never will be. Just 'cos my dad fancied a night with some bird years ago doesn't give you any claim on our business. We're just here to make sure you understand that.'

'Phil, you can rest assured that I've no intentions of laying claim to any part of your business. I've no interest at all in knowing what you do or being part of it. As far as I'm concerned, I don't want Terry Breeze in my life. So, you and your henchmen can just leave by the same door that you came in through.'

Steve quickly realised that Phil had come with an agenda to fulfil and that until he'd been roughed up a bit by Phil's lads, that agenda wouldn't be complete. The two thugs started moving towards Steve, coming in from different angles to gain most advantage. They were almost on him when...

'Steve? Any problem here?' A voice came from the doorway. Richard Whittle was standing there. How long he'd been there, Steve couldn't say, but he was a welcome sight.

'You'd better ask Phil, Rich. Phil, any problem?'
Steve asked in a much more reassured way.

'No problem, bruv, none at all. Inspector, I'm just
introducing myself to my new brother,' Phil said, turning
to face Richard. 'Welcoming him to his new family. All
done now. Come on, lads. Remember what I said,
Hamshaw. This isn't over yet.' With that, they turned to
go. Richard stood his ground, blocking their exit. He
stayed still for a few seconds, just to exert his police
authority. Then he moved aside to let them pass before
making his way over to Steve.

'Good job I was passing by,' he grinned.

'I think I had the measure of them,' replied Steve,
grinning back. 'But yes – it was a good job you were
passing. Or were you just passing? It's unlike you, Rich,
not to have a purpose for everything.'

'As it is, I had a reason for this visit. I wanted you to
hear from me that we've located Jock Crammie.'

'How is he?'

'He's dying, Steve. Cancer. He's living in Perth,
Australia – I'm booked on a flight later this evening.
Thought you should know, before it got out.'

'Thanks. Is he in the frame for the murder?'

'There's some DNA match from the tarpaulin,
you'd expect that.'

'Then it's the robbery, is it?' asked Steve.

'I can't give you that information, Steve, you know
that, but…' Richard said nothing more.

At that point Steve should have told Richard about
the photograph with the shadowy figure that he and
Gloria had found. But he didn't. He thought about it later
and realised the reason he'd kept quiet was that his
grandpa was still Rich's number one suspect for Terry

Breeze's death, and it was up to Steve to clear his name. Richard Whittle was a good bloke, but he always did things by the book. There was no evidence yet as to whether this mystery man was just a fanciful thought or a real lead. No, he'd keep that information to himself until he knew more.

'I must go, Steve, I've a plane to catch.'

'Tell Jock "Hi" from me, will you, Rich. Tell him I'm OK. He was always good to me.'

'Will do, Steve. See you later.'

Chapter 21
Tuesday, 18th January 2000

The following day was a real winter's day. It was perishingly cold with an icy wind blowing off the Irish Sea. There was a hint of blue sky in the distance, which gave promise for some better weather to come. Just for fun, instead of driving, Steve and Gloria caught a tram from Northcliffe centre. It trundled its way methodically along the length of the sea front, stopping every two hundred yards or so to pick up, or drop off, the odd passenger. They talked about classmates and shared memories of their school days.

Steve could barely remember Becca Boswell. She was never in his circle of friends, although she and Gloria were quite close. There were a couple of years between thirteen and fifteen, when Steve and Gloria's relationship cooled. They still got on and talked, mainly out of school, but in the confines of the classroom, they both had a different circle of friends.

Gloria enjoyed the company of girls, whose interests at that age were all things fashion and pop music. But she also liked to talk to other boys, much to Steve's irritation. Not that he had anything to worry about. He found it difficult to imagine talking to a girl without fancying her. Gloria, on the other hand, treated everyone except Steve as "just friends". Steve was into football and was the second-best player in his year after the captain, Teddy Watson.

The tram-ride took them through the town of Southcliffe to the south shore area which housed the Pleasurebeach complex. This fun-palace had been built by the Victorians to entice visitors to spend their money on what were seen in those days as scary rides. Some of the wooden structures that supported these rides still existed, although they'd been revamped and strengthened for safety.

Steve could remember the visitors to his nan's boarding house looking forward to their one and only visit in their week's holiday, because that was all they could afford. Only one trip during the week. He used to listen to them talking about their day of enjoyment when they got back to his nan's. Some would go Monday or Tuesday, as they were impatient for the action, but others would listen to their fellow visitors' exploits, knowing full well that their turn was still to come and hoping that the weather would stay kind to them.

Steve and Gloria walked past the entrance to the funfair, with the well-known booth containing the Laughing Man, although at this time of year he was far from laughing. His head lolled to one side and his clown outfit looked a little weather-beaten. Both of them burst out laughing. 'It's infectious, isn't it, Steve? He doesn't even have to laugh to set us off. It brings back happy memories, not just of here, but of me and you.'

Steve was taken aback a bit. He'd been wanting Gloria to say something like that, but never expected her to. He was just about to respond when…

'Hi Gloria, I'm over here.' Their gaze followed the sound of a woman's voice and they saw Becca standing outside a small booth, one without windows. 'I'm just starting to re-do the paintwork, ready for when we open again at Easter,' she said after they'd walked over to see her.

'Hi Steve, you've not changed much. Look – sorry about – you know, erm…'

'Thanks Becca, and don't worry, most people don't know what to say. A lot don't say anything but just think it. I'd rather you said it to me out loud. That way I know you mean it. But I'm glad you didn't say, "Sorry for your loss", because it's no loss to me.'

'Everyone knew what Terry Breeze was like, Steve, even over on this side of town. He caused a lot of trouble when he came visiting with his mates. My dad said everyone breathed a sigh of relief when he disappeared. Anyway, let's not stand here. The café's open, let's get a coffee and have a chat. I'm guessing from our conversation, Gloria, that it's not just a social call?' They got coffees and sat in a quiet corner of the café, overlooking the busy workmen, hard at their repairs.

'So, you took over from your mum here, Becca?'

'Yes, the gift was passed to my mum from my grandmother, and her mother before and beyond that probably. But in reality, everyone has clairvoyancy in them. It's just realising you've got it and understanding it.'

'You make it sound so easy.'

'It is, Gloria. Well, it is for me.'

'So, did your family come from Romania?' asked Steve.

'That's a common misconception, Steve… but I'll

let you off,' she continued, after seeing a look of unease on Steve's face. 'Romany families originally came from Egypt. It's where the name Gypsy originated. It started off as Gyptians and eventually became Gypsies. My surname's Boswell, which is as British Romany as you can get. My dad, Billy, married my mother, Elana Goralova in 1948. Her family had fled Czechoslovakia just as war was breaking out in 1939. That was the time of the round-ups of all Romany people by the Nazis. Just in time, she and her two brothers were sent over to family, who were living in Southcliffe.

'She never knew what happened to my maternal grandparents, but we can guess. After the war, there was plenty of casual work at the circus and funfair for my uncles, as the visitors began to come back. Sadly, one of my uncles, was killed in a fight years back. The other uncle, Valdo, helped my dad set up the Russian Club, not just for Russians, but also for all those people who felt they didn't belong here, or weren't made welcome.

'In the '50s, being ethnic was looked upon with fear and suspicion. Thankfully, those prejudices have eased but not gone completely. Every now and again, I get verbally abused, particularly if they've had a drink or two. So I need a minder on hand when I'm working, just in case. Mostly, I can defuse the situation with a careful word. It's amazing how just mentioning something about a person's future can make an aggressive one into a mouse. It can be good fun sometimes,' she laughed.

'When did you learn about using your gift, Becca?' Gloria asked her friend. 'You were so studious at school.'

'I learnt it during every school holiday. I was taught palmistry and fortune-telling until I knew every facet of the skill. A lot of its secret is just listening to people and then giving them advice. I'm doing the same teaching with my daughter and hopefully she'll take over from me some day. Anyway, Steve, I don't think it takes a clairvoyant to realise that you're here to talk about your dad.'

'You're right, Becca. But it's to do with finding my dad's killer.'

Steve told Becca about finding the body during the dig behind number 9, Nuttall Road. How the police had matched his DNA with that of Terry Breeze. How Terry Breeze was linked to the bank robbery at that time, and how, for want of any other suspects, his grandpa, Tom Hamshaw, was top of the list for the murder. He showed her the photograph that had been taken outside the boarding house, pointing out the mystery man.

'I know it's not politically correct these days, and I apologise immediately, Becca, but my recollection is that he sounded Russian or, I should say now, eastern European. I know it's a long shot, but we were wondering if you could show your dad this photo and see if he can recognise him from his days when he was running the Russian Club? Maybe they met.'

'Asking my dad won't do any good, Steve. He's got dementia. It's been over a year now and he can't even remember who I am most days.'

'Oh, sorry Becca, that was insensitive of me.'

'Not at all, Steve. You couldn't have known about my dad, but my uncle Valdo might know who the man on the photo is. He worked with my dad at the club and he's been around the circus and funfair scene all his life. He's away at the moment, but he should be back in a few days. Can I keep this photo?

'I must say, what a great idea it was for your gran to take a photo of her visitors every week. I should have started it with all my clients. I've had many a famous person come into the booth and some even before they became famous. I've got a few photos, but only those that they sent to me.'

'I bet you've heard some interesting stuff in your time, Becca,' said Gloria.

'I have, Gloria, but I'm like a doctor. Whatever is said between these four walls stays here. We're an honest bunch, us Romanies, whatever others might say!'

'I'll echo that,' said Steve. 'I met many Romany families in Bosnia in the '90s. They were being persecuted, terribly, along with the local Muslim population. But the kindness they showed me, even under terrible conditions, is something I'll never forget.'

There was a short silence, each deep in thought, then Becca said, 'Right. How about I do both of you a reading for free? Don't look like that, Gloria. You don't have to be a believer to listen to what I have to say. It doesn't take a clairvoyant to see that you two belong together. I can see it in how close you sit to each other, how you look at each other. I remember, at school, everyone knew you'd end up together. I remember giving you this advice then, Gloria, that Steve's the right one. Maybe it's taken longer than expected, but journeys have a funny way of not being straight or continuous. There are plenty of hazards on the way, but if it's somewhere you both want to get to, then it's all worthwhile.'

After Becca had given her advice, Steve and Gloria found it difficult to think of anything other than to mumble their goodbyes. Becca said she'd be in touch if she heard anything and they made their way across the road onto the promenade and stood by the railings, watching the waves crash into the sea wall below, sending spray up into the air to freshen their faces.

Steve broke the silence. 'Gloria, we need to talk. I mean really talk, not dance around it. It's all a mess and I messed it up.'

'No Steve, you didn't. I know what happened all those years ago, but now's not the time. Becca's right, you know. Just treat it as if it wasn't meant to be, at that time. We went our separate ways and made new lives for ourselves. You needed to get away, explore who you really were. You saw the world through a lens. Not many people could have taken those photographs, showing the plight of those poor people so well. And me, well, I wouldn't have had my two gorgeous daughters and my adorable Sophie. And soon that little girl will be standing at the school gates, wondering when her grandma is going to arrive to pick her up. So we need to get back. I promise you, we'll talk, very soon.'

They saw a tram almost at their stop, so they had to run to catch it. It was a double decker and they managed to get the front seat upstairs. The journey back to Northcliffe took them back to their teenage years. Both swapped stories of their previous tram trips to Southcliffe. Of them going to the cinema, or to a live summer show or, best of all, the weekly pilgrimage to the Twisted Wheel nightclub.

It was there that they watched live groups and danced the night away. Gloria remembered seeing the Kinks and the Yardbirds, before either of the groups became famous. It was a time when the onlookers would listen and enjoy the music, rather than shriek and scream. Steve remembered the Rolling Stones at the

Palace Theatre where the noise from the audience was so deafening, he could hardly hear a word that Mick Jagger sang.

They parted at the tram stop in Northcliffe, each going their separate way. The hug as they parted lasted a little longer than two people just saying goodbye. 'We'll talk,' mouthed Gloria. 'Promise.' She let Steve's fingers slip slowly from her hand and with a smile, she turned and walked away.

Chapter 22
Wednesday, 19th January in Perth

Jock Crammie was sitting up in bed. Well, propped up, more like. He was gazing vacantly out of his bedroom window at the sunlit garden which stretched down to the Swan River, with the stark outline of Mount Eliza and the city skyline in the background. He felt as if the side of a house had collapsed and fallen on him, pinning him to the ground. His breaths were short and if he coughed, he knew that the result would be searing pain with more blood brought up.

A combination of heavy smoking and the exposure to uranium from those mines was finally seeing him off. He would spend his last days in this room and he didn't think that there were many of them left. He glanced at his hand to see where, in about another hour or so, he'd get another intravenous shot of morphine to ease the growing pain. It was nagging at the moment, bearable, but it would get steadily worse. A lesser man would end up screaming. Jock liked to think that he was made of sterner stuff. These periods between his shots were, however, getting steadily shorter.

The door opened and he looked up, expecting to see one of the nurses, here to take his blood pressure or to plump up his pillows.

'Hello, Jock. It's been quite a while. You don't look good, my friend.' A man that Jock had not seen in over thirty years stood in the doorway. The shock made him gasp for breath and set him off in a coughing fit. The man moved across to the bedside to assist him.

'Sit up, Jock, and have some water.' The man carefully propped another pillow behind the frail Scotsman's head. The wheezing subsided as Jock sipped the water slowly, trying to slow down his breathing. Finally, when he became calmer, Jock had a chance to look at the stranger more closely.

'It's been a long time,' he spluttered, trying not to start coughing again.

'It has indeed, and time hasn't been kind to you, my dear friend.'

'I've done OK with my life. Better than some, not as good as others. But life's been good since I got me a wife, Evie, and a beautiful step-daughter called Lucy.'

'I know, Jock. I heard from Lucy that you were bad. I've been meaning to come over and see you for some time. But when Lucy told me how poorly you were, I wanted to make this final trip.'

'Yeah, thanks for coming. You've been a good friend to me all these years. I couldn't have afforded a place like this without your help.'

'That's what friends do, Jock. Look after each other. But I must say, I didn't expect you to look this bad.'

'Always direct, you were, weren't you? Thing about you I liked the best. Could have been a Gorbals' chap 'cept for yer accent.' Jock managed a bit of a chuckle which set off another bout of coughing. After another couple of sips of water, he started to tell his visitor about his past thirty years as if they would be his last words. 'I needed some work when I got here. That robbery only just paid for my ticket. What a shambles that was,' he joked. 'What were we thinking? Anyway, I got a job up near Batchelor in one of them new uranium mines. Pay was good, but the conditions? Well, you don't consider them at the time, do you? A few beers and a good laugh at the end of a shift, that's all you want.

'Finally got married to a local girl, Evie, and took on her daughter as well. Evie had a husband who'd knocked her about a lot, but he'd just scarpered. Good job, otherwise I might have done for him. Can't stand that sort of bloke. I think they both took me on, rather than the other way round. Made me appreciate the good in people again. They used to visit me most days but I don't want them to see me like this, so I've told them not to visit no more.'

He started wheezing again. The visitor made to stop him speaking to help the breathing, but Jock waved him away. 'Not got long for this world, so I better make the most of it. Haven't had such a conversation in months. Nice of you to visit, but can't think it's just to pay your final respects. I'm guessing our past is finally catching up with us.'

The stranger smiled. 'You guessed right, Jock. It has. The police have dug up Terry Breeze's body and they've reopened the robbery case. These new advances in DNA testing means they've linked you to the robbery and to Breeze's death. You'll be getting a visit from Southcliffe police very soon. So I thought I'd give you a heads up.'

'You don't have to worry about me dobbing you in. You've been a real pal to me, probably the only one I've ever had. Can't do much to hurt me now. Can they? I'm due my next morphine shot in an hour. The gaps in between hurt me more than that could ever do. I'm not one for death-bed confessions. The past is best kept there. It wasn't our greatest moment, was it?'

'No Jock. It wasn't. Nothing went to plan and we've both been paying for it with guilt ever since.'

'They must have someone good on the case, if they've managed to track me down?' Jock wheezed.

'They have. George Whittle's kid, Richard. He's leading the investigation. He'll be on a plane over here, before you know it.'

'George Whittle's son, eh? I heard he'd followed his old man into the force. He'll be good then. George was a top guy. I've never had many coppers for friends, but George... You knew where you stood with George.' The cough rattled round in his ribcage as if unable to find any way out except for a narrow exit via his throat. 'Anyway buddy, thanks for this chat, it's meant a lot to me, to see you again after all this time. I've put a bundle of things together – old photos, letters you sent. Evie has them, she'll post them unless you want to call and pick them up.'

'I'm leaving Perth this evening, Jock, so there's no time. The past is something I don't want to be reminded of.'

Jock looked at the stranger seriously. 'While you're here, would you do me one last favour?'

'Yes, I will, Jock. What is it?'

Chapter 23
Same day in Perth

The flight to Perth had been a horrendous journey. The best flights Richard and Daniel could get at short notice and with economy tickets took them via Zurich and then a long flight to Singapore. They had to kick their heels at Singapore airport for a further six hours before the onward flight took off to Perth. They arrived at Perth airport just after five in the morning, local time. Over twenty-six hours of almost constant travel and sitting, waiting at airports. Two days after setting off.

Both officers slept fitfully on the flights and they were mightily relieved to be met at the airport by Sergeant Gaynor Stanley, a liaison officer with the Perth police. She took charge, shepherding them to their hotel, waving away the registration process and assuring them she would deal with it. She promised to return at 2pm and take them to the hospice. Within an hour of their arrival both Richard and Daniel had showered and were fast asleep in their rooms.

At two o'clock, as agreed, Gaynor met them in the hotel foyer. The car waiting outside soon sped them across the city. Perth is one of Australia's major cities but it's very remote from the other major conurbations.

It's a sprawling low-lying city and was a favourite destination for many Scots who emigrated in the 1960s for the princely sum of ten pounds. Daniel had found out that Jock Crammie hadn't been living above his means – in fact, his existence seemed to be one of hardship. He'd worked in the notorious uranium mines to the far north of the city. Life appeared to be hard and not very rewarding. So if Jock Crammie was one of the robbers, it seemed the robbery was a one-off. 'Maybe killing Terry Breeze had made him change. Hopefully, we'll soon find out,' he thought.

The hospice was on the outskirts of the city in a leafy suburb and looked quite a plush establishment. Richard thought, 'If I had to finish my days somewhere then this would be as good a place as any, but it must be expensive. I wonder where Jock Crammie is getting that kind of money from?'

The summer sun was shining across the neatly manicured lawn, which was enhanced by a backdrop of different grasses and cacti. He could see some of the patients sitting out on the veranda, taking in the sun, chatting, or having a short nap.

The clinical director, Dr Forbes, met them at the front entrance and they made their way along the clean, bright corridors to Jock Crammie's wing.

'He's very weak, Inspector, and a lot of the time he's heavily sedated, but we've held back on the next dose so at least you can have a conversation with him. I'll stay in the room and stop you if it's getting too much for him. My patient's welfare must come first.'

'Understood,' said Richard, although visibly annoyed at any possible restriction to his questioning. There could be a major breakthrough in his investigations and he didn't need an officious doctor interfering.

They turned into a shorter corridor and then stopped outside a glass door. Dr Forbes opened it and walked in followed by the two English policemen. Jock Crammie lay under the sheets with his eyes closed, looking completely peaceful.

'Mr Cameron.' The doctor gently shook the patient's shoulder. 'Mr Cameron, these gentlemen are policemen from England, they'd like to ask you…' The words suddenly died on his breath as he leant over the patient and felt for a pulse at the side of his neck. He turned to Richard. 'I'm afraid he won't be answering any of your questions, Inspector. John Cameron is dead.'

They were ushered out in silence, back into the reception area at the front, as the nursing staff took over.

'There'll be a post-mortem, of course,' said the doctor. 'Although it will probably show that his heart gave out.'

Richard turned to the receptionist. 'Did Mr Crammie… I mean Mr Cameron in room 35, have any visitors today? Can you quickly look for me please?'

The receptionist looked at the doctor, who nodded, giving her permission to answer. She scanned the visitors' book, turning over the previous page.

'A Mr Alksnis visited him today about two hours ago.'

'Alksnis?' snapped Richard. 'Who's Alksnis?'

The receptionist was flustered. 'I don't know. I don't think I've seen him before,' she said. 'But he rings every week, to check on Mr Cameron's health.'

'Something's not quite right, Daniel,' muttered a concerned Richard. 'Doctor, this is potentially a crime scene. I must ask you to close the outside gates and not allow anyone in or out. Daniel, get back to Crammie's room and stop anything or anybody from contaminating the scene.'

'Inspector, I must protest. This is not England. I'm sure you have no authority to do this. This is a hospice where very ill people are trying to see out their lives in peace. Mr Cameron most probably died of a heart attack.'

'Doctor Forbes, I've come all the way from England to question John Cameron about a murder and a forty-year-old bank robbery. Cameron is now dead and he'd just had a visitor two hours previously. In my experience that adds up to being very suspicious. I don't believe in coincidences like this. So will you please do as I ask?'

'Ah, I see what you mean.'

Richard turned to the liaison officer. 'Gaynor, can you ring your colleagues and get a SOCO team out here urgently, and an investigating officer. As Doctor Forbes quite rightly points out, I have no jurisdiction out here, but I do have a "copper's nose" and I'd be amazed if this is just a straightforward heart attack.'

Richard paced around the waiting area with constantly changing thoughts swirling around in his head. He knew this was no coincidence and was just waiting for confirmation. 'If only we'd come straight here from the airport, or we'd flown direct.' Then he gained control and told himself, 'Stop it, Richard. You can't change this now. Concentrate, man. Someone knew we were coming. Someone from back home has associates over here and set it up. That must be it. We're getting close, I know it.'

'Daniel, get yourself off to the local station. Try and

identify who this Alksnis is. And get some background information on Crammie's time while he was in Perth.'

The SOCO team arrived and set to work. After the young forensic scientist had examined Jock's body, she approached an expectant Richard and gave her verdict on the likely cause of death.

'The deceased was suffocated, probably using his own pillow. I'll have to do some tests but it's covered with saliva, which would correspond with him choking. He's been dead for about an hour, but I'll be more exact in my report.'

'So this visitor for Mr Cameron, Alksnis, did you say?' Richard asked, turning to the receptionist. 'Do you think he was Australian?'

'That's difficult to tell. He spoke with a foreign accent. Yugoslavian or whatever they are now. There's a lot of them up here in Perth. It sounded like that sort of accent.'

'Latvian.'

Richard turned to the forensic scientist. 'What did you say?'

'Latvian. Alksnis is a Latvian name. I'm Latvian, so I know. It means Alder tree in our language.'

'Do you know him?' asked Richard.

'No,' replied the scientist. 'There are only three Latvian families in Perth, and none of them are called Alksnis.'

Richard looked out of the window at the setting sun, deep in thought. Finally, it all became clear. "The Russian!". He had his third man.

Whilst he was still at the hospice, Richard asked the receptionist if she knew how Alksnis had arrived. She thought it was by taxi but wasn't sure. 'I noticed some sort of car waiting outside for a while when he was here. There was someone in the driver's seat. But I didn't see Mr Alksnis get out or get back in,' she said.

Richard turned to Gaynor and said, 'Jock Crammie paid for his treatment from his own personal account. That makes me wonder if the cash was being provided by this Alksnis guy. Can you try and track it down, please?'

Gaynor replied, 'Yes, I'll start following the money trail back through the Australian banking system. I'll also get my colleagues to check out all the taxi firms in the city to locate the driver and the car.'

The Perth police were still checking things out when Richard and Daniel were airborne on the first leg of their long journey home later that evening.

Richard stared out of the window, looking at the fast-receding city skyline below. He felt so frustrated. This mystery man was beginning to annoy the normally unflappable inspector.

Chapter 24
Thursday, 20th January 2000

Steve's sleep was broken by the sound of his mobile phone ringing. He switched on his bedside light and as he reached to pick up the phone, he glanced at his alarm clock. It was two-thirty in the morning. 'Mr Hamshaw? Mr Steven Hamshaw?'

'Yes, what is it?'

'It's Sergeant Cooper, Sir – from the police. Do you own the chapel on North Drive, Sir?'

'Yes, I do. What's wrong, Sergeant?'

'I'm afraid that it's on fire, Sir. The fire brigade are in attendance as we speak. I wonder if you would come down here as soon as possible.'

Steve threw on some clothing and drove the five-minute journey to the chapel. He could see the flames flaring up into the sky as he turned into North Drive. Two fire engines were in attendance and the crews were busy trying to contain the blaze. Steve sought out the lead firefighter, whom he knew by sight as Trevor Perkins.

'It's nearly under control now, Mr Hamshaw. It looks worse than it is. The fire was confined to an area just behind the wooden front doors. My investigation team will have a good look, but to me it's a deliberate act. Can you smell the petrol in the air?'

'Yes, I can. I didn't keep anything in there that could trigger a fire. The building is just a shell really.'

'A good job you didn't. The fire had nothing to burn other than your doors and the frame plus what looks like a pile of wood and cloths behind the door. We should be finished within half an hour.'

'Thanks for coming out so swiftly,' said Steve. 'It could have caused damage to the surrounding houses.'

'Probably not,' said Trevor. 'The wind's not strong tonight. It'd probably have burnt out by itself eventually. By the way – the side entrance door was staved in. It's hanging off its hinges. Looks like it was the arsonist's method of entry.'

'That was a strong door,' said Steve. 'Someone really wanted to get in and make a point.'

'I'm sure the police will be wanting to ask you if there's anyone with a grudge, Mr Hamshaw,' Trevor said, with a smile, knowing about Steve's link to the Breeze family.

'And I'm sure I can give them one or two names to keep them going,' replied Steve.

Steve stayed around until the fire crews had left the scene. One of his builder mates, Jim, lived just round the corner and he was already there amongst the locals watching the events. Together they shored up the broken doorway with thick plywood and cleared away the remnants of the burnt joists. Jim's wife brought over some coffee and bacon butties when they'd finished. By the time Jim and his wife said their goodbyes, it was five-thirty.

Steve decided to stay on and try and clear things up a bit, before his crew came in later that morning. He checked that the front doors would still open and shut easily and that the locks worked. The doors were made from solid oak and had withstood most of the fire. There were a few scorch marks. 'It's given them some character,' thought Steve. 'I must remember to thank Phil, when I see him next.'

The whole chapel floor was clear now. The emergency lighting from the mobile generator gave off a bright glow to the centre of the floor, whilst leaving dark shadows at the edges. Steve thanked his lucky stars that the irreplaceable stained-glass windows had been removed and taken away for repair the previous morning, before the fire had been set. Surveying the scene inside the chapel, he could see only minimal damage caused by the flames. Some joists would have to be replaced, but structurally it was still sound. In fact, most of the damage was done by the water used to douse the fire.

Steve had spoken to Sergeant Cooper earlier and had been informed that there hadn't been any progress made on finding the culprit. However, the fire investigator had just left and he'd confirmed that the blaze had been started by burning petrol-soaked rags and wooden joists piled up behind the door. 'I'm going to have one hell-of-a-job convincing the insurance people to pay up,' thought Steve.

Just then, Steve turned towards a noise as the wooden front door opened. In the shadow of the door stood Gary Breeze.

'Oh no,' thought Steve. 'What does he want?'

'Hello Gary,' he sighed. 'Come to see your little

brother's handiwork?'

'That's a strong accusation, Steve. Have you got some proof he did this?... I thought not. It might have been one of your workmen not tidying up properly. Or it could have been kids. You know what they're like round here.'

'I'm afraid not. It's got all the hallmarks of a vindictive coward, who's trying to send a message to his half-brother to keep out of the Breezes' business. But then again – you fit that bill as well, Gary. It wasn't you was it, by any chance?'

'Not my style, Hamshaw. All our businesses are totally legitimate these days. We're pillars of society in Northcliffe – ask anyone.'

'So, if it's not gloating that you're here for, what is it? I've got lots of things that need my time.'

Gary Breeze walked up close. 'At least he's on his own,' thought Steve.

'I'm here to warn you to stay away from my wife. She doesn't want you around, and neither do I.'

'I think Gloria is old enough to know what she does and doesn't want, without her husband deciding for her. Don't you? Or are you going to fit me up again – you know, just like you did thirty-three years ago?'

'I don't know what you mean. Nobody set you up. You stole money from Don Ward. You were lucky he didn't press charges. All you did was run away like a frightened rabbit. Gloria was devastated by your deception. I had to pick up the pieces and we've done just fine while you've been gone.'

'And now I'm back, Gary. Gloria's a friend from years back. If she wants to see me, then it's down to her. Not you. And definitely not a husband who's well-known around here for his numerous affairs. That doesn't show much respect to someone like Gloria, does it? Or any feeling towards your daughters.'

'Leave my family out of this, Hamshaw.' With that, Gary lunged forward, attempting to hit Steve. But Steve was ready and Gary was unfit and carrying excess weight.

'It's like being attacked by a beached seal, wafting a flipper in my direction,' Steve laughed to himself. He managed to catch Gary under his arms as he stumbled past. A quick flip and Gary fell on his backside on the wet floor. Steve tried to help him up, but was pushed away.

As Gary rose, he stared daggers at Steve. 'Just like your grandad, you are. Is this what he did to my dad? Beat him up. Killed him. They'll prove it now. And when they do, maybe you'll turn tail and run off again. Good riddance, I say. And stay away from my wife. Last warning.' With a final jab of his finger in Steve's direction, Gary turned round and left.

Steve watched the door for a few moments, then went over and closed it. He replayed this confrontation in his mind. Why was he back? Really? Was it to settle old scores, reclaim an old flame or relive those lost years? Maybe he was better on his own. He'd never been good at relationships. He'd messed up any hope of settling down with somebody special. Maybe Gary Breeze was right. Steve Hamshaw had run away thirty-three years ago and he'd been running ever since. What right did he have to come back and disrupt Gloria's life? She seemed content and happy. She had two lovely daughters and a grand-daughter she adored. Why should he mess that up for her?

Maybe it would be for the best, all-round, if he left Northcliffe. But not before he'd cleared his grandpa of Terry Breeze's murder. He owed that to his grandpa's good name within this community. 'I'll clear Grandpa's name and then sell up and leave. That'll be the best thing for everyone,' Steve thought with increasing resolve.

Chapter 25
Saturday, 22nd January 2000

'There's a photo doing the rounds, an old one with you on it. Do you know what I mean? Someone's looking for this person, and they're asking me if I know him.' The voice on the other end of the phone paused, to let the effect of his words sink in. 'My guess is, it's worth a favour or two for me to keep quiet again.'

'I've helped you enough in the past, Valdo. I've put my neck on the block for you more than once. You've done all right by me, keeping my secret. That illegal planning permission on your farm. If the council found out the truth, then they'd make you demolish it... I'm tired, Valdo. Tired of all the deception and secrets. So, go ahead, make it known if you really want to, but make sure you realise that there can be no winners here.'

'Fair enough,' came the voice from the other end, 'I won't say anything. But you can't fault a man for trying.'

'No, you can't, but I can give you something in return. Something that will maybe give you some peace at last.'

'OK, what is it?'

'Cristian's death in 1947. The police now know who

did it.'

Cristian Goralova was Valdo's older brother. Valdo had doted on him and when Cristian was killed at the Gala rumble all those years ago, Valdo had vowed to find the culprit. After the war, he'd settled in Southcliffe working at the circus, first of all cleaning out the animal cages and then at front of stage as one of the clowns. All that time he kept his ear to the ground, hoping to find a clue to the culprit's identity. Revenge had fired in his belly for many years, but as he grew older it mellowed. On hearing his brother's name, the fire burned once more.

'Who is it? Tell me.'

'The word is that it was Terry Breeze. He's been identified as the skeleton that was dug up three weeks ago. You must have heard about it – it's been all over the news. The police have a cold case open for that, and for the Southcliffe bank robbery in 1957. You know, the one where the bank guard was stabbed. Seems that they've matched the bank guard's wound with the one that killed your brother. Something about a chip on the knife's blade. It's not totally conclusive and I doubt it would have been enough to convict him in a court of law, if he were still alive. But the police are satisfied.'

There was a pause at the other end of the line and then a sound of a sharp intake of breath. 'Terry Breeze. That scumbag. I had my suspicions all along but the rest of my family said to let it go. Don't make trouble with the Breezes. They're still causing trouble today, well, one is, in particular. Thanks. That's payment enough. Your secret's still safe with me for now.'

The phone line went dead and Graham Atkinson stood there shaking. He'd been keeping secrets for all of his life, hiding, pretending to be someone else, sorting it out if those secrets were in danger of being exposed.

He'd kept secrets from his wife, until she'd prised them out of him. He'd kept secrets from his son which could have devastating consequences if they became public. He was tired, but he also knew what he had to do to keep Daniel safe. Hopefully the information that he'd passed on to Valdo about Terry Breeze would have bought him the time he needed.

Chapter 26
Sunday, 23rd January 2000

Richard and Daniel arrived at the police station almost at the same time.

'Daniel, you look like death.'

'You too, Sir. This jet-lag's a killer.'

'Right, Cora,' Richard turned to his sergeant. 'What have you got?' Richard had phoned the station back in the UK as soon as he had been given the details of Jock Crammie's death and the possible link to a person called Alksnis. Richard reckoned that this person was either an Australian or more likely, in his mind, someone from the Southcliffe area who'd got wind of their investigation and managed to fly over more quickly than he and Daniel.

'There's nobody with the name of Alksnis locally,' Cora said, bringing Richard's thoughts back to the job in hand. 'We've identified some families with that surname in the Northwest – one is in Blackburn and there are twelve in the Greater Manchester area. We're checking these out, before we start looking farther afield. There's only a couple more to go.

'We've concentrated on the UK airports with direct

flights to Perth and other Australian airports. We're waiting for them to get back to us. Perth are checking all flights at their end. And we've also got requests out with our EU friends to see if he's on their radar.'

'Good, concentrate on those direct flights. If he comes from round here, he'd have had to have gone direct to get there before us.'

'Unless he was on our flight, Sir,' Daniel wondered out loud. 'He could have gone straight from the airport to the home, whilst we caught up with our sleep.'

'All right, Daniel. If so, that was a major blunder on my part. The question is, how did he know what we were doing out there and get to Crammie before we did? I should have got the locals to put some protection on Crammie as soon as we located him. I made a big mistake, but I won't underestimate Alksnis again.'

Cora drew Richard to one side and quietly asked, 'Could we have a leak, Sir?'

'I hope not, Cora, but he seems to be one step ahead of us all the time. I think it might be wise to keep a few facts from the others for now. Just in case. Anyway, there's nothing else we can do, except to redouble our efforts.'

Turning back to the gathered officers, Richard started allocating the leads to be followed up.

'Get me a list of all passengers on our flight, will you, Daniel. We may need to eliminate every one of them. Barry, check the flights from the UK to Latvia, going back six months to start with. Yes, I know it's a busy route with all those stag nights going on in Riga, but get onto it all the same. We've identified that Alksnis is a Latvian name. He may have relatives back there, that he visits. But if he lives in this area, and my gut feeling says that he does, then he has to have a British bank account that paid for Jock Crammie's treatment. He knows we've unearthed Terry Breeze and he knows the heat's on. He took one almighty gamble going after Jock, so we know he's getting desperate.'

All that morning, the phone-lines buzzed with conversations as the team tried to locate any information that would give them a lead towards finding Alksnis.

Later that morning, Cora fairly raced into Richard's office and slapped down a sheet of A4 paper on his desk.

'Sir, we've got a hit from Heathrow airport in our search for Alksnis. Someone of that name caught the Qantas flight on the evening of the 17th from Heathrow. It was a direct flight, getting in to Perth at 1:30am on the 19th, four hours before you and Daniel arrived.'

'Damn,' swore Richard. 'I tried to get us on that flight but it was all booked up except for spaces in business class. Don't tell me he went business class, Cora, please.'

'He went business class, Sir, I'm afraid. Probably slept well and was fresh and ready to go on his arrival. It's not your fault, Sir.'

'Try telling that to the super, Cora. This case is a mighty big headache. Still, we can only crack on with what we've got. Can you get back on to Manchester airport and get all the passenger lists for flights on the 17th to Heathrow? He had to get to Heathrow airport somehow. Get on to the Passport Office as well and request an address. Let's keep doing the proper police-work and the results will come.

'I've got a couple of phone calls to make, then I'm heading for home and my bed.' Then turning to Daniel,

Richard said, 'You get yourself off and get some sleep as well. We both need clear heads if we're to solve this case and a few more hours isn't going to make much difference. I'll see you back here first thing in the morning. Cora, can I have a word – in the office, please?'

'Take a seat, Cora. So, what happened with the court case? I was hoping that Phil Breeze's people would have been banged up by now.'

'Me too, sir. Our whistle-blower got cold feet. He decided not to give evidence. There wasn't enough for the DPP to take it forward.'

'Was he got at, do you think?'

'Almost certainly, Sir. We think that they threatened his mum and dad. We'd got his wife and kids in protective custody, but we can't stretch it to everybody in his family.'

'So, Phil Breeze got away with it?'

'He did, Sir. I'd have loved to have wiped that smile off his face, but the queue would be too long! All that time and effort, gone to waste.'

'Not totally, Cora. You intercepted a big shipment of drugs that were intended for our streets. And you've brought Phil Breeze's activities out into the open. His paymasters won't be too pleased about that. You've caused him plenty of grief. A small win, but a win all the same. He'll slip up, sooner or later.

'Now, my cosy bed is calling me. No more major crimes until tomorrow. Do you think you can manage that, Sergeant?'

Cora smiled. 'I'll try my best, Sir.'

Chapter 27
Monday, 24th January 2000

'Sir, we've got a dead body, out on the salt marshes on the way to Braides, just off Back Sands Lane. The crew are already on their way... No. All I know is it's a male and it looks recent. Maybe just a drowning... Yes, Sir, I'm on site, but haven't had a chance to see for myself yet. It was reported by a local dog walker.'

Cora Stone got off the phone to Inspector Whittle, unfastened her seat-belt and got out of the car. She made her way over to the cordoned-off area, where a tent was being erected over the body, to shield it from the inclement weather. She couldn't do much until the scene of crime operatives had finished their preliminary investigation, but she could at least look at the body from a short distance away, to see if she could recognise him. He looked old, probably '60s or '70s. He wasn't really dressed for walking, though. The face was difficult to see as it was partially hidden by the bank of one of the deep channels which had been carved by the tide over many years. But from what she could see, she didn't recognise him.

Cora stood and faced the sea some fifty yards away.

151

The tide seemed to have turned and it would be a race against time to get the scene processed and the body moved before the site was once again covered in water. This area was a bleak part of the world in late winter, almost always buffeted by wind and rain off the Irish Sea. In the distance, across the estuary, she could just make out the ruins of Cockersand Abbey, a twelfth century building, housing an infirmary for the local peasantry at that time, and further to the east was a farm, with a group of outbuildings.

By the time Richard arrived, David Leadbeater and his forensic team had swung into action. The makeshift tent was keeping out most of the rain, but the tide was making its relentless progress towards the technicians.

Cora proceeded to fill him in. 'No news yet, Sir. Seeing as how the tide's on its way in, I've left them to it. I've sent one of the locals over to the farm to see if they saw anything. The lady who found the body has given a statement and she's being taken home. Nothing obvious, just taking her daily walk. She did the same walk yesterday and no body, so...'

'Male, late '60s I'd say. Looks like stab wound to the chest,' said David, interrupting the two police officers. 'The body's been submerged in water for a while. My opinion is that this happened here, or the body was dumped before the last high tide. Normally it would have been carried out to sea and washed up onto the shore further up the coast, but the jacket got hooked on a steel bar sticking up in the channel, probably some old fencing, and that kept the body here overnight. We won't know more until I get it back to the lab. We'll do that now.' He looked across at the ever-closer tide and set off to go back. He turned and smiled, 'Nice of you to find me a body with some flesh on it, Richard, for a change. See you in the morning for the autopsy. Bright and early, mind.'

Just then, Cora and Richard's mobile phones rang almost simultaneously. They both moved away, turning against the wind, straining to hear the voices on the other end. Cora's call ended first and once Richard had put his phone away too, she spoke.

'Nothing from the farm, Sir. They don't often come out here except to round up any stray sheep.'

'Better result for me, though. I noticed a car parked off the roadway on the way up, just off Back Sands Lane. Sent the reg. number through. It's come back as being owned by a Valdo Goralova, who lives in Burlington Road, Southcliffe, at the back of the Pleasurebeach. He's had the odd misdemeanour – affray, possession, but nothing else on his record since 1984. Apparently, he worked at the circus for years, as a clown.'

'Have we got our third robber, Sir?'

'Whoa, let's not get too excited yet, Cora. Jock Crammie's dead and there's an Eastern European connection. And now this. Is it a coincidence or is it connected? More legwork, I'm afraid. Let's get back to the station, give the team a ring and get them all back in for a two o'clock briefing.'

On the drive back, Richard mulled over all that had occurred on the case over the previous few days. 'Jock Crammie's murder came as a big shock', he thought. Until then he'd felt he was in control of the case, that it was moving along in a linear way – find body, locate suspects, get confession and somewhere in that process, determine motive.

'A policeman should always expect setbacks, but these setbacks have a strange feel to them,' thought Richard. 'Does someone know what my team are doing and what progress they're making? Because it seems that someone is one step ahead. And now, another murder… Is this definitely linked to the case, or are we just jumping the gun? Am I trying to see a connection that isn't there?'

He got a grip. 'Don't get ahead of yourself, Richard Whittle. Stick to the facts and wait for David's findings tomorrow. This case has a long way to go yet.'

Chapter 28
Tuesday, 25th January 2000

Richard was joined by Cora at the forensic lab at 8:15 the following morning. As they entered the lab, it was already a hive of activity, almost as if no-one had been to bed the night before. David Leadbeater was taking a telephone call in his office so they had chance to watch the technicians at work.

In the far corner, the remains of the Terry Breeze dig were still bagged and stacked. Other bits of debris had been tagged and were on separate desks, being analysed. Richard marvelled at the amount that had been reclaimed from the burial site over the previous three weeks. The site had now been released from police control and Steve was allowed to do what he wanted with it.

Steve had made it clear to Richard that he'd no intention of doing anything with the site for the foreseeable future, other than to fill in the accursed hole, level the surrounding area and remove any dangerous rubble. Already, the site had become an attraction for morbid voyeurs to visit. Not just locals, but those from much further afield with a penchant for the macabre. The local café owners joked that this had given them a massive boost at a time of year when this small seaside resort was scarcely visited.

David came out of his office with quite a spring in his step. 'Whether it's just the new millennium or a sign of things to come, but this case, Richard, it gets more interesting to us forensic guys every day. We've got three major findings, so get yourselves comfortable.'

'Ah-ha,' thought Cora. 'The famous Professor Leadbeater's three findings.' She was getting used to it by now.

'First finding. The body is indeed that of Valdo Goralova. We've checked his dental records. Formal identification will be done by his niece later today. He was stabbed with a thrust from the front in a downwards direction. That would be consistent with a taller person being the culprit. Look, you can see the entry wound.'

'So, what was Goralova? Five feet nine... ten?'

'Good guess, Richard. Five feet nine and a half, or one point seven six metres in new money!'

'Would I be right in assuming, from the angle of entry, that the attacker was right-handed, David?'

'Well spotted, Inspector,' David observed dryly.

'He also got close up as well,' added Cora, 'so they probably knew each other.'

'But that wasn't the cause of death,' David said. 'We found water in his lungs, seawater to be precise.'

'So he drowned?'

'Yes, Richard, he drowned. The exact time of death is a little difficult to ascertain, but I'd estimate between midnight and two in the morning.'

'And high tide was when?' asked Richard, turning to Cora.

'High tide last night was 11:59pm,' said David.

'I've already looked it up.'

'Of course, you have, David,' replied Richard, dryly. 'Any idea of the high tide yesterday morning at all? As if I need to ask.'

'That would be 10:03am.'

'Sir, we took tide measurements at the location where the body was found. That area is submerged under water for about two hours before and after high tide.'

'This means that any altercation must have happened between... What – 1pm and 10pm? Do you agree with my maths, Cora?'

'Yes, Sir. I do.'

'So, in that nine-hour window, some meeting between Valdo Goralova and his assailant took place. Goralova was stabbed and, although not dead, was either dumped in the channel or staggered off and collapsed. The incoming tide would drown him and then the outgoing tide would be expected to do the clearing up. Can we narrow the time frame down any more?'

'Yes, we can, Sir. I talked to the farm owner again. He'd been muck-spreading in a field opposite the spot where Goralova's car was parked. He was on his way home at about 6:30pm on his tractor. He says he'd have noticed the car if it was there then. And he didn't. So, that narrows the time frame down to about three hours.'

'It'd be dark by then, Cora. Can he be sure of that?' asked Richard.

'Yes, Sir, he can. The tractor's lights were on and a hare ran across the road in front of him. He had to brake hard. Then he watched the hare as it ran into the bushes, exactly where the car was later found. It's a popular place for couples to stop. A quiet place, a bit remote. You know, Sir,' smiled Cora.

'I do indeed. OK, so that's progress. I presume that was the second finding. Was it, David?'

'Correct. Even better than my estimate.'

'And the third finding, then, David?' He hoped that the pathologist was saving the best until last again.

'The third finding, Richard, is that there were fragments of skin under the fingernails of the victim's right hand.'

'What, they weren't washed off by the seawater?'

'No, not totally. I found the hand caught up in his jacket, probably clutching his wound after the stabbing. That seemed to protect it from the buffeting of the tide. Anyway, not all fragments were washed away.'

'So, David, tell me you have a match.'

'Indeed, I do have a match. Someone on the police DNA database. A total match.' The chief forensic scientist passed a sheet of A4 paper over to Richard, and with Cora looking on, announced, 'Phil Breeze's DNA matches the flesh found under the dead body's nails.'

It took a few moments for it to sink in. 'Richard, I swear, this is the most convoluted case I've ever come across. I could write a book about this case alone and retire rich and happy.'

'Not until we've solved it, you can't, David. It might still be two cases not even connected. Cora, could this be linked to your case? When the county police intercepted the drug delivery to Phil Breeze?'

'It could be, Sir. It could be someone demanding some hush money to keep quiet about Phil's drug activities. But Valdo Goralova has never been on our radar. I'll check with the drugs squad, but I'm pretty sure he's not an active player.'

'Right, we'd better be smart how we play this, Cora.

As soon as we make our move, Phil Breeze will be on the phone to that smarmy lawyer from Manchester. We need to have all the facts and have them straight. We mustn't allow any wriggle-room. Get back to the station and see if we can pull any records of his car's movements yesterday. Check all the traffic cameras. That's a swanky car he's got, so it's bound to show up on one of them.

'He'll be pretty confident that the death can't be attributed to him. He'll think it's already in the sea, ready to be washed up further up the coast near Morecambe. He's not the brightest, our Phil. If we can goad him into talking, we may just get somewhere. We also need to dig and see if there's any link between Valdo Goralova and Phil Breeze, any run-ins they may have had in the past. We might just get a result on this now.'

Richard turned to David once more. 'David, Jill and I owe you and Mary a slap-up meal after this. With you buying those two paintings last weekend, you were already the flavour of the month in the Whittle household.'

'Happy to oblige, Richard, and we look forward to the meal, but no more bodies, please. My workload has sky-rocketed. However, I have kept something back. It's purely conjecture on my part, and I need to do some more testing and even then, it will be quite difficult to prove…'

'David, for pity's sake, put us out of our misery. What have you got?'

'Well, as you know, I've been looking closely at the entry wounds of that chap that was killed at the Gala in 1947. The photos were quite detailed for the time, I have to say.'

'Yes, you managed to match that wound to the wound that Arthur Dowling, the bank guard, suffered. You told me it was the same knife.'

'Most probably the same knife, Richard. Without having the knife in front of me, I couldn't be certain.'

Richard knew he couldn't rush David. He'd find out in David's own time.

'Valdo's knife wound had similarities to the other two wounds. So, I did some further analysis.'

'Don't tell me this is the same knife?' Richard asked eagerly.

'Yes. I can't be more definite but all three wounds show a knife with serrated edges and a notch of missing steel near the top. I would even go so far as to say, there are strong similarities in all three wounds. If I had the knife, I could be more certain?' David looked inquiringly.

'Wow,' said Cora. 'It looks like the knife was passed down from Terry to his son. If we search Phil's house, we'll probably find it. Have we got enough evidence for that to happen, Sir?'

'I'm not sure yet, Cora. It could be a difficult thing to prove, but we can run with that and see where it goes.' Turning to David, Richard asked, 'Anything else before we go?'

'Nothing else, Richard, except maybe an extra brandy after the meal you promised.'

Back in the car, Richard mulled over the new revelations. 'The same knife was used in three stabbings over a period of forty-three years. This is not a coincidence, Cora. I agree, Terry Breeze's knife has been passed down. We never found it in the search of his burial site. So it's come into the possession of his son, Phil. He's probably been carrying it for years. But we're still no clearer as to why Phil met Valdo in such a remote place. Could it be something to do with the collapsed drug trial? Maybe Valdo had information and was trying to blackmail Phil? Phil wouldn't play ball, and then it all kicked off?'

Cora organised the team to concentrate on details of Valdo Goralova's life and any cross-overs with Phil Breeze. There were many tenuous links, as there would be in a town this size and with the similar company both kept. Cora wanted desperately to take Phil Breeze down after the humiliation she'd suffered in court, where her witness refused to testify. Something nagged in her brain, something to do with the case, but she just couldn't drag it to the fore. She started reading the files from the beginning, and it made her realise that as a case evolves, small details could be easily put aside as irrelevant or less important.

Chapter 29
That afternoon

Daniel Atkinson had been kept busy on his favourite job, following any leads and crossing off names. In reality this meant working his way through the passenger lists on possible 'mystery man' suspects that had flown into Heathrow from Manchester in time for the Perth flight. He'd had no success so far, but that didn't deter him at all. He knew that painstaking checking was required for any breakthrough. As usual, he'd worked through his lunch break, stopping only to munch a sandwich that had been brought from the canteen by a colleague.

His thoughts were interrupted by a phone call on his personal mobile. It was his father's neighbour, Ken Barton.

'Dan, it's Ken here. Sorry to bother you at work, but your father's burglar alarm is going off. It's been like that for the past hour or so. I've checked the doors and the windows and there doesn't seem to be any sign of a forced entry. I rang your dad quite a few times but couldn't get an answer. I've left him three messages. I just thought I'd let you know in case you know where he is?'

'No, I don't, Ken. I'll come over and turn it off and have a look for myself. Thanks for ringing.'

'Don't mention it, Dan. I just thought you should know.'

Daniel quickly tidied his desk and turned off his computer, and after clearing it with Sergeant Stone, he was soon off to his father's house.

As he drove there, he thought about his relationship with his father. Angie had said before the Perth trip, that his father had something on his mind. Daniel had promised to address her concerns when he got back, but the workload had increased and he'd put it off. Deep down Daniel knew that was an excuse. An excuse not to ask his father too many questions. All his life, he'd never seemed to have really known his father. There was always something that appeared to be hidden in the father-son relationship. Not knowing, and therefore not asking, was the simplest solution.

'It's much easier, as a policeman, to delve into other people's problems and try to solve them, rather than those of your own family,' he thought.

Daniel reached his father's home. A large, detached, mock-tudor style house overlooking Stanley Park. It was an exclusive area of Southcliffe where wealthy people lived. Two doors down, there lived a retired British and Commonwealth boxer, who now ran a successful nightclub on the sea-front. Growing up, Daniel would watch from his bedroom window as the athlete set off on his early morning training run. He'd watch the mighty man as he disappeared beyond the park gates into the trees and then Daniel's eyes would focus beyond there, to the distance, where he could make out the shapes of the larger wild animals of the famous zoo. Elephants would parade majestically, waving their trunks as they became impatient for their morning feed. Giraffes would chew lazily at the straw bales. It had been a lonely but satisfying childhood for Daniel, and he loved this house and all its memories.

He used his own key to gain access and turned off the alarm, situated behind the door. A quick scan of all the rooms confirmed what Ken had said. There was no forced entry or anything out of place.

'A faulty alarm,' thought Daniel. He quickly texted Ken to put his dad's neighbour's mind at rest.

Daniel couldn't resist climbing the stairs again to his old room. It hadn't changed much from the time he lived there. The view was different now though. The zoo had relocated to the edge of town and new housing had sprung up in its place. Other than that, everything else had remained the same. He reflected on his life, with just him and his father. His mother, Irena, had died when he was twelve and it had affected him a lot. She'd been ill for as long as he could remember.

He loved her name, Irena, and would sometimes call her that instead of 'Mum'. She said that it meant "Woman of Peace" in Czech, her native language. He knew little except that her family had fled Košice, near the Hungarian border, after the war and just before the Russian army had arrived. She'd told Daniel that her father had fought in the resistance and that he had made some British contacts who helped his family get out of Czechoslovakia and make the long and dangerous journey to the safety of England and then Southcliffe.

She'd said that both her parents had died before Daniel was born and there were no photographs. All he had were the memories his mum had told him growing up.

Daniel's thoughts were broken by the chimes of the front door-bell. He made his way downstairs and on opening the door saw the postwoman, holding out some letters and a large manilla envelope.

'I need a signature on this one, please,' the postwoman said, passing him the big envelope. 'A quick squiggle here… Thanks. See you.' …and she was on her way.

Daniel put the post on the hall table in a neat pile and was just turning away when his eyes locked onto the larger envelope. It was quite bulky and had a large gaudy orange, blue and yellow stamp with exploding fireworks on it – as well as the word "Australia".

'Who's sending Dad something from Australia?' he thought. Then, turning it sideways, he checked the return address. It read "From Lucy Siddall, 139 Post Road, Perth, Western Australia".

'Lucy? That's a bit of a coincidence. Didn't someone mention a Lucy when I was in Perth?'

Daniel's mind wandered back a week or so. 'I'm sure Jock Crammie was living with a woman named Evie. The Perth police had interviewed her and her daughter to see if they knew who the mystery visitor was. But they said they didn't. Wasn't her daughter's name Lucy, I seem to remember?' And if her name is Lucy Siddall, why would she be sending my dad an envelope? Daniel – stop this,' he cried out loud. 'It's a coincidence, it's your police-mind working overtime,' he told himself.

Daniel left the post on the hall table, set the alarm, and locked up the house. It was only when he was back in his car driving to the station that the nagging thought returned. He spoke out loud. 'The inspector always says that you should question coincidences, don't ignore them. I'll find out who this Lucy Siddall is and put my mind at rest. Dad couldn't be involved in this case. No chance.'

But at the back of Daniel's mind was his father's secretive and evasive nature. And it worried him. 'Where is Dad? And why didn't he answer the phone when Ken rang him about the alarm or pick up his messages?'

Daniel's drive back to the station was full of gloomy and dark thoughts.

Chapter 30
The same day

When Daniel got back to the station, he set about trying to catch up on lost time. But for the first time ever, he wasn't able to focus on the police case. His mind, usually so resolute, kept wandering back to the strange envelope that lay, unopened, on his father's hall table.

He looked back through the notes he'd taken whilst over in Perth and checked the statements received from the police over there.

He reproached himself. 'Why didn't I follow this lead while I was over in Perth? Why didn't I interview his wife and check on any children? It's not like me to miss something like this. I didn't do it because it wasn't on my patch – that's all.'

'You can't interfere with another country's policing,' were the words the inspector had used. 'We wouldn't stand for them coming over here and putting their size nines in our investigation. No, Daniel, we take a back-seat. Just chivvy them along, if possible.'

And that's what he'd done. He'd chivvied them along as best he could, always keen to get back to Southcliffe, where he could do his own digging in more favourable surroundings. But he'd messed up, and with the time in Australia after eleven at night, he couldn't do anything until morning. Unless...

Daniel glanced at the clock again and then picked up the phone and rang Gaynor Stanley, the liaison officer who had been assigned to them in Perth. She answered her mobile phone on the eighth ring.

'Hello?' said a tired and irritated-sounding voice.

'Gaynor – erm, it's Daniel Atkinson from the UK – Southcliffe. Look, I'm really sorry to ring you at this time, but – well, it can't really wait until tomorrow.'

'Do you know what time it is over here, Daniel?'

'I know it's after eleven...'

'It's one-fifteen, Daniel – and I'm knackered. Just a minute while I get up and move to somewhere that won't wake the whole household.' The line went quiet and Daniel waited, hardly daring to breathe, waiting to see if Gaynor had calmed down. She had. When she spoke again, it was the professional Gaynor Stanley he'd met when he'd been over there. 'Right, Daniel. What's this all about? Has there been a development?'

'Look, Gaynor, I'm really sorry, but I just needed some clarification. Yes. There has been a development, of sorts. But it's a bit too early to confirm anything. You remember that Cameron had a wife and a step-daughter. Can you remember their names?'

'Let me think. His wife was called Evie and his step-daughter's name was... Yes, that's it. It was Lucy.'

Daniel took a deep breath. 'Do you know her surname, Gaynor?'

Well, she's his wife, so it's probably Cameron!'

'No – sorry. I mean the step-daughter. Do you know the step-daughter's surname?'

'Oh! You mean, she might be married? No, I don't,

I've not got the file to hand so I can't look at any statement she made. Look, give me half an hour and I'll ring the station. Get the duty officer to check it out and I'll get back to you.'

'Thanks, Gaynor. I really appreciate this. I'll hang on in the office until you ring back. Thanks again.' With that, the call was finished. All Daniel could do now was wait. Wait until he had confirmation that Lucy wasn't married. That she was called Cameron or Smith or whatever.

Daniel tried to work, but he couldn't concentrate. Cora came past his desk on her way home and commented on his dedication, telling him not to work too hard. The other members of the team had left the office to go home. Daniel had been waiting for over two hours, when at last the phone rang. It would be well past three in the morning in Perth. He picked up the receiver.

'Hi, Daniel. Sorry I've been so long, but there was an incident overnight and the duty officer has only just come back to his desk. Anyway, I've got what you want. The step-daughter, Lucy, is married although she's not living with her husband any more. Her married name's Siddall. Does that help? Daniel... Daniel... Are you still there?'

'Yes... Sorry, Gaynor. You said her surname is Siddall?'

'Siddall, yes, Lucy Siddall. Hope that helps. Good luck with the enquiry. I'm off back to bed, Daniel.'

'Thanks again, Gaynor. Really sorry for the late phone call. Hope you can catch up with your sleep.' With that, he hung up the receiver.

Daniel sat there in a daze, all the old doubts from his early life about who he was and where, and who, his grandparents might be, resurfaced. His father had brushed all his questions off. Daniel now felt that maybe he'd been quite content with no answers at the time, in case they were answers he didn't really want to hear. But now Daniel Atkinson was a police detective and it was his duty, however unpleasant, to find the real truth and his training kicked in. He reached for the passenger lists for the flights from Manchester to Heathrow on the evening of 17th January. There on the 7:10pm flight he found the name Graham Atkinson.

'Dad flew to London that night. Maybe it's just a coincidence. It could have been for a meeting, something to do with his work. There might also be some innocent explanation for the envelope from Australia.' But no matter how hard he tried, Daniel couldn't convince himself.

Daniel realised that his father would probably be home by now. He would have found the envelope and opened it and he would have known that someone had been into his house and picked up the post and put it on the table. That someone would almost certainly be Daniel. And Daniel would have noticed the return address on the envelope. 'I need to get home, to Angie,' Daniel thought. 'I need Angie to sort this out for me. Tell me if I'm being stupid.'

'Hi Dan. Had a busy day, love?' Angie asked, as she lifted her head from marking homework.
'Angie, I need to know. Did you go round to see my

dad whilst I was in Australia?'

'What? Oh – well, yes, I did. You asked me to go round, love, while you were away. Remember?'

'Yes, I remember. So, you went round.' Daniel relaxed a bit. 'He was OK. Was he?'

'I don't know, Dan, he wasn't in. I spoke to Ken next door. He said that your dad had gone away for a couple of days on some business. So, I thought he must be OK, and that it was some business problem that had been bothering him. Why?'

Daniel blurted out everything. The mystery man who got to Jock Crammie first. The name on the return address on the envelope. The phone call with Gaynor and finding out Jock Crammie's step-daughter's name. Those names being the same.

'On top of all that, Dad was on a flight to Heathrow the same time that I set off for Perth with Inspector Whittle. And he was also away for a few days.

'Please tell me I'm being daft, Angie? Tell me I'm overreacting?'

'Look, love, if you'd told me all this about someone else, I'd have said that your suspicions were right. But it's your dad, Dan. There's got to be some simple explanation for all this.'

'I know, but all the same…'

'What're you going to do, love?'

'I really don't know, Angie. Confront him. Ask him where he was, while I was away? Ask him about the envelope and how he knows Lucy Siddall? It's all I can do. Let him explain.'

'Yes. That's what you should do, Dan. But not tonight. I know you won't sleep much, but you need to process everything. Clear your head, and be a policeman.

Father or no father, that's what you have to do. Now come here and I'll give you a hug.'

Graham Atkinson got back home at about six-thirty in the evening from his business meeting. He'd read the four texts from his next-door neighbour, Ken. The first three telling him that his house alarm had gone off, and a fourth to reassure him that everything was OK, as Daniel had been round to check and reset it.

It had been a long and arduous meeting, and all Graham wanted to do was have a lovely, warming drink of his favourite whisky. With a half-full tumbler in his hand, he picked up the post from the hall table and wandered into his conservatory. Sitting down, he began leafing through the post. His eyes were immediately drawn to a large manilla envelope bearing an unmistakable Australian stamp. He checked the return address and realised it was the stuff Jock had said he'd get his step-daughter to send him.

And then... he realised that it was Daniel who had put the post on the hall table. That Daniel would have seen the envelope and, almost certainly, that Daniel would have read the return address and come to a shattering conclusion.

Years of lies and half-truths were about to be revealed. Graham had met with his solicitor that day to prevent the truth coming out in this way. He'd already resigned himself to confessing. It was just a matter of finding the best and least hurtful way to do it. Now all that had been taken out of his hands. Graham had no doubt that his son would be round here first thing in the morning. What he had to do before then was to think of the best way to approach giving this news to his son.

Nothing would be held back, but Graham's main aim must be to protect his son from any backlash.

Chapter 31
Wednesday, 26th January 2000

The next morning, after a sleepless night, Daniel rang the police station. He spoke to Cora and requested a day's personal leave. Cora didn't ask questions, but she recognised from Daniel's voice that her constable was distressed.

'Ring me if you want to talk, Daniel. OK?'

Daniel mumbled some thanks and then after an especially long hug from Angie, he drove to his father's house. He arrived just before eight and, as usual, let himself in with his key. He found his father sitting at the breakfast bar in the kitchen. 'There's a pot of coffee ready, Son,' said his father. 'I think we both need one.'

There was no need for any other words at that point. They had both lain awake most of the night, preparing in their own minds, how to say the things they needed to say. Graham poured the coffee and placed a full mug down on the breakfast bar in front of Daniel. His son watched, and then, when his father had taken the stool opposite, Daniel asked, 'What's all this about, Dad?'

'Son, I want to tell you everything. All the secrets that I've kept from you. All the lies I've told you while you've been growing up. But I would like to explain it my own way – to you. Then we'll decide how and when to tell Richard Whittle.' Daniel nodded, and took a sip of his coffee.

'My real name is Gregor Alksnis. I was born in 1930, in a small city called Rēzekne. It's in the east of Latvia and about forty miles from the Russian border. In July 1940, when I was ten, the Russian red army invaded, with, it seems, the blessing of Germany. To start with, the Russians were very friendly as most lived just over the border. But a year later the Germans invaded the south-west and things changed. Latvians from that region were conscripted into their army. So, we had Latvian fighting Latvian. My father and my uncles were taken to fight for Russia. I never saw them again.

'I was kept on the farm to work, along with my mother, elder brother, Bruno and younger sister, Anastasia. We got help from the old men in the village. The crops were taken from us to feed the Red Army. The Rēzekne area was bombed, almost to oblivion, first by the Germans, and then later, by the Allies. When Bruno was fifteen, he was conscripted into the army.

'Later, the Jewish population was annihilated and the majority of the remaining grown-ups were sent to the gulags in Siberia. My grandfather and grandmother were amongst them. I never heard from any of them again. When the Germans were defeated, the Russian army went on the rampage. My mother and my sister were killed whilst they were working in the fields. I can only hope that their deaths were quick.

'I ran away and joined the resistance – I was just fifteen. We hadn't any weapons, other than the ones we took from those we killed. I lost a lot of friends and we were told to shoot ourselves rather than get captured and tortured. Eventually, two of us made it to the north-west coast port of Kolka, where we stole a fishing boat and made it to Sweden. From there we planned to work our way to England.

'My friend, Ivo, had a brother who lived in Southcliffe. So we aimed to get there. But Ivo died in a storm on the way across the North Sea, He was swept over-board, as I watched on, helpless. I arrived in Southcliffe in 1948. I was eighteen. I couldn't find Ivo's brother, but luckily for me, there was a growing population of eastern-European people in the town. All refugees from the war. They took me in, and that's where I met your mother.'

'Why did you never tell me all this, Dad? I can't imagine how awful your young life must have been.'

'I wanted to, Son, I really wanted to. I told your mother. She also knew about everything that came after. I never kept anything from her. But we agreed that you should never know anything about our past. It was wrong, and I've had to live with it since. I made mistakes, but it wasn't right that you should suffer because of them.'

Daniel's coffee had cooled somewhat, but he mechanically drank from the mug all the same. 'Go on, Dad. What happened next?'

'What happened next, Daniel, was your mum, Irena. I met her the day that I arrived in Southcliffe. Her mum, Triska, took me in and gave me shelter and food. They had nothing, really, just the clothes they'd left Czechoslovakia in, after the war. They'd come over here to try and find Irena's father, Ondrej – your grandfather. He'd served with the RAF during the war at nearby

Warton. But he was killed at the tail-end of the war when an American B24 bomber crashed on landing. Ondrej is buried in the church graveyard in Warton. Triska had no proof that she was married to Ondrej. So they had no entitlement to any pension or anything. Like me, they had to be taken in by the community and looked after. Irena was only seven when I arrived but in the years, to come, after being like big brother and little sister, we fell in love.'

'I remember mum had an accent,' said Daniel. 'But you never did, Dad? All this history about my family. All this suffering. It's a lot to take in.'

Graham got up and started making a fresh pot of coffee. Whilst he did, he continued. 'I worked at the Pleasurebeach in Southcliffe during the summer. During the winter months I helped Tom Hamshaw on his building sites in Northcliffe. Tom and Dorothy took me in – let me stay in his house. He was a good friend. But I always kept in touch with Irena.'

'And was it there that you met Jock Crammie? asked Daniel.

'Yes, and Terry Breeze. We used to spend time together in the snooker hall. It was there that we hatched the plan to rob the bank.'

'Dad!'

'Let me tell it all, Son... please... Terry had got inside information from Arthur Dowling, the guard, about a lot of money in the safe. It was easy pickings. There was no need for any violence. But Terry had a vicious streak in him that I didn't know about. It was straightforward until he messed it up.'

'Dad, you said Arthur Dowling was in on it. Why did he get hurt?'

'We'd agreed that Arthur should try some lame attempt to stop us and that he'd be pushed aside. But Terry lost it. That's why we got away without the safe contents, only with what was in the till.'

'So you and Jock Crammie killed Terry Breeze?'

'Daniel, I'll come to that. Please, let me tell it my way. I promise I won't leave anything out. Can I make some breakfast while I talk?'

Graham set to, toasting two teacakes and making another pot of coffee. Whilst he busied himself, he told Daniel of all his dealings with Terry Breeze and of his confession to Daniel's mother. 'I told her everything. She didn't judge me. She said that I should leave the area quickly. I went to Leeds, where there was a sizeable Latvian community that I could get lost in. I couldn't forget your mum and we kept in touch. Your grandma was very poorly, so your mum couldn't leave her.

I decided to change my appearance so that I could go back to be with her. Someone knew of a doctor that was doing cheek implants. It wasn't legal and it was 'back-street' surgery. He basically wanted a guinea-pig to try it out on. It hurt, but it was worth it to be able to be with your mother again. And I got a wig. I suffer from alopecia. It came on when we were trying to get out of Latvia. I was really ill for about six weeks. All my hair fell out and it hasn't grown since.'

'I know about your wig, Dad. That's a difficult secret to keep from me for all the years. I guess I just got used to it and then forgot about it. But what about your accent and your identity? You flew to Australia under the name of Alksnis?'

'I just learnt to speak like an English person. It

didn't seem hard. In the early days, I sometimes forgot, but your mum was very strict on this. She made me remember. She used to say 'If you speak like an English person, you will always be accepted. If you speak like a Latvian you'll never be accepted.' Those words have always rung true, even today. And as for my identity, I got a new one whilst I was living in Leeds. Graham Atkinson was a really close English likeness to my own Latvian name. So that's who I became. I kept my old name and passport up-to-date, just in case. Our kind – Eastern Europeans – were looked upon with mistrust in those post-war years, so most of us kept dual nationalities as a safeguard.'

They talked for ages, about the life of Daniel's parents, both before Daniel was born, and their life as Daniel grew up. Daniel asked about his paternal grandparents, about any uncle or aunties – or cousins. All Graham could say was that he didn't know what had happened to anyone.

'I've really tried to make up for what I did, Daniel, I honestly have. I've worked hard for this town, built up a business where all the employees benefit. I know it'll never make up for what happened to Arthur Dowling but I've provided for his widow over the years...'

'And you paid for Jock Crammie's care as well, didn't you, Dad?'

'Ah, Jock. It was my fault he was there in the bank robbery. I talked him into it. I convinced him how easy it would be. The money was there for the taking. He'd be able to do anything, go anywhere. Be somebody. That's what I told him, because I believed it – at the time. I've regretted it every day since. I tried to make it up to him. I sent him money when he went to Australia. Only a bit to start with, because we hadn't much spare. But as I got more successful, I sent him a bit more. So at least in the end, he had enough to be a bit more comfortable.'

'In the end, Dad... In the end you killed him!'

'Yes, I did, Son. I killed him. But I want to explain what happened.'

Daniel looked at his father and couldn't really see the man who'd brought him up, given him so much love – so much care. This was a stranger, who talked of killing people as if it was a natural thing to do. 'Oh – I've no money – so I'll rob a bank. Oh – someone might tell on me – so I'll kill him.'

'How many more times will this man, who is sitting opposite me, cause suffering and destruction? Who is he?' Daniel thought. 'I don't recognise him.' Yet Daniel was in conflict. Part of him was beginning to understand what his father had been through. It was difficult to comprehend the suffering and danger that his dad had been forced to face in those war years. 'I owe it to Dad, to listen to what he has to say,' thought Daniel. It seemed like an age since anyone had spoken, and Daniel could see his dad watching his face waiting for a reaction.

'Go on, Dad. Tell me what happened,' Daniel said in a very quiet voice.

'Jock got in touch about three months ago to tell me he had lung cancer, caused by exposure to gases in the uranium mine. It was incurable and he had been moved to a hospice in Perth. I had already planned to go over there. Then Terry Breeze's body was dug up and as soon as you told me you'd found where Jock was, I felt I had to go straight away and tell him what to expect.'

'You used me, Dad. I told you something in

confidence and you used that for your own ends. How could you?'

'I know, Son. My intention was to get to Jock and tell him that you and the inspector were on their way. I wanted to tell Jock to tell you everything about the robbery. But when I got there, I realised that hearing that about your father from a stranger, was not the right way. It had to be from me.

Jock said that he wouldn't tell you anything about the robbery but would take it to his grave. I said that I'd tell you when the time was right. I wish I'd told you earlier.

'These last few days, I've been completing the hand-over of the business to the staff, I didn't want them to suffer for what I'd done. I know you don't want anything from the business, Daniel. And I've always respected your wishes. Your career is in the police. Yesterday I completed the transfer with the solicitors and I was ready to tell you everything and hand myself over to the police.'

'But – I don't understand, Dad? Why did you have to kill Jock Crammie?'

'Because he asked me to, Daniel. Because he begged me to put him out of his pain and suffering. He hadn't got anyone else who could help. He was hardly coherent. The only time he was lucid was when he was in pain. The rest of the time, he was drugged up with morphine. Jock begged me to put a pillow over his face, to press it down until he stopped breathing. I did it because I loved him as a friend. I'm sure I'm not the only one who would have done that, if they'd seen a close friend in the same state.'

They stopped talking, each thinking of what had

been said. Each trying to come to terms with what was now out in the open. Daniel felt numb – no – he didn't really know how he felt. This was still his dad.

Graham felt relieved that all his secrets were finally being let out. It hadn't played out the way he had hoped. Telling deeply-held secrets never does. He'd hurt his son badly. He wouldn't have been surprised if Daniel had just walked out the door and gone straight to the police station. But his son just sat there looking out through the window into the garden. Finally, Daniel turned to his dad and said, 'Other than Mum, did anybody know about your past?'

'Only Valdo Goralova. We were good friends, early on. He recognised me when I'd changed my appearance, but he never said anything to anyone about it. I know Valdo, he's true to his word.'

'Valdo Goralova was murdered two days ago. Dad, please tell me you had nothing to do with it?'

'Oh my god! Daniel – I had nothing to do with it. You've got to believe me. What happened?'

'I can't tell you that, Dad. I've told you enough already.'

Graham then told Daniel about his phone call with Valdo and the information that they'd exchanged. They talked for more than two hours about everything. Daniel asked questions and Graham held nothing back. Finally, when both father and son simultaneously felt that all had been said, Daniel asked, 'What now, Dad? What do I do?'

'Son – you have to arrest me. But before you do, I want to say to you how immensely proud I am of you and what you've achieved. You have a wonderful, loving wife, just like I had with your mum. Angie will be your rock, not just through this, but in the future. I hope there may be a grandchild that I might meet one day. That's only if you still want contact with me?'

'You're my dad. Of course we'll still want contact with you. But now I need to ring Angie to tell her what's happened and to say that I'll be staying the night here. I think we should have one more night together. Then tomorrow we'll both go to the police station. OK?'

Chapter 32
Overnight

That night stayed in Daniel's memory forever as one of the happiest times he'd had, irrespective of the impending action to be taken the next morning. This was a time to put all those thoughts out of his mind. They talked long about Daniel's family – a family he never knew he had. His dad told him about growing up in Latvia before the war – about how his family all lived on and worked the farm together – Daniel's grandparents, his dad, his three uncles and two aunts. How they grew wheat and barley and kept a flock of sheep. How each autumn all the farmers would help with the cropping and the sheep shearing. Then they would have a festival of food, music and dancing. The winters were cold but the summers were hot. There was no inkling of what was just around the corner.

'I often think back to those days, Daniel. Simple, but happy times. It helps to try and block out the following years of hell that we had. We had Russian neighbours. Alex was my age. We'd go swimming and fishing every day, climbing trees and chasing rabbits. We were inseparable. Then in 1940, that all changed. Russia invaded. Alex's parents took over our farm and made us work in the fields. Our family had to all live in the barn – our barn. Alex wasn't allowed to come near me, or talk to me. I think that soured my thinking about friendships. How brittle they were, given the ever-changing circumstances. That's why I've kept everything secret, I think, in fear of spoiling everything.'

Daniel pondered those words from his father, still trying to comprehend how it was possible to live through all that. 'I wish you'd told me all this earlier, Dad.'

'So do I, Daniel. But the time was never right. First you were too young, then, all of a sudden, you were a teenager and you had other things to cope with. And then you joined the police and I knew that if I told you then, you'd hate me. Your mother was right. She told me never to tell any of this to anyone. To keep it secret. It was mine to live with and mine alone.'

'Yet you told Mum?'

'I told your mum everything. She was only seven when we met and I loved her like a brother does his sister. It was only after the robbery, when she told me to leave Southcliffe, that I realised my feelings had changed. There were eleven years' difference in our ages, but it never mattered to her. I thought she would outlive me and I always planned it so she would be taken care of. But plans don't always work out as you expect, Son. It tore my heart out when she died.'

'I know. I remember hearing you crying in your bedroom. I couldn't do anything to help.'

'But you did help, Son. By being you. That brought me through it all.'

'Look – here.' Graham passed his son a photograph. 'It's a photo that Jock's daughter sent me. It's one of Jock, me and your mum, when she was sixteen. I'd forgotten it had been taken. Jock had it all this time. It's the only one I've got of her when she was that young.'

Daniel looked at the photo, taken on the North Pier, showing three young people, seemingly without a care in the world. His mum looked radiant and she seemed so happy. He'd never really seen her like that. She'd fallen ill during his birth and had never really recovered. 'She'd been loving and caring, but never carefree and happy like this,' he thought.

'I wish I'd known Mum when she was like this. When I was young, I used to envy all the other kids whose mums would run around on the beach and go in the sea with them. But I know she loved me. I miss her, Dad.'

'I miss her too, Son. Every day. All you have left are memories, so never lose them. You have to treasure them instead.'

'Dad, whatever happens, I'll always be here for you – and so will Angie.'

'You've got a pearl there, Daniel. Look after her, won't you?'

They both dozed in their armchairs overnight, neither wanting to break the bond by going to bed. About sixish, Graham announced, 'I'm going for a shower and to get dressed before breakfast. You should ring your inspector. Give him a heads-up before we go to the station.'

Daniel knew that his boss would be up and about even at this hour, so he made the call. Richard listened without comment, until he'd heard all Daniel wanted to say. 'Right, Daniel, you should both come in at nine and make sure your dad brings his solicitor. I'll be there to take a statement. Once he's booked in, I want you to hand in your warrant card and leave the station. I'm placing you on indefinite leave, Daniel. This is standard procedure in these circumstances. Do you understand?'

'Yes, Sir, I understand.' And with that the telephone call ended.

Richard stood cradling the phone in his hand not wanting to let it go. He was full of mixed emotions. Graham Atkinson was a well-liked and respected person in the town. Daniel Atkinson was a promising and diligent police officer who was unwittingly connected to an investigation concerning murder and robbery. From what Daniel had said, Graham Atkinson was going to cooperate fully, but with the presence of a solicitor everything could change. He rang Cora Stone to give her a heads-up. 'There can be no favours shown to anyone in this case, Cora. It's got to be handled right. I want you to keep me focused on that.'

'Digging up that body, was like opening Pandora's box, Jill,' he said to his wife as he hung up the phone. 'I'm not sure what else we'll find, but I have a feeling that there's plenty more that will shake this town before this sorry episode is finished.'

Chapter 33
Thursday, 27th January 2000

At 9am sharp, Graham Atkinson walked into Southcliffe police station accompanied by his son, Daniel, and his solicitor, Robert Bramble. Daniel stood aside whilst the other two were signed in by the duty sergeant. They were then escorted into an interview room. Daniel waited until the door was closed, then stepped forward to the desk and, as his inspector had ordered, handed his warrant card to the sergeant. He then left the police station and met up with Angie, who was waiting outside in their car.

'How was it?' she asked nervously.

'OK,' said Daniel. 'They just booked Dad in and took him to an interview room. We just have to go home and wait.'

Angie knew that waiting was the last thing Daniel could do at this moment. Two of the most important things in her husband's life had just been taken away from him. His father and his work. 'Look, your dad rang me this morning while you were on the phone to Inspector Whittle. He wants you to go to the warehouse and tell the staff what's happened and what's going to become of them. He left this folder on the seat.' She held it out to Daniel. 'It outlines who will be running the business from now on and how the business will continue. Your father wants you to tell everyone, Dan. He wants the people who work for him to have secure employment. Are you up for going there now?'

Daniel smiled for the first time that morning. He knew what Angie was trying to do and he loved her for it. 'Yes, this needs to be done, love. Let's go.'

Inspector Richard Whittle had got into work at seven to allow himself plenty of time to prepare for the upcoming interview. Cora arrived a few minutes later. 'Right, Cora, as soon as the team's assembled, I want to brief them. I'll be starting the interview at ten. I'm not sure at this moment how much this will impact on our investigation. I deliberately told Daniel to keep it vague on the phone so that that we didn't draw any conclusions. Graham Atkinson is involved in some or all of this. I believe that he will co-operate, but no mistakes. OK?'

Cora nodded. 'Could be all wrapped up by lunch-time, Sir. Or it might open up a whole new can of worms.'

'Exactly,' replied Richard. 'Keep concentrating on collating the evidence, ready to interview Phil Breeze as well. I'm not sure if these two are connected, but I've a strong feeling they are. It should become clearer later.'

With the team briefed and the time now 10am, Richard and Cora entered the interview room. With the formalities done, Richard was about to start with his first question, when Robert Bramble intervened. 'My client would like me to read a statement he has prepared and signed. This may save time and make the facts clearer.'

Richard nodded. Go ahead.'

The solicitor picked up his papers, and began to read.

'I, Graham Atkinson, formally known as Gregor Alksnis, confess that on 8th August 1957, I was part of a gang that held up the National Bank on Corporation Street in Southcliffe, at gunpoint. In that hold-up, the bank guard, Arthur Dowling was seriously injured. I had no part in that attack. It was carried out by Terry Breeze and was not at all expected by myself or Jock Crammie, the other member of the gang. But I am truly sorry that it happened and so I bear the responsibility for his subsequent death.

I also confess that on 19th January 2000, I held a pillow over the face of Jock Crammie and suffocated him. Because of the pain he was in, he begged me to do it. I did not do this action to prevent Jock Crammie talking to you and implicating me in the robbery. I had already decided to confess to my part in the robbery and I went to see him specifically to tell him that and to see an old friend before he died.

'I want to exonerate my son, DC Daniel Atkinson, of all knowledge of any of this. I used my office as chair of the Police Liaison Committee to find out the status of the investigation by talking to the chief constable. At no time did my son, Daniel, divulge any information that I did not already know about the current standing of the case. He has acted with total professionalism and propriety throughout

the whole investigation.'

Graham Atkinson sat quietly whilst the statement was read. The solicitor finished, then passed the signed statement over to Richard. 'We shall of course have to take our own statement, Mr Atkinson, but this will be used as part of the evidence against you.'

There followed getting on for two hours of questions and answers between the participants. It became clear to Richard very early on that Graham Atkinson was willing to co-operate fully. Although it was difficult to extract the personal details and life of the original Gregor Alksnis, Richard suspected that Daniel had been told more about his father's early life, but it wasn't pertinent to the case, so that information was left unsaid.

Richard glanced at his watch, 'This interview is suspended so that all participants can rest and recover. It will reconvene at 2pm. Cora, can you arrange for sandwiches and drinks to be brought in. Then, can I see you in my office, please. Thank you, gentlemen.'

'That went well, Sir,' said Cora as she entered Richard's office.

'Yes, it did, but no mention yet of Terry Breeze's death. We'll tackle that straight after the break. We also need to broach the Valdo Goralova death as well. I know we've got Phil Breeze in the frame, but it's back to coincidences. There's too many for them not to be linked in some way. Now, let's get some lunch, Cora. My feeling is, it's going to be a long afternoon.'

Reconvening at 2pm, Richard reread Graham Atkinson his rights and then launched straight into further questioning. 'On, or around, 18th November 1957, Terry Breeze was murdered and dumped in a hole behind number 9, Nuttall Road in Northcliffe. The body was subsequently covered with a deep layer of concrete. This body was unearthed on 6th January 2000. Mr Atkinson, what do you know about these events?'

'I don't know anything about these events, Inspector, other than I know that he was dug up three weeks ago. I was as surprised as everyone else. After the robbery we'd still meet in the snooker hall. There was never any inkling that any of us were suspected. The money was split three ways. It wasn't that much, so our spending habits didn't change significantly. I did hear at the time that Terry was catching a lot of grief from his dad, Jed, about his wild ways. Soon after that, Terry disappeared. I can't say when exactly, but life became quieter and safer. The rumour was that he'd run off to Spain. It was generally accepted to be the best solution all round.'

'Did you talk to Jock Crammie about him, when you went to Perth?' asked Richard.

'I told Jock about the discovery of Terry's body, but that was because of our involvement together in the robbery, not because I suspected that Jock had had any hand in Terry's death. I can safely say that the Jock I have known for a large part of my life wouldn't have killed anyone, even such a lowlife as Terry Breeze.'

'So, you can't shed any light on who killed Terry Breeze and buried his body?' asked Richard.

'Inspector, I'm answering all of your questions honestly. I hope it's something you can believe? What I can add is that Jock was aware of Terry Breeze's death. He said that he helped someone else bury the body, but more than that, he wasn't willing to say. I respected that and didn't push him any further.'

Richard and Cora exchanged glances. This was proof that Jock Crammie was at least involved in disposing of the body and that another person was involved as well. Most probably the killer.

'Leaving that to one side, Mr Atkinson, what can you tell me about Valdo Goralova?'

'Valdo was a good friend of mine from the time I first came to Northcliffe.'

'You say – was?' said Richard hurriedly. 'Not is – are you saying that you know he's dead?'

Graham was shaken. 'I heard about it last night, Inspector. I'm not sure from whom.'

Richard paused the tape machine, holding the button down with his finger. 'Did Daniel tell you?'

'Yes, he did. He asked me if I'd killed Valdo. I told him "No". And I'm telling you "No" as well. I pressed Daniel to tell me what had happened to Valdo. But he wouldn't say any more, because that information was restricted.'

'Ok,' said Richard as he released the button. 'When was the last time you spoke to Valdo Goralova?'

'Last Wednesday. He rang to tell me that someone was showing an old photograph of me around.'

'Do you know who that someone was?'

'Yes. It was Tom Hamshaw's grandson, Steve. It seems it was a photo that was taken of me in a holiday group outside number 9, Nuttall Road in the 1950s. Valdo said he wouldn't tell Steve it was me, and I believed him. So, I gave him some information – as a thank you.'

'What kind of information?'

'I told Valdo that the police were fairly certain that Terry Breeze had killed his elder brother, Cristian, back in 1947 – the Gala murder.'

That news stunned Richard. 'That lad that died? Valdo Goralova was his brother?'

'Yes. It was before I came to Southcliffe, but Valdo had always sworn vengeance on whoever killed Cristian. It's a Czech thing. Honour in the family. For years he talked of nothing else.'

'So you knew what he'd do when you told him?'

'What? Go after Terry Breeze's son? No! I only thought he should know after all this time. It didn't seem that the police were going to tell him anything.'

'That's because we hadn't made the connection. So we couldn't inform him. All we had in the files was the name Cristian. There was no surname written down. We didn't know they were related. Until now,' said Richard.

Cora took down the statement and Graham signed it. The charges were laid against Graham for his involvement in the robbery and the unlawful death of Jock Crammie. As he was led away to the cell, Graham turned to Richard and said, 'Daniel's a fine young policeman, Inspector. I hope the sins of his father don't prevent him from doing what he's cut out to do. That war and the aftermath made people take decisions that they will regret for ever. It's those mistakes that they can never rectify. In the 1950s, folk – upstanding folk – did things and kept secrets that they wouldn't do today. That was the way of life then. It's different now, thank goodness.'

Richard reflected on what his prisoner had said for a long time afterwards. He couldn't help but be moved by the early life that Gregor Alksnis had suffered. At the same age, Richard had been enjoying a carefree childhood in the loving care of his parents. He had been shown what was right and wrong by his father. If he'd been Gregor Alksnis, would he have acted any differently? It was a question he wasn't able to answer.

Back in Richard's office, Cora said, 'At least we now have a link between Valdo Goralova and Phil Breeze, Sir.'

'Yes, we do. It could be that Valdo met with Phil to confront him, or even to kill him. Vengeance of some kind. But Phil Breeze got in first. It's good information for our interview with him, Cora. He won't be expecting that we've found a link. Where are we up to with his movements?'

'Traffic information puts Phil in the area of the attack at the time that the pathologist estimated. It's a remote area, so I can't think of any other reason for Phil Breeze to be there at that time.'

Chapter 34
Monday, 31st January 2000

Richard had arranged details of the arrest and search operation the previous day. At 7am they raided Phil Breeze's house and took him into custody. They had a search warrant and needed to take as much time as possible to complete it. The timing was specific because Richard knew Phil would contact his solicitor in Manchester and they were aiming to make their interview happen at the most inconvenient time. Because of the rush-hour traffic, it would take at least two hours for the solicitor to arrive.

'Let him stew for a bit on his own,' said Richard. 'We need to play this just right. This is a good chance to get a major drugs player out of the game. Give them an hour together and then we'll go in at ten. Phil's not the most patient person. It'll make it more likely he'll slip up.'

At ten o'clock sharp Richard and Cora went into the interview room. They followed all the usual procedures regarding interviewing a suspect and then Richard opened up the questioning.

'How do you know Valdo Goralova?'

'I don't. Never heard of him.'

'Valdo was found dead on the salt marshes near Braides on Monday, 24th January. He'd been stabbed.'

'As I said, I don't know him, and if you think you can pin this on me, then I've plenty of people who can say I was with them all Sunday evening.'

'We never said a time. What makes you think it was the Sunday evening, Phil?'

'Morning…afternoon… evening. It doesn't matter. I wasn't there.'

'Between 6:30 and 10pm last Sunday, some sort of altercation took place between Valdo Goralova and his assailant. We have a traffic report from the toll bridge. The one that spans the river Wyre. This photo shows your car, Phil. It's crossing at 7:08pm. But you say you weren't there.'

'OK. I went for a ride to clear my head. Had an argument with the wife – you know. It happens.'

'That's a nasty scratch you've got on your face, Phil,' said Cora. 'How did you get it?'

Phil touched his cheek and answered, 'It was the cat. She can be a bit lively sometimes.'

Cora laid out two DNA reports in front of Phil. 'DNA result from skin fragments found under Valdo Goralova's finger nails on his right hand, match those in a DNA report from police files belonging to a Phillip Breeze.

'So, are you still saying you don't know him? Your car was seen in the vicinity at the time of his death and then there are the records from your mobile phone number. Valdo Goralova telephoned you on the morning of the 23rd. The call lasted one minute, twelve seconds. Still don't know him?'

Phil looked anxiously at his brief, who just nodded to him. 'OK. Yes, I know him. He rang me and asked to meet. I didn't know what it was about. When I arrived, he came at me with a blade. We struggled, I got the upper hand and somehow the blade slid into him. It was self-defence. The guy was a nutter.'

Richard took over the questioning. 'So someone you don't know wants to meet you in a remote location to talk to you about something you know nothing about? Do me a favour, Phil.'

'It's true. I thought it might be a business opportunity. The way things are, I can't afford to turn anybody down at the moment.'

'And was there a business opportunity?'

'I didn't get chance to find out. He just came at me with a knife. We fought, he scratched me.' Phil felt his face again. 'That's the truth.'

Richard settled himself. 'I think that you did have a conversation and that Valdo Goralova told you that he knew your dad had murdered his brother, Cristian at the Gala in 1947. He may have been meaning to kill you in an act of revenge, but you went there carrying a knife – the same knife that was used by your dad to kill Cristian Goralova.'

Richard produced the knife in a sealed evidence bag. 'We found this knife during a search of your house. We've done preliminary tests and it shows that this is the knife that stabbed Valdo Goralova. It has your fingerprints on it and remnants of blood traces on the shaft. I'm sure further tests will confirm that its Valdo's blood. Maybe there's some blood from its previous use back in 1947 as well?'

'Look Inspector, I'll own up to stabbing this guy –

in self-defence, mind. I don't know anything about this knife being involved in any other crime. If it was from when this Goralova guy's brother was killed, then maybe he picked it up at the scene and kept it, waiting to use it again on some innocent guy who happened to be in the wrong place. It's only my guess – I'm not the detective here.'

'So how come it was found in your house during the search, Phil?'

'OK. After I'd managed to turn HIS knife away from me and it accidently stabbed him, I panicked. I took his knife and scarpered. I knew you'd try and pin it on me. Anyway, he got up and staggered off over the marshes.'

'Word on the street says that you often carry a knife, Phil.'

'Word on the street isn't always right, Inspector. I don't think you've got anything on me at all. It all seems to be just a load of fairy stories. Can I go?'

'Right,' said Richard, stopping the recording machine and getting up from his chair. We'll take a break here.'

Back in the office, Richard looked rueful. 'It's not going well, Cora. Breeze has been well briefed and he's sticking to his story. Valdo could have picked up the knife in 1947 after his brother had been killed. I'm not sure we've got enough to make a murder charge stick. His brief's pushing for self-defence and leaving the site of an incident.'

'But, Sir. If the same knife was used in the Gala murder back in 1947, in the bank robbery, and in the stabbing of Valdo Goralova, then it must have been in the Breeze family possession all this time. Valdo couldn't have picked it up in 1947.'

'I know what you're saying Cora. But we've no concrete proof it's the same knife. David can't confirm one-hundred-percent that all three stabbings were done with this knife. He's only working off photographs. It's enough for us to close the cases but not enough for a court of law.'

'Let's get a cup of coffee and we'll go back in at twelve-thirty. They'll be a bit hungry by then and maybe we'll catch them off-guard.'

Chapter 35
The same day

Gary Breeze had been a great dad to Samantha and Heather, Gloria conceded. Much more, he'd kept them all away from the dodgy businesses that the Breeze family had been involved in for a great many years. A nice house in the best part of Northcliffe, private education and a lifestyle many would dream of, didn't come without a cost. That cost was something that Gloria had ignored all her married life.

She always told herself that it was for her girls, but in her bad moments she secretly thought of it as punishment for having the temerity to love someone so much that every day hurt. She'd been brought up with the post-war mantra of "get on with life, make the most of what you've got, you're lucky to have anything at all".

So as time went on, Gloria got on with her life and made the most of what she'd got. She was, after all, lucky to have two loving daughters whom she adored and a little grand-daughter, Sophie, who melted her heart every time she saw her.

Of Gary, well – she'd always suspected he'd set Steve up somehow all those years ago. How he did it, she was never sure? But she also knew that Steve would have never stayed in Northcliffe forever without resenting the fact. The death of his grandfather, Tom, in 1966, followed shortly after by his nan moving to South Wales, gave Steve the reason he needed to get away and spread his wings.

This small corner of England was Gloria's home. She couldn't imagine being anywhere else. She loved the family-run shops and the local vegetable market. All her friends were here. Sure, they'd gone on holidays as a family, some of them to exotic places. But the packing of the holiday clothes for their return journey at the end was always something she looked forward to. It meant her home was calling her again and soon she'd see the familiar sights and sounds, and most of all she'd see the sea.

She often thought back to that day, the 7th May 1967, when Steve left. She'd often re-read the letter that he'd sent to her two weeks later. 'I've let you and your dad down', it read. 'I never meant to hurt anyone, but it seems I've hurt everyone that I care about. I'm going away for a while to see if I can understand what I've become. I'll let you know when I'm settled and then we'll talk.' But he never let Gloria know where he'd gone and they had never had that talk.

Steve had tried two weeks ago when they'd gone to see Becca, but Gloria had made an excuse about having to pick Sophie up after school and the moment had gone. 'I'm frightened of opening myself up to him and then he ends up leaving again,' she'd said to Becca on the phone earlier that evening. 'I don't know whether I could ever recover from losing him a second time. I'm fighting it, Becca, and it hurts so much.'

'But if you don't tell him how you feel, Gloria, how will he ever know?' Becca replied.

'If I tell Steve how I feel, he may think he has to stay for me. To make up for what he did. I don't want that. He'd only come to resent me. Oh – I'm in a mess.'

'Take a bit of advice from Gypsy Rosa Lee. Concentrate on sorting out what you can do and what you have control of. Once those are sorted, then the other things will take care of themselves. Now, we both know what the first thing you need to do is, don't we Gloria? Something you should have done a long time ago.'

'Thanks, Becca. You're a good friend and a brilliant counsellor. Ever thought of doing it professionally?' They both laughed.

'Gloria, you and Steve belong together, but you both have to make it happen. Do what you have to do. That's the start.'

After she'd finished the phone-call, Gloria looked around a room that had been part of her life for over thirty years. But now her girls had moved on, this was not a home any longer. She realised it was not the house, but who you shared it with that mattered. That's what made it into a home. Not the bricks and mortar, but the people that live in it. She smiled. That was what Steve's grandfather used to say. And it was true – this house was now just bricks and mortar.

Gary always worked late these days, or that's what he'd tell Gloria. But she knew different. Northcliffe was a small close-knit community and not much got past the gossip brigade. Sally Briggs had been in Gary's life now for over five years. One day Gloria had suddenly realised Sally had lasted longer than all the others. But Gary seeing Sally, suited Gloria. And part of her believed that it suited Gary as well.

After Steve left Northcliffe, Gary had been wonderfully attentive and made her feel important again. And, she thought, he does love me, in his own way, although maybe the act of stealing Gloria from Steve had thrilled him the most. But she didn't love Gary. How could she? She was still in love with Steve.

Over the years, that drains someone, so when Gary's affections moved elsewhere, Gloria was actually both relieved and happy for him. 'Why make his life a misery just because mine is?' she often thought. The situation suited them both, or it did until now. It was time to do something about it. It was the time to confront Gary. It was the time for Gloria to take control of her life.

Gary arrived home that evening about ten-thirty. Normally, Gloria would have gone to bed by then and have feigned to be asleep as he eased his way into the king-size bed. He'd always lean across to give her a kiss on the cheek as if that very action wiped away his infidelity. That night, however, Gloria was still up, sitting in her favourite armchair.

'You're still up?' asked a surprised Gary.

'Yes, I am. Gary, we need to talk. Not tomorrow, not next week, but now. Please sit down.' A sheepish Gary sat on the settee and looked towards his wife with an expectant gaze. 'I know where you've been, and I know where you go nearly every night and I know who you've been with. So, no games – eh? I think you should go and live with Sally. Our marriage is over, isn't it?' Gary nodded. 'We can both blame each other – you did this, I did that – but in the end we're both unhappy.

When the girls left, we had nothing left to give each other. We've drifted apart and to tell you the truth, it hasn't bothered me. If we can stay amicable then we can both get what we want. We can tell Sam and Heather together. We'll explain the situation. I think they both suspect something already...'

'Sally's pregnant.'

'What?'

'Sally – she's pregnant. I didn't know how to tell you.'

Gloria was shocked. She'd been planning what to say all evening. She was willing to take the blame to help them both move on. But now this. This revelation should have made things easier, but somehow it seemed to complicate it more.

Chapter 36
Tuesday, 1st February 2000

Phil Breeze was feeling pretty chipper with himself. He'd been grilled by the police for most of the previous day and they'd decided to keep him in overnight. But thanks to his brief, he'd warded off all accusations that it was his knife and that he'd gone to the meeting with the intention of doing this guy, Valdo, some damage.

He'd managed to convince Inspector Whittle that it was self-defence and that this Valdo guy had got up and staggered away. 'It seems to me he was trying to avenge his brother's death, which you lot are trying to pin on my dad,' Phil had made out. 'If my dad had done it then why should this guy want to kill me?' he thought. 'Why not Gary? Or better still – why not Steve Hamshaw? That would have been the best outcome, all round.'

That stuff about his knife being used previously had come as bit of a shock. But he'd thought on his feet and given a plausible account. 'Phil Breeze didn't get to where he is, without being quick-witted,' he thought. But the same knife being used to kill two brothers, fifty years apart! Wow! That's a tale he could tell for years to come.

It was a shame that he had lost that knife, though, after owning it for so long. Phil had taken it from his dad's secret hiding place after Terry had 'disappeared'. He remembered, one day, when he was only five. He watched his dad remove a loose brick from the back wall of the outside toilet wall and fish out the knife. His dad had turned and seen his young son watching. With a smirk on his face, his dad had put his finger to his lips. 'Shh!' he had said. 'Our secret.'

His dad was gone and now his knife was gone as well. 'Steve Hamshaw's going to pay for what his grandad did,' Phil vowed. 'Just as soon as I get these charges sorted.'

The worst-case scenario, his brief had told him, was that Phil would be given a suspended sentence for leaving the scene of a crime, instead of ringing the police. His brief had served him well. He made out that Valdo, although stabbed, had got up and walked away. Phil said it had only been a flesh wound and he didn't think much of it. Also, it was fortuitous that the police couldn't prove that the knife wasn't actually Valdo's... that the Czech guy hadn't picked it up in 1947 after his brother Cristian had been killed, and held on to it, ready for the time that he could exact some form of retribution. 'That was clever,' Phil thought, 'reckon I even impressed my brief with that reasoning.'

Anyway, he was out on bail so no harm done. These skirmishes with the law were an occupational hazard in his line of business. He didn't really need a brief there but the guys in Manchester had insisted. 'As if I'd say anything to incriminate them,' he thought. 'What do they take me for?'

His brief had left him on the steps of the police

station, with a message. 'Your presence is requested over in Manchester this evening. Eight o'clock. Usual place. They'll make the arrangements for an overnight stop.'

Phil had asked if he could cadge a lift to Manchester. Then he could get the train back the following morning. But his brief said that he was off to another job, further south, so Phil would have to drive. 'We'll have the meeting, then I can get off to the club,' thought Phil. 'Not a bad night to be looking forward to. I wonder if Claire will be working there tonight? Today hasn't turned out so bad after all.'

Back in Richard's office, things weren't quite as buoyant. 'He's slipped through our fingers again. Cora. In fact, he's made a bit of a mug of me. We went in too quickly with not enough hard evidence.'

'We couldn't have done it any other way, Sir. We had what we had, and nothing more. Breeze is a slippery customer. But it's only a matter of time before he slips up. We just need to keep the pressure on. Make him realise we're still around. He'll slip up eventually.'

'I hope you're right, Cora. Set-backs like this are part of the job. But two in a week, with that failed court case. Well… it's a bit much. Let's get proactive. We'll get it into the press and local radio. Surely someone saw or heard something that could help. Let's get off home and hope we have a better day tomorrow.

'I don't know,' Richard mused. 'Four weeks into the new millennium, and this town is strewn with bodies. What happened to the quiet time of the last century?'

Chapter 37
Wednesday, 2nd February 2000

Richard overslept the following morning, after an almost sleepless night. His mind was so active that he was watching a re-run of the 1999 snooker World Championship final at three in the morning. He saw his favourite player, Stephen Hendry win his seventh title, but even watching that couldn't distract Richard. It made him think again about the old snooker hall at the back of Nuttall Road and the ongoing investigation that didn't seem to be getting anywhere. It was only after he returned to a sleeping Jill, well after five o'clock, that he fell into an exhausted sleep.

Cora was there to meet him when he arrived at his office at 10:15, with a freshly-brewed mug of coffee.

'Inspector McCloud, Manchester CID rang you, Sir, at about 9:30. He asked that you ring him back as soon as you get in.'

'Thanks Cora. And thanks for the coffee, it's just what I need. Stay here will you, please. Connor McCloud never rings just for a chat.'

Richard rang the number and the phone was picked up almost immediately. 'Rich, I recognised your number. Thanks for ringing back, although it's nearly lunch-time. Didn't know you were semi-retired!'

'It's the sea air, Connor. It does that to you. Anyway, I assume this is not just a social call?'

'I've got some news, Rich. News that might just make your day.'

Connor McCloud and Richard Whittle were at Hutton police training college together where they formed a formidable tennis doubles team. They were unbeaten in all their training years and had cups and medals to show for it. They even beat the Met Training College team, who had as one of their duo a future British Davis Cup member, although Richard could never remember his name. After graduation, they never totally lost touch. But as is the case for a sizeable number of men, they only talked now and again. Each time one contacted the other – and almost invariably it was Richard contacting Connor – they fell into conversation easily.

'OK, mate. Make my day,' said Richard affably.

'Phil Breeze. He's one of yours, isn't he?'

Both Richard and Cora perked up, 'Yes, he's definitely one of ours. What's he done?'

'Only got himself killed. That's what he's done. And on our turf as well. Fished him out of the water at Salford Quays early this morning. Throat cut. No wallet, so it could have been robbery, but with his background, I suspect not. Is he active with you at the moment?'

'Very much so, mate. We had him in here yesterday. Possible murder suspect but not enough evidence. Also, a drugs trial collapsed because of witness intimidation. Our Phil has been sailing close to the wind for some time now.'

'Tell me a bit about this murder, Rich, will you?'

'We've enough proof that Phil Breeze stabbed a guy, who's not known to us, but he claims it was in self-defence. His explanation is hard to disprove. The guy was a Czech. Came over here just after the war. Name of Valdo Goralova.'

'Spell that, Rich,' came a curt reply.

'G O R A L O V A.'

'Wow! That is a coincidence. A guy named Simon Goralova is a major drugs player over here. One of the top ones in Manchester. I'm pretty sure his gang sources the drugs for the Fylde coast. And your man Phil Breeze was most probably the buyer.'

'Makes sense,' said Richard. 'They hear about Valdo – could be a relative? Phil Breeze is summoned to his supplier. Supplier enacts revenge.'

'And everyone's happy,' said Connor.

'We can't condone a murder, but… What do you know about this Simon character, Connor?'

'Mother and father came over from Czechoslovakia in 1949. Settled in Levenshulme in South Manchester. Always boasted that he had family who worked on the fairs – dodgems, coconuts, goldfish... You know the thing. And he had an uncle who was allegedly murdered in a gang fight somewhere up your neck of the woods.'

'There's the link,' shouted Cora. 'We believe Phil Breeze's dad, Terry, murdered Cristian Goralova in 1947 in a gang fight in Northcliffe at the summer Gala. Revenge all-round it seems. Cristian was Valdo's brother.'

'Is Terry Breeze that skeleton you dug up a few weeks back, Rich?'

'Yes, he is, and it's been mayhem over here ever since.'

'Well, if revenge is the motive,' said Connor, 'then we have an unsolvable murder on our hands. There's no way we'll be able to get Simon Goralova for this. We can rattle his cage, let him know that we know. But it sounds like a 'crime of honour' to me, so I'm guessing he did it himself. He'll have twenty or more alibis set up already to prove he was nowhere near. I hate it when we have to waste our resources on scum like that, but a murder is a murder, I suppose. Any progress on this Terry Breeze murder yet?'

'A bit, Connor, but forty years is a long time. People have died and forgotten things in the meantime. But we've cleared up that bank robbery in Southcliffe in 1957.'

'And now you've got a major drug dealer out of the way, Rich.'

'To be replaced by another one, I'm sure. Probably hand-picked by Manchester. It doesn't get any easier.'

Cora went back into the main office to brief the team on the new developments. Richard and Connor chatted on for another five minutes, catching up on their lives, and the call ended with promises to exchange file notes and to meet up for a game of tennis. The former would happen as soon as the phone call ended... The latter... Hmm!

Chapter 38
Saturday, 5th February 2000

Following the events of the previous two weeks, Richard had given all the team a well-earned weekend off. The chief super would be pleased – he'd been complaining about the amount of overtime. So much had happened in such a short period of time that some of them were well-nigh exhausted. The bank robbery crime was solved and Phil Breeze was off the radar. But they were still no further on with the "Skeleton case".

The national newspapers and TV channels had given a lot of coverage to the events as they unfolded and Richard thought that they were beginning to get in the way of his investigations. He was definitely in the chief super's good books, but the original crime of Terry Breeze's demise still bugged him. This was close to home and personal. It also affected a close friend of his, so he rang Steve and arranged to meet for a pub lunch in the Victoria Hotel.

'The pie's supposed to be really good in here, Steve. That's what I've been told.'

'Then it's pie for me, please, Rich. And I'll have a pint of that Epic cask beer. It's supposed to be from round here. That's if you're buying?'

They talked about general stuff whilst eating the food but when Steve had bought a second round of drinks, he said. 'Right, Rich. Why did you really want us to meet up?'

'You heard about Valdo Goralova, Steve?'

'Yes I did. Gloria heard about it from her friend, Becca. She was Valdo's niece and his closest relative so she had to identify his body. Becca was in our class at school, Rich. Did you not recognise her?'

'Oh! Now you come to mention it, I thought she looked familiar. Cora organised the identification, so I only saw her from a distance.'

Richard took out the photo of the mystery man that Steve had given to Becca. 'Yours, I believe?'

'Yes, it is. Becca said she'd ask her uncle if he knew who this guy was – here,' said Steve, pointing to the person on the back row.

'We now know that this chap is Graham Atkinson.'

Steve was totally taken aback. Graham Atkinson was often in the local paper, owing to his work on the council and advertisements for his carpet warehouse.

Richard then related all that had gone on with regard to Gregor Alksnis, the mystery man in Steve's photo – changing his appearance and his name to Graham Atkinson and Valdo phoning Graham to warn him about the existence of the photo. He also told Steve about the meeting on the sand marshes between Valdo and Phil Breeze, about how Phil had stabbed Valdo and then how Phil had also met his sticky end.

'Graham Atkinson was the third robber, Steve. He also smothered Jock Crammie, although he says it was at Jock's behest. And I believe him.'

'Jock wasn't the type to hang on if he knew he was close to the end of his life,' said Steve. 'But I don't think I could have done that. If he'd asked me.'

'Steve, we now know that Jock was one of the people who disposed of Terry Breeze's body in 1957. But Graham Atkinson wasn't the other one. Before he died, Jock had told Graham there were two men that night. But he wouldn't elaborate any further.'

'So, you still think the other one was my grandpa?'

'It's not what I think, Steve. It's what the evidence points to.'

'What evidence, Rich?'

'The fight between your grandfather and Terry Breeze two weeks earlier. We think your grandfather found out about Terry and your mum.'

'But you've no proof yet?'

'No, no proof, but we have to keep looking. I hope you can understand that, Steve.'

'It's a long time ago, Rich. Everybody's dead. Can't you just leave it?'

'I'm afraid I can't, Steve. It's my job.'

Chapter 39
Monday, 7th February 2000

The following Monday morning, Richard met up with his team for the morning briefing. They were all in a more jolly and relaxed state.

'We've had a hell of a month, folks, but we've come through it in a very professional way. I'm very proud of you all. We've solved the 'crime of the century' as far as Southcliffe is concerned by identifying the bank robbers, and we got a major drug baron, and all-round bad egg, Phil Breeze, off the streets – albeit in dubious circumstances. All as a consequence of finding Terry Breeze's skeleton. But we still have his murder to solve, which has had to take a back-seat of late. Cora, can you familiarise us all again with the case? It's become quite complex.'

'Yes, Sir. I'll try my best.'

'The skeleton of Terry Breeze was dug up on 6th January 2000. We've established that he was killed sometime in the period before the morning of 19th November 1957. His body was dumped in a hole forming the foundations of an extension to number 9, Nuttall Road, Northcliffe. We are certain that the hole was filled in with cement early on the morning of 19th

November because we have the receipt from the cement company. The builders involved in the extension were Tom Hamshaw, the owner of the property, who died in 1966, and Jock Crammie, his brickie, who died, as we know, two weeks ago on 19th January 2000.

'We've also established from Graham Atkinson's confession, that Jock Crammie was one of two people who put the body in the hole. We don't yet know who the other person was, or whether either of them was actually our killer.

'Our chief suspect is Tom Hamshaw. We now know that Tom Hamshaw's grandson, Steve, is Terry Breeze's son. DNA tests have established that. We know that Tom Hamshaw confronted Terry Breeze two weeks before Breeze's death, in the old Anvil Snooker Hall. Mr Hamshaw had to be restrained according to a local police report.

'Now, did Tom Hamshaw know that Terry Breeze was Steve's dad when that altercation took place? If not, then what was the fight about?

'Tom Hamshaw could have motive, certainly had opportunity and undoubtable had the means to kill Terry Breeze. But as yet, we haven't got the evidence, Sir.'

'Thanks, Cora, for a very succinct appraisal of where we are. We still haven't got a murder scene. Cora, how are we going on with finding old contacts of Terry Breeze and Tom Hamshaw?'

'There aren't many left alive, Sir, I'm afraid – and what with all the other stuff that's been going on, we've not really had the manpower to do it.'

'Yes, I know, but we can concentrate all our resources on this now. Can you follow up on this old snooker hall angle. Find anyone who used to frequent it around that time. Right, people, do your best. Cora, a word in my office, please. I'll get the coffees.'

Once they were seated, Richard said, 'Daniel Atkinson is coming in today to discuss his future. I'd like you in on the meeting as well so we can to keep it as informal as possible. I've still a phone call to make before that, but right now, I'd like to talk about how you're doing. It's been a rollercoaster of a month and you've performed superbly. Anything worrying you?'

Richard and Cora talked for a good half hour about how the events of the past few weeks had been handled, particularly the collapse of the drugs trial, which, Richard recognised, had hit Cora quite badly.

'You handled it as best you could, Cora. As best as anyone could, given the circumstances. All we can do is follow procedures, use our experience, and most times, it works out. If sometimes it doesn't, take it on the chin, and move on. How are things outside of work?'

Cora smiled, 'Well, if you want to know about my love life, Sir, there isn't one. But I have two adorable cats that I can go home to every night, who calm me down and make me forget about all the bad things. At least until the following day.'

'That's good to hear,' said Richard. 'By the way, I don't know if you like art, but it's Jill's opening night of her exhibition on Friday. You're more than welcome to come. That's if you want to, of course.'

'Thanks, Sir. I'll bear it in mind.'

At two o'clock, Richard, Cora and a perturbed Daniel Atkinson sat down in Richard's office.

'How are you doing, Daniel?'

'Not great, Sir. I'm not sleeping much. Spending a lot of time at my dad's. He's out on bail and there's no date set as yet for a hearing, pre-trial. I just want to get back to work, to do what I'm good at.'

'That's why we're here, Daniel. I have a proposal for you. You heard about what happened to Phil Breeze in Manchester?' Daniel nodded. 'Well, I've been talking to an old colleague of mine in Manchester CID – Inspector McCloud, a good bloke, meticulous, a lot like you. Anyway, he's got a spare place on his team for a young recruit. I've put your name forward and sent over your file. He's just got back to me and now I can offer you a transfer to Manchester CID.

'It's not Southcliffe, I know, but it's not prudent for you to be here at the moment. Manchester's not far away, so that you can be close to your dad. And just like me, when you climb the ranks and make inspector, you can come back and take over if you want to. I'll be ready to retire by then. What do you think? You can talk it over with Angie if you need to and get back to me.'

'Thank you, Sir. That's more than I expected, to be honest. I don't need to talk to it over with Angie. Her last words before I left were to take anything that was offered, no matter what or where. She knows that without this job, I'd just mope around. I'll be sorry to leave Southcliffe, but this is a wonderful opportunity, better than I could have hoped for. I can't thank you enough, Sir. When can I start?'

'Easy, Daniel. It'll take a few days to sort the paperwork out, but Inspector McCloud will expect you to report to him a week from today. You've got a good one in Angie. Unfortunately, police work can make you very selfish and having someone who understands is so important. Just remember that. Now, off you go and say your goodbyes to the team. We're all going to miss you. Remember, wherever you go in the future, don't lose your attention to detail. That's your strength.'

'Thanks again, Sir – and you too, Sergeant. For all you've done for me. I won't let you down.'

As Daniel was getting up to leave, he turned to Richard.

'Sir? While I've been busy doing nothing, I had a chance to look at my notes and I have an idea which may help the investigation.'

'Go on,' said Richard, intrigued.

'Whilst in the lab, I noticed there were some scraps of wood in all the debris. In the stuff that they still hadn't managed to analyse.'

'There's a lot still to go through, yet,' commented Cora.

'Sir. The shape of the wound on the side of the skull could indicate a blow with a snooker cue. If so, the snooker hall could be the scene of crime. We need to test the wood... Sir. In my opinion...Sir.'

'That's what we're going to miss without you, Daniel. Thinking outside the box. I'll get on to David Leadbeater and get that wood tested. If you're right, Daniel, then it could prove a big breakthrough. Now off you go, and keep in touch.'

Chapter 40
Friday, 11th February 2000

'Jill, this is wonderful. So many lovely exhibits including some from artists I've not heard of.' Mary Leadbeater raised her glass to the beaming gallery director. 'David and I are already arguing about which ones we should buy. It's high time a bit of London came up north and recognised the talent that we have.'

'A lot of this is thanks to you, Mary. You pointed me in the direction of Angus Breen. He's a rare talent. A couple of art dealers have come up from London especially. They've snapped up most of his exhibits.'

'I know, Jill. I was wavering over which one of two to buy, and one was suddenly bought! I snapped the other up immediately.'

'It helped you make your mind up though, Mary. Didn't it?'

'Yes, I suppose so, although I'd just decided to buy both. At least David won't be complaining about his wallet being emptied again.'

Mary rushed off across the room to meet up with David and review their purchases. Jill surveyed the room and the smartly-dressed throng milling around the exhibits. She exuded a quiet glow of satisfaction. It had been hard work convincing her boss that some of the artists were well worth their place in the show. But she'd stuck to her guns and he'd been really impressed. Sales were going well.

Richard watched his wife from across the room, feeling immensely proud of her. Too often in their marriage, she had been the one who supported him in his work. She'd been there when he'd had a rough day. She'd picked up the pieces when his investigation had led to some gruesome find. 'A police officer's life – eh? Nothing but torment,' thought Richard. 'But now it's Jill's turn to bask in the limelight, if only for this evening.'

They had never had any children. Neither had shown any preference one way or the other. It had just happened that way. Time had moved on. Both had jobs they found fulfilling, but also time-consuming, not leaving much remaining to bring up children properly. Now this was the moment for him to take a back seat and allow all the focus to be on Jill.

He noticed Cora had come in and was standing on her own. He picked up a glass of orange juice from the drinks table and walked across the gallery towards her.

'Thanks for coming, Cora,' he said, offering her the glass. 'I presumed you drove?' he asked. 'It's just orange juice.'

She nodded. 'Thanks, Sir. Yes, I did.'

'We're off duty, Cora, so it's Richard, not Sir. OK?'

'Yes, Sir... I mean Richard. There are some nice pictures here, but they're a bit outside my price bracket.'

'Mine too, but there's plenty of people with deep pockets in this room and Jill's doing well with sales. Speaking of which, here comes David Leadbeater. Hi

David, I thought you'd be busy buying up most of the exhibits?'

'That's Mary's forte really. We talk about what's good and what isn't, but at the end of the day, Mary decides and I agree. Luckily, she's got a good eye and I have a deep bank account. I'm glad I've got you both here. Can we talk shop?'

Richard smiled, 'Neither of us are ever really off duty are we, David? So go ahead.'

'Your PC Atkinson is a gem, Richard. I'd been putting off searching through all those items from the dig. Probably your fault for keeping me so busy. However, the wood samples he talked about are ash, which marries with the wood used for a normal snooker cue in the '50s. They're all coated with thick layers of beeswax, so they must have been cleaned regularly. I've managed to fit three pieces together and the tapered shape they made would indeed indicate a snooker cue. In fact, in my humble opinion, the wooden samples were almost certainly part of the same snooker cue. Whether it's the murder weapon, I can't be sure, but it could have caused the blow to the side of the head. And because they were found next to the skeleton, that makes them relevant.'

'That means we can tie the murder scene down to the snooker hall, doesn't it, Sir?'

Richard smiled. 'Sir,' he thought – 'Cora's back on duty.'

'I don't think it's enough evidence for a court of law, but it's definitely enough for us to turn our focus to the snooker hall again. It's a good breakthrough. The investigation was flagging a bit, but now with this new lead, it may be able to move forward.

'We need to revisit what happened out of the ordinary in the snooker hall on or around the day of the murder. But that's for Monday, Cora. Now, David, let's join Jill and Mary. I see they're deep in conversation over by the window. Let's see how much you have to fork out this time.'

Chapter 41
Monday, 14th February 2000

'Margaret Bowler was the cleaner at the snooker hall around the time Terry Breeze disappeared. She's living up near Lancaster.' Cora had burst in on Richard with this news after she had just put down the phone from a call to a potential witness. 'She seems to have a really good memory of another altercation between Terry and Tom Hamshaw, and it was on the morning of Terry Breeze's death! It had something to do with Tom's daughter, Rose... and I didn't have to prompt her.'

'Excellent news, Cora. When can we interview her?'

'If you're available, Sir, we can head off now. It's only an hour away.'

'Right. Let's go now. Where in Lancaster does she live?'

'Just outside. Some place called Sunderland Point – on The Lane.'

Richard smiled. 'Have you checked the tides, Cora? Sunderland Point can only be reached by a causeway that's under water twice a day at high tide. It's something that us locals have been brought up with.' Richard tapped into the computer and quickly announced, 'Good. It's on its way out. Should be low enough by the time we get there. Just let her know we're on our way.'

In fact, they arrived in Richard's car while the sea was still covering the causeway and had to wait nearly thirty minutes for it to recede back into the mud channels that skirted the road. They talked about the case all the way up, but when they got there and had to sit for a while, it gave Richard chance to reflect on times gone by.

He'd cycled up here when he was ten, with his two best school friends, Bobby and Derek. Richard's dad, George, had made the bike up from parts that he'd found at the local tip, and it was Richard's pride and joy. His friends both had new bikes with Sturmy-Archer gearing systems – three actual gears, which allowed them to climb hills much easier than his bike. His bike had a fixed wheel and no brakes!

That meant one gear only and when the wheels went round, the pedals went round as well. To brake, he would stamp on the pedals. So it was much harder to climb hills and the other two would race away. But coming down was another matter. He went whizzing down the hills at breakneck speeds, his feet splayed out so that the fast-rotating pedals didn't clatter his ankles. He had to judge carefully when to catch the pedals to get back control of the bike. It took some learning, with many falls and bruised ankles, but Richard had mastered the art. And it had given him very strong leg muscles. He'd had other bikes since, but that was the one he'd treasured the most.

The wintery sun glistened on the folds of mud as they formed channels like guards of honour for the outgoing tide. With his window open, Richard could hear the gurgling of the water as it lapped across the mud banks. Meanwhile, the ducks and seabirds joined in, their voices in harmony, as they floated on the water searching for tasty morsels, just below the surface.

'This is so peaceful,' Richard said as he filled his lungs with another deep breath of cold, clean air.

'It is, Sir. I didn't know places like this existed. I'm too much of a town girl, I'm afraid. And before you say it – yes, I should get out more.'

'I wouldn't dream of saying anything of the sort, Cora,' replied Richard, laughing. 'I think it's the lure of this coast that brought me back here. On a crisp winter's day, there's nowhere better. Now, it looks like the water level's low enough for us to cross. The only trouble with coming at this time is that the car ends up totally splattered with mud.'

'How long before the causeway is flooded again, Sir?'

'Oh, we're all right. It's only covered for about three hours each high tide. So we've got plenty of time to talk to our witness and get back across.'

The residents of Sunderland Point are well known for their hospitality, so Richard and Cora were soon seated with a steaming mug of tea and a generous wedge of fruit cake by a jolly-looking Margaret Bowler. Richard was trying to gauge her age. Margaret must have noticed as she said, 'I'm eighty-nine next birthday. Born in 1912, I was. I can't really remember the Great War, but I remember growing up afterwards, when there was a lot of poverty. As children, though, we were always happy and looked after by our parents. It was a good childhood, not like today's kids. They've got too much and always want more. Anyway, you're not here to listen to an old woman ramble on about her memories.'

'We are, actually, Mrs Bowler. You told Sergeant Stone that when you were working at the snooker hall in Northcliffe in the 1950s, you overheard an altercation between Terry Breeze and Tom Hamshaw. Can you tell us something about that, please?'

'Well, yes, I can, Inspector. You're probably wondering how I can remember something as far back as that, when I sometimes can't remember what day it is or what I had for lunch an hour ago. Well, it's 'cos I kept a diary. Always have done. One for each year since I was twelve. So I've got seventy-six upstairs, all kept in date order, my daughter sees to that. She makes me write something in it each day, still. Helps keep my mind active.

'Anyway, when she hears that you're looking for anyone who worked at the snooker hall around that time, she comes round and she makes me look in my diaries and we come up with this entry.' Margaret picked up a dark blue-covered book from the coffee table and opened it at a marked page. She passed it over to Richard, who turned it around. He saw a page full of beautiful handwriting, headed "Monday, 18th November 1957" and began to read out loud.

'Annie didn't want to go to school – AGAIN. Said she had tummy ache, but I knows it's just an excuse cos Susan's fallen out with her. Packs her off with a Milky Way for her elevenses. Said I'd pick her up at dinner-time and take her to see Doctor Peters. When I got to work, Don was in his office. Was hoovering when Tom Hamshaw

comes in. He was blazing. Made straight over to Terry Breeze and grabbed him by the throat. Couldn't make out all that was said, but was something to do with Rose. How Terry needed to stay away from her, or else. Could guess the rest, knowing Terry Breeze's reputation with young girls. Don comes out and managed to calm things down. Told Terry to leave, then he and Tom went into his office and I couldn't hear anything else. Finished as quick as I could then went to meet Annie from school. She needs my help at the moment. Doctor said there was nothing to worry about and to give Annie some cod-liver-oil twice a day. Mince and onions with mash for tea with some of those nice sprouts from the Co-op that have just come into season. Then listened to The Band Waggon and then The Archers on the Light programme. Ted got in at eight-thirty. He smelt of booze – again!'

'This is really useful, Mrs Bowler and, I might add, beautifully written. Do you remember anything else about what happened?'

'Inspector, I don't remember even this happening. It's only 'cos I wrote it down at the time that I even know about it now.'

'That's OK. This is a great help. Would you mind if we borrowed this for a while? Cora can write you a receipt and we won't lose it.'

'Of course, you can, Inspector. I'll be glad if it helps, although if Tom was still alive, I wouldn't be showing you this at all. Wouldn't be wanting to get Tom Hamshaw into trouble. If he did for Terry Breeze, then it's only what the scumbag deserved. Pardon my language, but he was a nasty bit of stuff. Good riddance, I say. Northcliffe was better off, the day Terry Breeze disappeared.'

'You're not the first to say that, but I'm afraid justice doesn't work quite like that, Mrs. Bowler,' said Richard.

Margaret wrapped a couple of pieces of fruit cake up in tin-foil. 'Just in-case you get peckish on the way back,' she smiled. 'It's so nice to have visitors. I love this place, but it can get a bit lonely in winter. Come back if you want anything else.'

'We will,' smiled Richard. 'Goodbye, and thanks, you've been really helpful.'

Back in the car, they crossed the causeway without problems and were soon back on the deserted lanes.

'So this latest argument between Tom Hamshaw and Terry Breeze took place the morning of the day Terry was killed,' said Richard.

'And it follows on from a similar fight two weeks previous at the same place. The one your dad broke up, Sir.'

'Yet Margaret's diary reads that Terry left before Tom. So Terry was still alive at lunch-time on the 18th.'

'Maybe they both came back in the afternoon and it all kicked off again? The evidence is mounting up against Tom Hamshaw, Sir. He could have found out that his grandson was Breeze's? That's motive enough for anyone.'

'It's still conjecture, Cora. We don't really have any hard evidence yet. I think it's time I had another chat to Don Ward. I'll drop you at the station and head out there.'

Chapter 42
The same day

Richard arrived at Thurnham Grange and was greeted at the door by Kathleen, Don's wife. She wasn't pleased to see him.

'Come in, Richard, if you must. I'm afraid if it's Don you've come to see, you'll have to wait. He's asleep. Would you like some tea?'

Whilst Kathleen busied herself in the kitchen, Richard thought over the fact that being a policeman meant you sometimes had to make choices when it came to friends and acquaintances. He'd always got on well with Don and Kathleen. She'd been one of his teachers at primary school, and they'd both been close friends with his dad. Don and his dad had both sung in the local operatic society, only as part of the chorus, and he'd often been taken to see the shows by Kathleen, with their Gloria.

He remembered vividly the time when they performed The White Horse Inn operetta, the last number the cast sang was the 'Goodbye' song. As they sang the final chorus, every one of the company whipped out a white handkerchief and waved it to the audience.

Some of the audience, including the chap next to him, did likewise, although Richard remembered that the handkerchief didn't look very clean. 'It's funny how you remember small things from your childhood,' Richard thought. 'I'd love to chat with Kathleen about the old days, but I've got a job to do. More's the pity.'

So after Richard had sipped his tea, he went straight into it. 'I've just been to see Margaret Bowler up on Sunderland Point. She sends her love, by the way. I've seen some information in her diary about a set-to between Tom Hamshaw and Terry Breeze that took place in the snooker hall the day that Terry was killed. Don apparently broke up the fight. So I've come to ask him if he can remember anything about it.'

'Richard, Don is dying of cancer. He's only got a few weeks at most. Can't you leave things be? Let him have this short time in peace.'

'I can hear all that, Kathleen,' came a voice from the bedroom. 'I'm not dead yet. Richard, come through, and bring your cuppa with you.'

Richard thought Don looked very frail. 'I'm sorry to disturb you, Don, but I have to follow this up.'

'I know, lad. Kathleen's only trying to look after me. So Margaret's old diaries, eh. She always said what she'd written would come in useful some day. I can't add much to what Margaret's told you. My memory's no better than her diary. But, yes, there was a set-to between Tom and Breeze, and, yes, I did pull them apart. Although I can't for the life of me remember when it was.'

'Margaret's diary says it was Monday 18th November. The day Terry was killed,' said Richard.

'Can't argue with that, Richard. Anyway, as I

remember, Terry left and I took Tom into the office to calm him down. He'd got wind that Terry was sniffing after Rose. And being Rose's dad, Tom was livid, and rightly so, given Breeze's reputation. Any parent would be. But I can assure you, Richard, that if Tom Hamshaw had killed anyone, he'd have gone straight to the police afterwards and confessed. That was the nature of the man.'

Secretly, Richard had been thinking the same all along. Tom Hamshaw would never hide a crime like that. He'd have confessed to Richard's dad and suffered the consequences. But he had to follow the evidence, and the evidence was still pointing in Tom's direction.

'My advice to you is the same as last time you visited, Richard. Let it go. You've solved Southcliffe's crime of the century, you've got a major drug dealer off our streets, you've even solved the killing of that poor fairground boy back in 1947. Some things can't be solved or are not worthy of being solved. Breeze was scum. Even his own father, Jed, thought so. Northcliffe lived easier after he'd gone. I know he's Steve's biological father and Steve's been fighting this torment ever since he found out and he's finally coming to terms with it. Some advice from an old, dying man – let it go. But you're like your dad, Richard, you won't. Now, I'm feeling tired again, so can you go?'

Richard got up and by the time he'd reached the bedroom door, Don was asleep. He said his farewells to Kathleen and was soon in his car heading home. 'It doesn't get any easier,' he thought. 'I have an obligation to find the truth. But at what cost to me, or the people around me?'

Chapter 43
Friday, 25th February 2000

Steve was looking over some plans that he'd drawn up for the renovation of the houses, ready for council approval, when he heard the doorbell. It was eight o'clock at night and as he walked down the stairs to open the door, he secretly hoped it was Gloria.

And it was her, standing in a glow of what looked like moonlight, but was actually the light above his door. 'I'm smitten,' thought Steve. His heart fluttered as he showed Gloria up the stairs. When she was seated in his lounge, he asked, 'Can I get you anything?'

'A glass of red wine would go down a treat, Steve, if you've got one?'

'Coming up.' After he was seated and they'd sipped their wine, Steve dared to say, 'I haven't seen you since Phil was killed. How's Gary doing? I didn't think it was right to come to the funeral, even though Phil was my half-brother.'

'I know, Steve. You wouldn't have been welcomed anyway. Gary's doing OK. I guess he half expected something like that would happen to Phil one day. It's actually news about Gary that's brought me here tonight. We've split up. More than that, we're getting a divorce.

Becca made me face the fact of what I really want, so I confronted Gary about his affair a few weeks ago.'

'And?'

'He admitted it, but then hit me with a bombshell that his girlfriend was pregnant. Yeah. Suddenly he seemed to be the one dictating our break-up. That's Gary all over. What a fool.'

'Him or you?' ventured Steve. Gloria looked quizzical. 'A fool – him or you?'

'Oh. Both, I think. Him for getting Sally pregnant, and me for putting up with things for so long.'

'You must have loved him? After all, you've spent over thirty years together. From what I see, you have two wonderful daughters.'

'Oh, I have. Well, we have. He's a good father, is Gary. Always there for the girls as they grew up, taking them to clubs and school events. Never missed one, even though he was really busy.'

'What about you? Had he time for you?'

'Steve, I know what you've always thought about Gary. But you left and I was here, making a life for myself. He was attentive, thoughtful, caring. But did I love him? I don't think I did. We were – still are – a loving family unit and nothing will take that away, whatever he's done. I've talked it through with the girls and they're old enough to understand and not judge.'

Steve sat motionless, clutching his drink, deep in thought, his emotions all over the place.

'Say something, Steve.'

'I can't deny, this has confused me totally, Gloria. I never got on with Gary, but I'm sorry it's not worked out for you both. Sorry, especially for you. I've always wanted you to be happy, but I didn't realise until recently how much I hurt you and made you unhappy by going away.'

'Did you come back hoping I'd still be here waiting for you?'

'To be honest, yes. Part of me hoped we'd just pick up from when we were a couple, but I didn't think it through at the time. I've had time to think about all the disruption that I've caused since I got back. I've managed to rake up bad things from the past and I'm still none the wiser.

'Half of me wants to find out who killed my real dad, that swine Terry Breeze, just so I can close that chapter of my life. The other half doesn't want to find out, in case it was my grandpa. And I've managed to hurt you again by declaring my feelings for you. I bring chaos to everything.'

'Steve, are you feeling sorry for yourself?'

'Yes, I probably am, but your marriage is over and your dad's ill. You've got more to worry about than me. I'm sorry.'

'I think we both have an equal number of problems to contend with at the moment. It helps me to talk them through with someone close. I hope it's the same for you. The Tom Hamshaw that I knew as a child couldn't kill anyone, even Terry Breeze. You've got to keep believing it.'

'Oh, I do, Gloria. But I keep having this recurring memory from the past. You know when I told you I had toothache the night before the body was buried and my grandpa had to take me to the dentist the following morning?'

'Yes, and Jock took delivery of the cement. What of it, Steve?'

'Well, during the night I heard an engine sound. I looked out of my window and my grandpa's van was driving into the back yard.'

'What did you see, Steve?'

'Nothing. That's it, I saw nothing. After a few minutes, I went back to sleep. It's so long ago that I'm not even sure it happened. It might just be my mind playing tricks. I don't know what to think.'

Gloria took hold of Steve's hand. 'It might be, but even if it happened, it doesn't mean to say that your grandpa was driving, does it?'

'But he probably was. Jock never learned to drive, so someone had to be driving.'

'Steve, you're torturing yourself. What time was it you saw the van?'

'I don't know. I didn't look at a clock.'

'Well then. You went to bed at what… eight, eight-thirty? I know I did when I was that young. It could have been around ten o'clock and your grandpa was coming home from somewhere. Something as simple as that.'

'I'm probably worrying over nothing. Thanks for explaining it.' Steve realised he was holding Gloria's hand and he gave it a gentle squeeze. You've helped me so much, since I found out who my dad was. But I haven't really given anything back to you. I'm sorry. I need to be there for you more. Especially whilst your dad is ill.'

'Steve, I know you. I sense, you're leaving Northcliffe again?'

'I made my mind up after the police solved the bank robbery and found Graham Atkinson was the third man. It meant at least my grandpa wasn't involved in that.'

'But we never thought he could have been.'

'I know, but it still didn't stop me thinking the impossible. I thought if I went away, then everything would die down.'

'They're not going to put the body back in the hole and fill it in, Steve. You can't pretend it all hasn't happened. You need to stay, and I'm not saying this for my benefit, but for yours. Anyway, where would you go?'

'No idea. Maybe you're right, Gloria. Maybe it's something I have to face, for once.'

'At least stay 'til your birthday, Steve. I've got something planned and I don't want you to miss it.'

Steve smiled, 'I will. I'll stay until my birthday, and if I do go, I'll not sneak off this time.'

'I'll have a refill, if that's OK, Steve. Are you going to Teddy Watson's funeral?'

'Yes, I am. Are you?' She nodded. 'Do you know what happened to him?'

'He was killed in a car crash on the promenade road on that awkward bend. He went straight into a lamp-post. The police said he was speeding. You knew him well, didn't you, Steve?'

'I did know him well, but that was a long time ago. We were best mates at school, but afterwards we sort of drifted apart. He played football for Rossport Town. He was always a good player. So he got to hang out with different mates. Before that, we'd spent a lot of time together. I think the last time we saw him was that night when the Yardbirds were on at the Twisted Wheel. He was there with Carole Jackson, I think. She was in the year below us at school. But after that, I don't know anything. Do you know any more, Gloria?'

'Yes, I do. He got a move to Arsenal. The contract

was almost signed and delivered and then in his last match at Rossport, he got a terrible injury. His knee, I think. The move fell through and Teddy never played again. He did bits of training and coaching, but he got very depressed. He married Carole and they had a son, but after a while, Carole couldn't cope with his moods any more. She moved back in with her mum and Teddy went back to his mum's. It was all very sad.'

'I remember I got a wedding invitation, but I couldn't go. I think I was in Bosnia at the time.'

'You were. You sent a card and Teddy was dead pleased. I think we were all quite proud of what you were doing.'

'It's a shame I lost touch. I liked Teddy, I've been so wrapped up in myself that I don't seem to have had time for anyone else.'

Gloria finished her wine and then left. This time there was no 'Stay' from Steve. He needed to think hard about what he wanted and what he could give to people he cared for. At least he had his birthday to look forward to.

Chapter 44
Thursday, 2nd March 2000

At eight-o-clock sharp on the morning of his birthday, Steve's doorbell rang. He made his way downstairs and as he opened the door, he was welcomed by, 'Wake up sleepy-head. Happy birthday. Are you ready?'

Steve smiled and replied, 'Of course. I've been up since 6:30 and I've made up a flask of coffee and some sandwiches as ordered.' He let Gloria inside and she followed him up the stairs to his kitchen. 'I've got a warm pot of coffee ready. Have we time for a quick drink, boss?'

'Yes, we have. But we need to get off soon. There's a jam-packed day ahead of us, Steve. No slacking allowed.'

'Am I allowed to know where we're going?'

'All will be revealed in good time, Sir. But we might need waterproofs,' said Gloria, looking out of the window far across the sea.

'Yes, I reckon there'll be a few squalls, but look on the horizon, how much brighter it seems. And the wind's dropped. I think it will clear up pretty soon.'

'You don't change, do you?' laughed Gloria. 'Every time we walked on the prom after school, you'd tell me to look at the horizon. "It's brighter, it's going to clear up soon," you'd say.'

'And was I ever wrong?'

'Nearly always, dear. But I just loved you for your optimism. Anyway, let's get going. We've a boat to catch.'

'Intriguing,' said Steve, grabbing his rucksack. Steve was probably right about the weather this time. As they walked along the promenade, the sky above the sea did become clearer, although not before some drizzle had slightly dampened their clothes, but not their spirits.

They walked on, chatting about nothing in particular and everything in general. Since Gloria had told Steve about her and Gary splitting up, it had made it easier for Steve to be open with her. Although he still found it difficult to tell Gloria what his true feelings were, he didn't feel he needed to be guarded about what he said. Gloria chatted about things they'd done together and places they'd been to all those years ago. She talked about her two daughters and the kind of holidays that they had together as a family, including many mentions of Gary. 'It doesn't seem to worry her, talking about Gary,' thought Steve. He loved to hear her voice, her enthusiasm, the way she used her hands to gesture when describing events. But most of all he loved her laughter.

Gloria felt exuberant. She knew it from the moment Steve opened his door. She'd not felt like this for a long time. She knew she was wittering on, but it felt right. She and Steve felt comfortable together. She'd been playing it over in her mind most of a disrupted night of sleep. But suddenly out in the open air with the sea wind blowing through her hair, she felt that nothing would be a problem they couldn't overcome together.

They walked out of Northcliffe on the coastal path, past the impressive Victorian buildings, Rossport Hospital and Rossport Public School. 'I used to visit my great-grandfather in the hospital,' said Steve, pointing to an imposing building across the fields. 'The place used to scare the living daylights out of me. I can still remember the smell of antiseptic. Yuk! I'd be about four or five.'

'Do you remember him much, Steve?'

'No. Not really. What I remember most is the tram ride with my nan. I think she used that to convince me to go. It was a relief when we said our goodbyes to my great-grandfather. Is that a bad thing?'

'I don't think you can say anything you thought or did at that age could be classified as bad. I'd call it brave, more like. I don't know if I could have done it. But then – for a promise of a tram ride we'd do anything in those days,' she laughed.

'What about the school?' asked Steve, pointing in the direction of an imposing group of stone buildings just past the hospital.

'It's still a boarding school, but it takes day pupils as well. It's also co-ed these days. Do you remember when the lads used to do cross-country running on Sundays?'

'Yes, I do.'

'My auntie lived on Thornton Gate and they'd run past her house every Sunday afternoon. I used to stand at the front gate and tease them, by trying to get them to speak. They weren't allowed to talk to any locals on pain of detention or worse. It was fun, but maybe I was behaving badly for trying it. I'm so glad that I got a normal upbringing with two loving parents... Oh, Steve, I'm sorry... I didn't mean...'

'Gloria – stop. It's OK. Remember, years ago, we made a pact not be upset by anything either of us said. It's just words that come out wrongly, that's all. I'm so glad you had loving parents. They've made you who you are. I had loving grandparents and a mum who, I know, loved me in her own way. We were both lucky.' Steve took Gloria in his arms and hugged her tightly. Her warmth almost made him gasp. 'This feels so right,' he thought. They separated and looked into each other's eyes, but didn't kiss. Neither seemed to think this was the right moment.

'Come on slowcoach,' said Gloria. 'We've still a long way to go.'

They walked briskly into Rossport past the marine gardens with its lake, where Steve once sailed his toy yacht, then past the short pier with its amusements and cafés, already bustling with visitors, and towards the ferry terminal which carries freight to the Irish Mainland. Just before they reached the terminal, Gloria steered them towards a small jetty where, at the far end, there was a tug boat, its motor already chugging away. 'The ferry to Knott End,' said a startled Steve. 'And it's running too. What a lovely surprise.'

'I was so thankful that the wind had dropped this morning,' said Gloria. 'They often suspend sailings if it's choppy. We're in luck. Come on, hop aboard. It looks like the ferryman is ready to cast off.'

'Aye-Aye, captain,' laughed Steve. The ferry only took five minutes to complete its trip to Knott End on the other side of the estuary. But it was five minutes that stayed in Steve's memory for the rest of his life. 'I've never been on this ferry,' he said. 'I've always wanted to, but the chance never materialised.'

'Well, it has now, so sit back and enjoy the trip.'

There was a small café, overlooking the estuary and the town they had come from. There they enjoyed a cappuccino and a huge slice of lemon drizzle cake each. 'Is this my birthday cake?' asked Steve.

'No, it's not,' replied a smiling Gloria. 'But this is your birthday present,' she said, handing over a well-wrapped small parcel. Steve ripped open the present to find a small, square leather box. He flipped open the lid to reveal a watch. Not any watch, but a watch that looked like the one he'd lost a long time ago. A watch given to him by his grandpa for passing his O-level exams.

'An Omega Seamaster – it looks just like the one my grandpa...'

'It doesn't only look like it, Steve. It's the actual one your grandfather gave you. My dad found it down the back of the sofa, years after you left Northcliffe.'

'I couldn't remember what I'd done with it. The strap was worn and I thought it had broken and fallen off outside somewhere.'

'I remember. We looked everywhere.'

'Except down the back of your parents' settee, of course.'

'I think with all the canoodling that was going on, it would be easy not to feel it drop off,' said Gloria, with a twinkle in her eye. 'I didn't replace the strap. It's not broken, just very worn and loose. I thought it was down to you to decide whether you wanted it just as it is, or if you'd like me to get a new strap fitted.'

'I can't believe it. It's the best birthday present ever, Gloria. I certainly wouldn't want to lose it again, but don't worry, maybe we could choose a strap together.'

Steve looked longingly at the watch face as its second finger ticked round. He shifted his sight to look at Gloria. 'And you kept it all this time. Did you think about me as well?'

'Almost every day.'

Steve knew that this was the time for them to really talk. No more pussyfooting around. 'Me too,' he said. 'I can't even begin to think how to apologise for running away. But perhaps 'sorry' is a good start. It got too much for me, Gloria. Losing my grandpa. The look of disappointment on your face when you found that pass book with your dad's money in it.'

'Steve. I just wanted you to explain. If you'd said there and then that you hadn't taken the money, I'd have believed you and we'd have sorted it out. My dad never, ever thought it was you. He knew it was Gary, but left me to make up my own mind. He told me that it wasn't you years later, when Gary and I were having problems. But you'd left by then and no-one knew where you'd gone. Gary was kind to me and attentive. It seemed right to marry him and I'm glad I did, otherwise I wouldn't have had Sam and Heather. They're my world.'

'I know, Gloria, and I don't want to do anything that would affect that. I've thought long and hard about selling up and going. It seems like I'm causing problems for everyone by staying.'

'Steve, you're not going anywhere. Not if I've got anything to do with it. I still love you to bits even after all these years. I want you to stay and get to know my girls.'

Steve was speechless. He'd caused so much heartache for the woman he loved, and she still wanted him to stay. Despite what he'd done all those years ago,

Gloria still loved him and he still loved her. So, he said it. He said, out loud, in a crowded café, those three words. 'I love you.' The words came out much louder than he expected and the eyes of all the customers and all the staff behind the counter turned to look. There was a moment of quiet in the café, followed by some happy chortling and shouts of 'well done' from a group of walkers sitting close by. 'I love you,' repeated Steve, but in a quieter voice.

'And I love you too.' Then they both burst out laughing. 'Was that your "When Harry Met Sally" moment, Steve?'

'At my age, yes, I think it was the best I could do.'

They left the café and continued their walk north, following the coastal path. A usually reticent Steve was now in full flow. He told Gloria about everything he'd done since leaving Northcliffe. What his thoughts were at the time. The way he threw himself into his new career. The dangerous places he'd been sent to and the wonderful, down-to-earth, ordinary folk that he'd come across. 'It made me humble, I think,' said Steve. 'I always thought I was the lucky one. Being able to walk away, back into safety and security, while they had to stay behind to face whatever troubles and atrocities were waiting for them. But I think, in some ways, they were the lucky ones. They had friendship and comradeship with each other in their communities. I missed all that when I left.'

'Did you ever get married? Or have someone special?'

'No, I never married, but yes, I did have someone special. She's walking alongside me at this very moment. I had a few relationships, but they fizzled out pretty quickly. I suppose after I left, I was married to my work. As long as I never missed a deadline, I couldn't let anyone down. But that's not really living. I know that now.'

Time just flew by and so did the miles. Soon they had arrived at Glasson Dock, an old port built in the mid-eighteenth century. Steve had always loved this place and his grandpa used to bring him here often. 'It's a unique place is Glasson Dock,' his grandpa would say, almost every time they came here. 'Look, that's the dock where the ships arrive to discharge their cargo, and there's the canal where, in the day, slate and coal and potatoes would be loaded onto barges bound for Preston. And that's the freight train, just leaving the station bound for Lancaster and beyond. And look, here comes a bus as well. If you want to see all the different forms of transport working in one place, then come to Glasson Dock.' Steve smiled as he related this tale to Gloria.

'Do you think we've become too nostalgic?'

'Probably, love. But then, so much has happened that everything has been turned upside down. It's not surprising that we cling onto anything that reminds us of happier times.'

Lunch was a sumptuous all-day breakfast, served in the Lantern café, overlooking the Lune estuary. Afterwards, they sat idly chatting, each comfortable with the other, just like they used to be. Gloria got more serious. 'What do you remember about your mum, Steve?'

Steve thought for a moment. 'Whenever people ask me that, I'm never sure how to reply. I can't differentiate between what's truth and what I believe is truth. I know that doesn't make sense, but I grew up not knowing who my father was, and my mother was ill for as long as I remember. So I think I made things up, just so that I could be more normal.

'I remember my mum reading a bedtime story or singing me to sleep – I think. I remember her taking me to school and being there when I got home, or if I fell and bloodied my knee, she'd clean it and put a plaster on. She died when I was fourteen, but I can't remember with any certainty many moments we shared in those later years. It was always my grandpa or nan I did things with. When I was old enough to face it and want answers, it was too late. My grandparents had gone by then. Whenever I asked my Uncle Brian about my mum, he'd say, "Our Rose? She was always a bit strange." So I just have vague memories, which are either true or just my imagination hoping that they are true.'

'She drowned at sea, didn't she?' asked Gloria.

'Yes, she did. She was a very good swimmer. She made the county team. I've still got a few of her trophies at home. My nan used to say that swimming was all that kept my mum going, until I came along. She'd go swimming in the sea most days. One day she went for a swim and never came back. They found her two days later, up the coast opposite the hospital. We passed the spot this morning, but I didn't want to say anything.'

'Oh Steve, you should have done. You quite clearly needed to tell someone. Don't bottle it up. You know you can tell me anything.'

'I know now, Glo – Wow, I haven't called you that for thirty-three years. I've missed calling you that so much.'

'And I've missed being called that as well, love,' said Gloria, clasping Steve's hand across the table. 'Now let's not get all sentimental and gooey. We've got a bus to catch and a place to be this afternoon. Come on. If we miss this bus there isn't another one for two hours.'

The bus that ran from Lancaster to Preston arrived just on time. They climbed the stairs and sat on the front seats enjoying the views of the Lune valley and surrounding countryside. Some early lambs had been born and were frolicking in the fields. 'Rather like Gloria and me,' thought Steve. 'Two fifty-year-olds acting like starstruck lovers. And why not?' At least for a while, he could forget about dead bodies and burnt-out chapels.

Chapter 45
The same day

They got off the bus at a stop directly outside Thurnham Grange.

'Isn't this where your mum and dad live?' queried Steve.

'Yes, it is,' replied Gloria. 'We're going to visit them for afternoon tea. My mum's baked you a birthday cake 'specially. And I think you and Dad have lots to talk about. After I tell them about us, he'll want to make sure you're going to look after his little girl,' Gloria teased.

'Seriously though, Steve, my dad has deteriorated a lot. We're not sure how much longer he's got. But he so much wants to see you. I've kept this from you, 'til today, as I wanted us to sort ourselves out. And yes, I've talked about us with my parents and it's what they wanted, too. So don't feel scared. Come on, let's go and eat that cake.'

Steve was shocked to see how ill Don looked, but he was greeted by both Don and Kathleen like he'd never been away.

'Sit down here, Steve,' said Kathleen, pointing to a chair next to where Don was sitting. 'Gloria and I will get the tea and cake.'

Steve sat down and looked at the man he'd let down all those years ago. 'I'm sorry Don...'

'Stop there, Steve,' said Don, holding a hand up with some effort. 'There's nothing to be sorry about. Whatever happened, happened for a reason. You weren't ready for Northcliffe and Northcliffe wasn't ready for you. It was always obvious you had things you needed to do. Otherwise it would have eaten away at you. Some people are programmed to let life meander, and good for them, I say. Others, like yourself, have a hankering to do something different – sort of getting something out of your system. But now you're back and I can tell that it's more settled between you and Northcliffe. After everything that's happened, you're still here. It couldn't be something to do with my daughter, could it, Steve?' asked Don, smiling.

'Yes, it could, Don. I think I've realised what I gave up, or should I say, ran away from, all those years ago. If we could turn back the clock, eh?'

'Don't say that, Steve. One thing that this illness has shown me is to always look forward. To make the most of what you've got left. So make sure you look after Gloria for me. That's your job from now on. OK?'

'OK,' said Steve, nodding.

The tea and cake arrived. Steve even had "Happy Birthday" sung to him. They chatted for about half an hour about him and Gloria growing up together until it was apparent that Don had drifted off to sleep. Steve and Kathleen moved to the kitchen, whilst Gloria stayed with her dad.

Kathleen had been a teacher at Beach Road Primary School when he and Gloria were there. She'd been their form mistress when they were seven and Steve always remembered her as a kind and caring teacher. He'd so many questions he wanted to ask her, but couldn't find a way to ask any of them. Finally, Kathleen, sensing the dilemma he was in, broached the subject. 'Your mum was a lovely person, Steve. I'm saying that because you were maybe too young to remember how she was, when she was well. She'd come into our classroom one afternoon a week and help with the craft work. Your mum never showed you any favouritism. She treated you just like any other child in the class. She was very artistic, was Rose. And I can tell she passed that on to you from the way you compose your photographs.'

Steve was quiet, thinking back. 'I remember once, we each made a glove puppet, didn't we?' Kathleen smiled and nodded. 'We modelled the heads in clay and then used papier-mâché to cover them. Then, when they were dry, we painted them and sewed up some material so it would hide our hand. Is that really true? Did that really happen?' Kathleen nodded again.

'I remember, there was a lad in our class called Bobby Hunter. He was disabled, wasn't he? He'd got something wrong with one of his arms, couldn't use it very well, I think. My mum used to help him. She'd spend more time with him than all the others. I think he had the best puppet of all at the end. I can remember that all the class were really pleased for him.'

'What you don't know, Steve, is that Bobby Hunter did nearly all of it himself. He just needed some encouragement from someone. And that someone was your mum. That was Rose Hamshaw to a "T". Always trying to help others. But she got really ill soon after, so she had to stop coming.

'Bobby still sends me a Christmas card every year, you know. After he left school, he got a job at the council. He's still there, working in the planning department. I've always thought that those sessions with Rose gave him the confidence he needed to face any difficulty.'

'Thanks, Kathleen. I don't know how that memory came out of nowhere. I've hidden so much for too long. Thanks for helping me remember that about my mum. It means so much to me.'

'Think of it as a payment, Steve, for making our daughter the happiest girl in the world.'

Chapter 46
Friday, 3rd March 2000

The following day was Teddy Watson's funeral. It started damp and cold, with a strong westerly gale blowing in that mixture of rain and sea spray, which quickly soaks into your clothes. Steve entered the church at the last moment so that there were fewer inquisitive eyes watching him as he aimed for a seat in one of the back pews. He looked up along the pew to the next vacant space only to see that his neighbour would be Gloria.

She smiled and her look said, 'Just sit down, will you.' Before he could decide otherwise, some movement behind his right shoulder indicated that Teddy's coffin was already making its way down the centre aisle, carried by six former colleagues from his footballing days.

The service was short for a Catholic one, but still quite lengthy. Steve shared Gloria's order of service pamphlet and tried to join in the singing of the hymns and chosen songs. "Morning has Broken" by Cat Stevens and "Amazing Grace" by Joan Baez were two of Teddy's favourites that Steve approved of. Steve's singing wasn't up to much, but Gloria more than made up for it with her sweet, tuneful tone. She looked nice as well. It reminded him of the previous day and the lovely time they'd spent together.

As they left the church, they paused to pass on condolences to Teddy's mum, Theresa, his wife Carole and his son, who were all shivering in the cold wind.

'Hello Steve,' said Theresa. 'I'm glad you could come.'

'I'm so sorry, Mrs Watson. I always liked Teddy and now I feel sorry that we didn't keep in touch more.'

'I know what you boys are like,' she replied. 'Talking was neither of your strong points. Teddy always kept up with your exploits when you were in those war zones. He'd say, 'That's my friend Steve Hamshaw. We went to school together.' And I know he was dead chuffed with the card you sent him when he played his first senior game. I think secretly, you were his hero.'

'I didn't know that,' said Steve. 'That means a lot to me.'

'You'll both come back for some food, won't you?' she asked.

'I don't know,' said Steve, looking at Gloria. 'We're not close family, or anything. We don't want to intrude.'

'You won't be intruding, and I want to talk to you, Steve, away from all these people. It's about what's going on – I need to tell you something.'

Steve, taken aback, said, 'OK – yes, in that case, we'd love to.' And with that he pecked Theresa on the cheek and they moved away.

'What was that all about?' asked Gloria when they were out of earshot.

'I don't know. She said that she wanted to tell me

something – to do with finding the body, I think.'

'Or maybe it was something about your dad?'

'Or my mum? They were close friends.'

'Look Steve, my car's just around the corner. We can either walk and get drenched, or I can give you a lift. So, what's it to be?'

Steve was secretly pleased about the lift. Any chance to be in the same space as Gloria filled him with joy. They'd decided not to broadcast that they'd got back together yet. Gloria wanted to tell her girls first and for Steve to meet them. They chatted about Teddy and things they all got up to at school. Gloria, as always, had kept in touch and knew Teddy's wife quite well.

'I'm useless at keeping in touch with friends,' admitted Steve. 'Teddy was my best friend at school – after you, of course, Glo.' Steve remembered his days playing with Teddy in the school football team. Teddy was the star player of course and Steve was a lumbering right back. Or if the case arose, an emergency goalkeeper. In fact, Steve would always be willing to talk to anyone about the time in the area semi-final, when, because of sickness to the number one goalkeeper, Steve had gone between the sticks and saved a penalty. They had still lost 4-1, but he'd lived off that save for months.

They timed their arrival at Theresa's house so that most of the guests had already gone in. They both helped themselves to some food from the buffet. Gloria admitted that she was ravenous. After Theresa had announced a toast to 'Young Teddy' as she called him, she took Steve's arm and led him into the quiet of the front room, shooing a few guests out, before closing the door.

'Steve, I'm sorry about the news of who your dad is and all that's going on around it. I've been wanting to tell you something since Terry's body was found, but with Teddy still alive, it didn't seem right.'

'OK,' said Steve warily. 'Do you know something?'

'Steve, it's not easy for me because I've never told anyone else, not even Teddy, and not even your mum who, as you know, was my best friend.'

'Mrs Watson... Er, Theresa, you're not making much sense, I'm afraid. What is it that you've kept secret all this time?'

There was a pause. Steve could see Theresa was half-inclined to clam up and not say another word. He fully expected her to say, 'Never mind, it'll keep for another time,' or 'best left as a secret'. In fact, he half hoped that she would say one of those two things. But he wasn't prepared at all for what Theresa finally revealed.

'Teddy was your half-brother, Steve. His dad was Terry Breeze. I've kept it secret for nearly fifty years, but I have to tell someone now.' Theresa burst into tears. Steve tried his best to comfort her, while at the same time trying to understand the words she'd just spoken.

'Hold on,' Steve said eventually. 'Let me get this right. Teddy's dad was Terry Breeze as well?'

'Yes, he was. I'd put it all out of my mind, until I heard about the body being found. That brought it all back and I didn't know if I should say anything or not. But with Teddy gone...' Theresa burst into tears again, and Steve started crying too. How much more could life throw at him? He held Theresa close to him, both consumed in different ways by grief and incredulity.

Minutes passed and neither moved. Then they both

broke off at the same time. Steve found a box of tissues and handed a couple to Theresa. He didn't... no, he couldn't think of what to say. Finally, as if wanting to understand, he asked, 'But I thought Teddy's dad died in Israel? He was in the army. Teddy was dead proud of him. He even showed me a photo of his dad taken in uniform.'

'Yes, that's what Teddy had been told. I don't know who the soldier in that photo is. There was a story in the paper about some terrorists who blew up a train and a lot of soldiers were killed. It suited us to say his dad was one of them. You've got to understand, Steve, that my family is Catholic and they couldn't have anyone having a child out of wedlock. I was seventeen and didn't have a say in it. Father Cromer, who was the priest then, came and convinced me and my parents to stick to this story. In the end, I just chose to believe it was true. That way nobody got hurt.'

'Wow – but how have you managed? You've got a nice house. I was always a bit jealous of Teddy's big bedroom.'

'It was Jed Breeze's doing. He was really good to us. Jed, Terry's dad, wasn't a bad sort, really, unless you crossed him. He was always clearing up the messes that Terry left behind. Jed bought me this house. He gave me some money and got me a job. Made me promise not to tell anyone, and I'd had no reason until I heard about you being Terry's son. I meant to tell Teddy sometime, but you know, time just goes by and he worshipped his dad's memory. I just couldn't do it.'

'Yeah, I can understand that, and you never had an inkling from my mum about who my dad was?'

'No, nothing at all. I think she was just like me.

Didn't want anyone knowing. Strange how we were best friends and yet neither of us confided in each other. I know it's something I've had to get used to living with. It was harder for your mum. She wasn't really as resilient as me, as you know.'

'Do you think my grandpa knew who my dad was, Theresa?'

'I don't know, Steve. I've been wondering that since I heard about it. Rose never said anything, and if he did know then he wouldn't have accepted a bean from Jed Breeze and I think he'd have given Terry a good hiding or even worse and not worried about the consequences. She was only seventeen when Terry got her in trouble. Same as me – a mere girl.'

'Blimey,' thought Steve. 'It gets more incredible every day.' Those dark thoughts quickly returned. 'Could my grandpa actually have killed Terry Breeze? Surely not? He always valued life and it would have devastated my nan and my mum. But, in the heat of the moment anything could have happened. No,' thought Steve. 'No way would he have done it. I'll have to dig deeper, even if worse things surface.'

He turned back to Theresa and said, 'Do you think he's got any other children out there that we don't know about? Maybe half my old classmates are his?'

'I don't know, Steve, but I'll regret telling you this if it gets out and besmirches Teddy's memory. You don't have to tell the police this, do you?'

'Theresa, if there's one thing you can take as read, Richard Whittle won't find out from me. You have my word. I can't see how it has any bearing on the case, but it just adds to how difficult it is to come to terms with who my dad was. I'm glad Teddy never had to go through this. What was Terry Breeze like? I don't have much of a memory of him.'

'A charmer, a troublemaker and a man with a filthy temper. He'd hit me sometimes – that's before Teddy was born. After that, Terry's dad, Jed, saw that he didn't go near me. He didn't want to anyway, what with me having Teddy to look after. When he disappeared all that time ago, I could gradually forget he existed. I even got to believe about Teddy's made-up dad.

'I was swept off my feet by Terry. He had money and a motor, scarce commodities in those years after the war, when most things were still rationed. He took me dancing and bought me presents. I'm afraid he seduced me.'

'And I bet he seduced my mum just the same. I'm actually pretty glad I didn't have Terry Breeze as my dad when I was growing up, but I regret every day digging his body up.'

'Keeping it a secret was Rose's doing. She mustn't have told anyone about her and Terry. She knew Terry would run a mile when he found out she was pregnant, and I bet she was worried what your grandfather would do if he found out. So she kept that secret from everyone. It must have cost her. I can see now why she changed so much.'

'Theresa, you knew my mum well. What was she like?'

'Rose? Rose Hamshaw was fun, Steve. During our teenage years we'd sneak off and go dancing. The war had just finished and we were fifteen. Southcliffe was still full of army chaps and some from the American air base – well… It was dancing every night. She laughed a lot. Everything was fun to Rose. She made me laugh and we were inseparable.

'But when she got pregnant, Rose changed. She went into some sort of shell and didn't allow anyone in. I asked her who the father was, but she wouldn't let on. We drifted apart and then Terry started taking an interest in me. He took me dancing and the like. And before you know it, I'm pregnant.

'Terry had a way of controlling you, if you let him. With me it didn't work, but with your mum, she was a bit more fragile and I think it affected her. So when I did get pregnant, I went to see Jed and he saw me right, giving me money to look after Teddy. But one thing I do know, Steve, is that your mum loved you to bits. You were the centre of her life. We didn't meet up very often after you and Teddy were born, but she doted on you. I saw it. What you are today, young man, is because of your mum, not your dad.'

'Thanks, Theresa. That means a lot to me. I'm beginning to understand a bit more. What can you tell me about her swimming accident?'

'Oh, Steve! I couldn't believe it when I heard about it. Rose was such a strong swimmer and she loved being in the sea. I'd seen her the day before and she'd blanked me completely. As if I didn't exist, or as if she didn't realise I was there. No-one saw her go into the water that day she disappeared.'

'What do you think happened, Theresa? – Please, it's important that I know what you think.'

'Steve – I've always thought this and when I heard about Terry being your dad, it made me more certain. When Rose went into that water, she didn't intend to come out of it. That's what I think.'

'Me too, Theresa. Me too.'

Chapter 47
Thursday, 9th March 2000

'Steve, my dad's dying. He wants to see us both straight away. Can I pick you up?' It was a sunny morning in early spring, usually a sight to behold in the countryside. Gloria and Steve were oblivious to their surroundings as they sped their way across the toll bridge and into the grounds of the nursing home at Glasson. Don Ward had been moved there when his condition had deteriorated so much that he required a machine to assist with his breathing.

'He wants us both here and he asked me to ring Rich as well. I'm not sure what this is about. But you know Dad. Always liked a bit of the dramatic.'

Steve knew as well as Gloria that her father had something final to say before he departed this earth. Whether it was something he wanted to hear was not an issue – it had become something he needed to hear. Those weeks since the unearthing of the body had played tricks on his mind. He'd seen things in Kosovo that he thought would never be repeated – and yet they were. Seeing all those atrocities happen and keeping professional at the same time had been difficult, but somehow, he could detach himself from the human suffering. These past nine or ten weeks had taught him a lot, yes, even at his age, about what he held dear, who he loved and how to protect them.

Richard was standing outside when they arrived. When he'd got Gloria's phone call that Don had something final to say, Richard was filled with apprehension. This case had taken its toll on him. The dash to Perth in Australia, only to be thwarted with the early death of Jock Crammie. The revelation that his constable's dad was the mastermind of the bank robbery in 1957 and Jock's killer. The death of Valdo Goralova and subsequent demise of Phil Breeze. And the possibility that people he loved and admired were caught up in the death of Terry Breeze forty-three years ago. Was Don Ward finally going to reveal all? He was soon to find out.

After a quick greeting, the three made their way to Don's room. As they entered, they saw a shrunken man swathed in tubes. Next to his bed was a bank of monitors. Remarkably, he was awake. His sunken eyes greeted them and he beckoned them over to three chairs laid out neatly. Don had prepared this well. Kathleen moved over to the back of the room to allow the three to take the seats. Gloria kissed her dad's forehead and squeezed his hand gently, then lowered herself into the chair next to him to join the others.

'I'm glad you could all come. Richard, this is not a statement, I won't sign anything and you won't record it, OK?' Richard nodded. 'You're here as George's son, not a policeman. Gloria, a sip of water, please.'

'Don's definitely in charge,' Steve thought. Gloria

administered the water like a priest does the communion cup – gently, carefully and just a sip.

'What I have to tell you is what really happened on 18th November 1957. I'm dying, I think we all know that.' Don turned to Gloria and she squeezed his hand a little more. 'I've held this secret for over forty years. I could take it with me. I probably would have done, except for that damn body being dug up. Richard, you're a persistent customer and I realise that you won't rest until you know what happened. Steve, you have a right to know whether your grandfather was involved in Terry Breeze's death. In fact, you all have a right to know everything, then you can decide what you want to do.'

'That Monday morning, as Richard knows from Margaret's diary, there was an argument between Tom and Terry Breeze. I broke it up and Terry left the hall. Tom and I sat talking for an hour or so and then he left. I think he said he'd got some supplies to pick up.

'After lunch, Terry had come back into the club and was having a game of snooker with Jock Crammie. The club had closed at 2pm, but Jock and Terry were finishing off a game on the table by the bar and having a couple of extra drinks. That often happened. It'd rained heavily that morning and seemed set for the day, so Tom had laid Jock off. As for Terry? As usual, he was at a loose end.

'He was easily bored, was your father, Steve. Unless he had some scam running. You're totally unlike him. I sometimes think you got every gene in your body from your mum. She made you what you are – you remember that – not your dad. Anyway, there was no trouble at all from either of them, so I let them play on. Then in walks

Dorothy, your nan, Steve. She'd been in the hall maybe twice in all the years I'd been there, so I was surprised.

'She was not in a mood for pleasantries. She walked straight over to Terry and accused him of trying to seduce her daughter. Seems Terry had got together with Rose and they had been seen canoodling, for want of a better word, in one of the arcades. Dorothy warned Terry off in no uncertain terms. I remember her saying, "You've ruined many a young girl's life round here. I'm not going to sit around and watch you ruin our Rose's life. She's got a young lad to bring up and I'm not going to let the likes of you mess it up for her." I saw Terry's mouth turn from shock to a broad grin.

"Mess her life up? Her life's messed up enough already thanks to you Hamshaws. Always telling her what to do, treating her like she's your skivvy. No wonder she's a bit funny up here. As for her lad, what, young Steve? Who d'ya think his dad is – eh? Well, it's me, I sired him. A chip off the old block, if you'd let him be. I've taken a shine to Rose. Maybe we'll go away together. Take young Steve with us. Me be a dad to him. Who'd empty the bedpans then, Dorothy?"

'Well, you could hear a pin drop. Dorothy stood there aghast. She obviously didn't know until then that Terry was Steve's dad. None of us did. She'd just realised the big secret that Rose had kept from her. Rumour had it, Steve, that your real dad was a visitor that stayed in your nan's boarding house, not someone closer to home, and definitely not Terry Breeze. Anyway, Terry let out a chuckle and turned back to Jock and I remember his words, his last words, that is.'

Don's eyes closed and he sighed. 'Can I have another sip, please, love?' Gloria held the beaker to

Don's lips and he took a small sip. Then he continued, slower and more pronounced than before, conscious he wanted to make sure he told the story correctly, for all their sakes. 'Ah. Yes. Terry Breeze's last words. They were, "Women are so weak, Jock, me old mate. They just can't resist me."

'I've never seen Dorothy so riled up and I can totally understand what happened next. I only hope you all can as well. As Terry turned back from talking to Jock, she grabbed hold of a snooker cue left on a table and before anyone could stop her, she hit Terry on the side of his head. Here.' Don slowly lifted his free left hand and pointed in the direction of the side of his head. 'Terry lurched sideways and, as he fell, he hit the back of his head against the brass corner pocket of the table. There was a loud crack, I can still hear it now, and he lay on the floor, his head slumped forward towards his chest. He'd broken his neck and was dead. We all stood there. None of us dared move.'

'So, it was an accident,' said Steve, turning to Richard. 'You said that it was a blow on the back of the head that killed him, not the side blow. Poor nan – I can't begin to comprehend what she went through. She must have been in pieces.'

'No, she wasn't, Steve,' said Don. 'Your nan was made of sterner stuff. She was the one who told me to ring for George Whittle.'

'You rang my dad?' asked Richard, in disbelief.

'Yes, Richard, Dorothy's words were "Ring George, I want him to arrest me – nobody else."

'George arrived within five minutes. Your dad was a fine man, Richard. Straight as a die, he lived for the law, but what he did that afternoon made him a god in my eyes. You have to understand that this was an accident. Terry Breeze was a low life, he'd ruined Rose's life and he would have ruined Steve's as well.

'They hung people for less in those days. That Ruth Ellis case was still in everyone's mind. Ellis had killed someone in what they called a crime of passion and she'd been hung for it. Was this any different? I swear, I'd have done the same thing if I'd have been in George's shoes. Steve and Tom needed Dorothy. George understood this and he took charge. He told me and Jock to move the body into the back room. We sat Terry in a chair, locked the door and cleaned up the mess in the hall.'

'The body was in the back room?' asked Steve. 'That small room, the old office?'

...when I took a glance into a dark corner of the room. There, staring at me were the scariest eyes I have ever seen. The eyeballs seemed to poke out like sticks from their sockets. The grotesque shape of its face looked set to devour me. I heard a voice in my head telling me not to move. I stood still, froze more likely, trying not to meet its gaze. The eyes seemed to move slightly, as if now looking into another part of the room. I took that opportunity to make a dash for the inviting hole.

Steve turned to Gloria. 'The snooker hall. Do you remember? That day, when we went hunting, and we climbed through the hole in the wall? That image I saw of someone sitting in a chair looking at me with those strange eyes. The one that scared me so much. That must have been Terry Breeze. That was my dad, I saw. Crikey!'

Steve looked out of the window, reliving that day which had stayed in his memory for over forty years. 'I'd begun to believe it was my imagination – those eyes staring at me like they could see through me...' He paused and a silence came over the room, each of them deep in thought.

'What happened, Don? How does this finish?' Richard asked, nervously.

'George and Jock came back in the early hours and we loaded the body into Tom's van. They set off to take the body to Over Wyre somewhere, to dump it in the salt marshes. The tide would have taken it out to sea and it would have washed up further up the coast. But on the way there, it seems they had second thoughts. Nobody wanted Terry's body found. That would have meant a proper inquiry. Jock had a better idea. The concrete for the extension at Nuttall Road was due in the morning. Tom had told Jock that he was taking Steve to the dentist, so had asked if Jock could sort it out. It was the perfect solution. Well it was for over forty years. Until the dig started.'

Gloria looked at Steve. His dream about seeing his grandpa's van was real after all.

'The following morning,' Don continued, 'I watched the unloading of the concrete from the back window of the hall. I saw George standing at the edge of the arcade, watching until the hole was filled. I'm sure I saw Dorothy at the upstairs window as well. It was never mentioned again by any of us and we got on with our lives as best we could. Your nan never told your grandpa about any of this, Steve. She kept it to herself until she died. He never knew.

'Sometimes the secret weighed me down and I was desperate to tell someone. I eventually told your mum, Gloria. And Kathleen has helped me keep it secret all these years. It's her idea that I tell you all this now, before it's too late. This may seem selfish, but I've kept this secret for forty years. But for you three – well, it's part of your heritage. It's something you need to know and you're old enough now to make the right decision on what to do with it. At the time, Dorothy deserved better and George knew it. And now, so do their children.'

Don closed his eyes and slipped into what looked to Gloria like a peaceful sleep. Saying all that had taken a lot out of him both physically and mentally. 'He's at peace, probably for the first time in a long while,' she thought.

She was proud of her father, prouder than she had ever been. Gloria said out loud, 'All three of us sitting round his bed have been protected from bad things. It's what parents naturally do for their children and sometimes it can take until you're older yourself, to actually realise it.'

Chapter 48

Don Ward died the following morning. He'd lost consciousness during the night and Gloria and Kathleen were called to his bedside. Kathleen held her husband's hand until the beep of the machine sounded its last long, never-ending note. She would say afterwards that his face was calm and all his troubles had finally been lifted. But in reality, he'd transferred them to his daughter and the two men he admired the most.

Richard had left the nursing home that day without uttering another word. Steve and Gloria had driven back in almost complete silence, each consumed by their own thoughts. Steve had gone in that morning fully expecting to be told his grandpa had killed Terry Breeze, only to find out worse news – that it was his nan who had felt provoked into doing the deed. He began to realise that if Don hadn't kept silent or George had followed his police code, Steve's life would have been significantly different and a great deal worse.

Gloria was secretly proud of her dad for keeping the awful secret for such a long time. She knew that in the aftermath of Terry's disappearance all those years ago, not only had her dad to contend with the police investigation, but he'd also had a late-night visit from

Terry's dad, Jed. She remembered overhearing their conversation through the gaps in the landing banisters. She hadn't understood the words that were spoken but the manner in which Jed Breeze delivered them was not easy to forget and the worry on her dad's face at breakfast the following morning only reinforced the severity.

Richard was in pieces. Everything he believed in was now in question. George Whittle had instilled in his son that the law was the law and a policeman must uphold it without fear or favour. So how could George Whittle not only have covered up a crime, but committed one himself by burying Terry Breeze's body?

As a policeman, Richard had arrested people he felt sorry for – people put in all kinds of situations not of their own choosing. Mothers like Dorothy Hamshaw, trying to protect their children. Should he have made allowances? Should he have looked the other way? Like his dad did. For days, he talked it through with Jill. She listened as he often contradicted himself and still, he couldn't find an answer.

Gloria kept herself busy organising the funeral and receiving the sympathy of well-wishers, so she didn't see either Steve or Richard until the day of the funeral. Steve had kept in touch by telephone and they had talked for hours about everything. Steve felt that at last, he could be there for Gloria.

The church was full. Some people had to stand at the back. Don Ward had been a popular person in the town and the church. He'd chosen his favourite hymns, all upbeat, as he said, 'to keep everyone happy.' Gloria came to the front and did a lovely eulogy. 'Dad's been an inspiration to me all my life. I've tried to follow his lead when bringing up my two daughters. Dad used to say, "I'm not going to stop you making mistakes, otherwise you won't learn and making mistakes is part of growing up. I still make them now. But I'll tell you when I think you've made one, then it's up to you. As long as you do what you think is right, even if it's not right with everyone else, but it's what you feel in your heart, well, that's good enough for me." And he believed that right up until the end.'

They went to the tennis club where a good spread had been laid on for all those who wanted to pay their respects. Steve and Richard made small talk in different parts of the room, subconsciously keeping their distance from Gloria. But neither really wanted to be there and Gloria had her family nearby. Both left at about the same time, but heading in different directions. Steve made his way to number 9, Nuttall Road, where it had all begun three months earlier.

He leant against the metal barrier that still surrounded the place where the skeleton had been found. It had remnants of police tape flapping in the increasing breeze. 'The tide's on the way in,' he thought and smiled, ruefully. It's exactly what his grandpa would have said. Steve heard a crunch of gravel behind his left shoulder, but he didn't need to turn round, as he knew who the visitor was.

'I thought I'd find you here. Nice service for Don, and Gloria said some lovely words. But like you, I wasn't that hungry and not really up to small talk.'

'Isn't this what we're doing here, small talk?' Steve smiled as he turned to see his childhood friend.

'I was so sorry for you, Steve. When this was uncovered. I wouldn't have wanted to have been in your shoes for anything. But now I'm the same as you. Don's dead, but his secret lives on with us.'

'What are you going to do, Rich? You're a policeman. Don't you have to solve a crime if it's there?'

'Yes, I do, but it's the exact same dilemma my dad was in all those years ago. Solve the crime, or do what's right. Until now I thought they were the same thing. Now I'm not so sure. I keep asking myself. What if I'd just found out that your nan killed Terry Breeze and my dad didn't know about it? How would I react? Would I be a true policeman and investigate it, report it, put it on file? I honestly don't know the answer to that, Steve. But my dad did know and what's more covered it up – in there,' he said, gazing at the patch of earth below them.

'So, Rich, what are you going to do?'

'Nothing, that's what I'm going to do. Just nothing. A dying man's ramblings, and nothing on record. There's no evidence pointing to anything that we can take forward. The bank robbery's solved. Gary doesn't seem that interested in who killed his dad. That part of his life is closed. Phil's dead, and Gloria has said in public what she thinks of her dad. Imagine if it got out that he'd kept quiet about your dad's death. What would everyone think of him? No Steve, I think the secret is with us three until we die.'

'I suppose it's fate that neither of us have any children to pass it onto on our death beds, Rich.'

'Yes, the secret will stay with us and die with us. Until then, we just soldier on. I'm winding up the case. It'll go back into Cold Case storage. Maybe one day, some new evidence will be unearthed and it will all come out. But I'll live with that. So, what about you, Steve? Now it's all over, are you going away again?'

'No, I'm not, Rich. I ran away once and look where that got me. It seems I've only been delaying the inevitable. I came back here trying to find what I left behind – my idyllic childhood. And I've found a father and three brothers I didn't know I had. Only one of them, Teddy, is one I would have really wanted and I'm ashamed I didn't get to know him better. I've found my nan killed my father and I've found my mum was horribly mixed up and probably took her own life.'

'Has it helped finding all this out?'

'That's a good question, "Inspector Whittle". Has it helped? In a way – it has. It's given me closure on things that have made me shun people in the past. I can't blame my nan. In fact, I'm secretly rather proud of her for standing up and protecting her daughter. And for protecting my grandpa, because he'd have done just the same and probably hung for it. I'm grateful to your dad, Rich. For covering it up and doing what all three of us think was the right thing to do.

'I came back to Northcliffe to try and get answers. And I suppose I've got them. But you can't always get the answers you want, can you?'

'No – that's true. My dad was the best policeman in the world in my eyes, and he still is. Whatever decision he made at the time was the best he could do. Who knows what I'd have done in the same circumstances? I hope I'd have done the same. Anyway, what are you going to do with all this now that we've finished with it?'

'Nothing, Rich. I've sold this site on, to a mate of mine. He owns the other six houses on the block. Now he's got the lot, he's going to knock them down and build some new retirement homes.'

'Good place for them, Steve. It's close to the shops and just a brisk walk to the beach. He'll do all right.'

'It's time to move on, Rich. Look forward, not back. One good thing has come out of it all, anyway.'

'What, you mean Gloria? You two were made for each other. Whatever happened way back?'

'Don't go there – please. I was an idiot then, but she's finally left Gary. Their two children are grown up enough to cope with it and Gary has a new woman, who's expecting his child. So it suits both him and Gloria to divorce. It was just his male pride that got in the way.'

'We all have that, and it does get in the way, but that's who we are, Steve.'

'Gloria and I are going off on some travels. Doing a visit to the Belgium battlefields, going to find my Great-Uncle Billy's grave. Then on to Malta to look up Nan's relatives, and find her roots. When we get back, all this should have faded to a distant memory. That's the plan. I've still got the church renovation to complete and the houses to do up for the council. That, plus being with Gloria, will keep me here for a long, long time… What about you Rich, are you staying or do you feel you should get away after all that's happened?'

'No, I'm staying, Steve. I love it here. My dad kept this town on the right path and now it's my turn. As Don Ward said, "Do what you think is right." Good words.'

'Yes. That's all we can do, Rich. We do what we think is right.'

THE END